To Emma,

With Best wishes,

[illegible]

Christina

2024

CW01594384

María-Christina Migone-Benfield was born in Buenos Aires and lived there until 1994. She is a qualified multilingual Translator and Interpreter and a Spanish Language and Literature teacher, and has Diplomas in Creative writing and History of Art from the University of Cambridge.

She practises in all of the above disciplines and is a columnist for Argentine newspapers, radio and TV. She writes fiction, poetry and essays in Spanish, English and occasionally, in French.

In 2001 she was awarded the First Poetry Prize in Buenos Aires and the Third prize for Surrealist Poetry.
TALES OF MANY LIVES, a collection of short stories, was published in 2015 as well as GETTING A LIFE (CUARTO DE SIGLO), a bilingual edition of memoirs of her early years in Argentina.

Her INVENTARIO is a compilation of poems and short stories published in Spanish. María-Christina loves London, Cambridge, Copenhagen, swimming, tea and the rain. WHAT WE CAN FACE is her first novel in English.

Judith Kahn-Foster

WHAT WE CAN FACE
© Christina Migone-Benfield

ISBN 978-1-4466-4469-0
Published by lulu.com December 2023
Printed in the United Kingdom
Cover design: Christina Migone-Benfield

OTHER TITLES BY THE AUTHOR
Getting a life / Cuarto de siglo
Tales of many lives
Inventario

WHAT WE CAN FACE

Christina Migone-Benfield

What we can laugh at, we can face;
What we can face, we can conquer
Jonathan Sacks

Chapter 1

Awakening

I remember it clearly now that I have got rid of the effect of the drugs. My operation was a success, Mr Henriksen told me, but the pain is still agonizing unless I administer myself a dose of morphine. Quite practical this new arrangement, or not so new according to the nurses, but it works wonderfully. They attach a little pump with only the amount of morphine they consider appropriate for each patient and you administer it yourself every time your pain increases. So efficient. This is only the third time I have experienced the effects of morphine but I can fully understand the addiction it creates. On one hand, my body feels at its most relaxed, heavy and spread out like a cat lying in the sun; on the other, my mind is clear, creative, quick. The nurse told me this couldn't be the case. Morphine is an opiate, she explained, almost irritated. Morphine makes you lose your lucidity. You can't possibly remain sharp under its effect. Morphine kills people, she added in that kind of know-it-all tone I can hardly suffer. Never mind. I am lucid, whether the nurses like it or not. Perhaps it's just because the dose is minimal, or because of the combined effect of morphine and steroids, what do I know?

The night I came round after two days of post-operation intensive care was heaven. It was ten past two and there were four other patients in the room. One of them was about my age, I guess. His eyes protruded beneath bushy eyebrows, full of anguish and disorientation. He stood on his bed and treated us to an aria at the top of his voice. Only the one who wasn't in severe pain was able to laugh out loud and when the nurse rushed in, he explained that the tenor had been a famous singer once, pulling her leg.

Another bloke, the one on my left, was sick after the anaesthetic or sheer panic perhaps, but the other two were quite alert, hyperactive even, especially one of them, the thinnest of the two. A skinny chap with a red moustache, which emphasized his hollow cheeks and bony chin. He must have weighed one stone... He said he'd had a minor surgery, but didn't say what. He got up four or five times, bent forward to arrange his shoes under the bed, turned the lights on, then off, then on again; otherwise, he was fine and we chatted avidly, quite sensibly, -at least we thought so at the time- although the following day we could not remember a word of what we had said.

The other old chap's wife turned up the following afternoon with a jar of black olives and a slab of blue cheese because he had messaged her asking for those... except that he must've been out of sorts because he passionately hates olives and smelly cheese. I would've thought that after a lifetime living together his wife could've known his pet hates, but obviously not. The tenor, on the other hand, could not believe he had sung for us since he'd always been tone deaf. We assured him that his version of Tosca was like nothing we had ever heard in our entire lives. Cancer was turning out to be fun.

We were on the fourth floor and the wind howled like a Siberian wolf. There were times when I could have sworn that I felt the building swaying. The streetlights stretching into the distance looked like an enchanted maze. Hardly any car drove past. The outline of the Botanic Gardens beyond the canal and the top of Rosenborg's spires in all its regal splendour were clear enough to see in the night light. It felt reassuringly familiar, like being a child again and at the same time, it felt like being abroad, in some magical place. I know that at that moment I wished I were a poet, or a painter, or a musician because the lights and the darkness outside and the gales and the stars above were inspiring. I felt inebriated by that orderly, sober beauty.

Since then, I've been drifting in and out of consciousness. Sometimes, the voices around me say things that merge into my dreams, but once I am well awaken, I recognize the difference. I can even retell my dreams if someone wants to hear about them, so I must not be that bad. Not yet.

Today is exactly six days since I checked in at the hospital. Grette was upset when she came home and found out what was happening to me. I had told her that I only needed a few tests, which were going to be done on the same day so that she needn't worry about me while she was in Napoli or thereabouts, finishing one of her deals. It amazes me how much profit a bit of sunshine can bring along. The number of Scandinavians renting properties in Southern Italy has been rising considerably in recent years, she tells me. Apparently, we behave differently once we are there, more outgoing and carefree, but I have my reservations. I believe that people feel like that while they are on holidays regardless of where they are, but if they decide to stay and settle down in their new place, their own true self takes over, and why should they not be what they have always been like, I wonder. Why should we always feel the need to change our characters, to adapt to different partners, friends, peoples, societies? I cannot see the point of this pseudo- schizophrenic attempt at becoming someone else, someone different. I am not being arrogant or self-centred thinking that we are already too good as we are, nor do I think that we shouldn't try to be convivial and embrace other cultures, but I like a change provided it is motivated by a desire to learn, to improve ourselves as human beings, or educate ourselves in some new discipline, a new language, a new skill... Change in order to go forward, not sideways.

We, Danes, are often given to much introspection but our periods of melancholy and reflection do not last long. Or do they? We tend to look ahead, not backwards and yet we love to keep our traditions alive. How contradictory is that? In any case, we are not particularly chauvinistic, and yes, we are "officially happy", so why change for the sake of changing? Why should I, for example, not be entitled to keep my illness secret if I feel like it?

On the other hand, no matter how much all this nonsense annoys me, I might end up being the one altering my personality, becoming someone else, thanks to the tumour, the cancer and the drugs. My son Anders would tell me off for ruminating in this manner.

I raised the subject with Grette this morning, not about my changes but about the changes in young people's current attitudes. She just shrugged it off and said that the elderly (by which she meant me) have always reacted to the younger generation in the same way, and carried on waxing lyrical about the Danes abroad, without considering my point. That is what separates me from Grette at times. It is not a lack of intelligence, nor a lack of concentration on her part, but simply a question of sensitivity, or depth, or the lack of these two. She seems to live in a perpetual state of denial when it comes to human emotions. Perhaps she has taught herself to be that way in order to survive after all she's had to endure. Who cares what I think, anyway? What does my opinion, any opinion, matter?

Mean, selfish as it might sound, I wouldn't dare to live on my own at this time of my life, so I find solace and reassurance in letting Grette be, putting up with her flaws in the same way she surely puts up with mine. Who am I to pass any judgement, anyhow? Right now, when doctors cannot yet be confident that I will live a few more years or die in a few days, I should not contemplate the complexities of my third marriage. Or perhaps I should?

Grette will have the privilege of being my last woman, my last companion, unless she leaves me of course, but I don't see that happening. We care for each other enough and enjoy life as it is. Besides, caring for someone can, in some cases, be better than loving someone passionately, which can lead to falling out of love. Passion is for the youngsters, like summer. Caring is a more real feeling, more tangible, less brittle, less vulnerable. When I was young, love was driven by passion and exposed to sacrifice; gloom could taste sweet at times and doom was part of the game. Hurting and getting hurt, deliberately or innocently, are inevitable ingredients of young love but at this time of life I could not bear to disappoint Grette or break her heart. She has come to visit me every day, morning and evening, apparently. I only have fragmented recollections of the first few days.

'Anders phoned before I left. He'll pop round this evening' Grette said. 'And Torben phoned last night and will try to ring you up here later today. He thinks it's terribly silly of you not to tell anybody. And so do I. You could've died alone', she added.

'We all die alone'

'Don't be ridiculous. This isn't the time for your philosophy'

If not now, when, I wondered, but did not say it as I noticed her palm was damp as she held my left hand, my right one being taken by a canula. 'I just didn't want to cause any upset. Besides, I had William to consider. Last thing he needed was to hear his father was also about to die. I didn't want to worry him any further'.

I have always protected William. Perhaps because I was already getting sentimental and more careful about things by the time he was born. He was such an endearing little boy, with his grey eyes and his long curls. It's such a shame that he's never forgiven Anna for our divorce.

We chatted on, Grette and I, about this and about that. I suppose she was trying to make light conversation so that I would not think about my condition, but the truth is I am not fretting about it. I need radiotherapy, I know. If that fails, then I will need chemotherapy and if that also fails, then I shall die. Simple. There are still lots of things I could think of doing, of course. Places to visit. People to meet. Wines to taste. Mountains to climb, but deep down, I feel that I have frankly and truly had my time and must therefore get used to the idea that what awaits me is my past. A long, good look at my past before I die.

Meanwhile, I appreciate the sun coming through the window and lying in rectangles on my bed and the scent of freesias on my bedside table and the nurses parading to and fro, bright, young and crispy like in a cheap fantasy. What more could an old man ask for?

Grette bent forward to drop a kiss on my forehead and promised to come back later, after attending Kar's funeral on my behalf. She said this from the door before leaving the room, in a slightly casual tone, but I ignored it, because on hearing of Kar I was overwhelmed by gloom and nostalgia. I remembered the last time I saw him, only a few days ago. Were I to have a heart attack right now, I thought with amusement, we would make a dynamic duo, Kar and I, knocking on the gates of Heaven, suitably naked and pale for the occasion. Goodness me.

I shall miss Kar. If only I had ever told him how much I valued his loyalty all these years! I had gone out for a deliberate, conscious stroll, admiring the light that bathed the harbour so broadly, so powerfully. The air was clear, pure. (My sons tease me about my obsession with light and air). There were seagulls around and the sky looked immaculate. Cafés had their tables out and people sat laughing, chatting, not rushing, drinking the sun. It was a familiar summer scene and I was still part of it, just as I like it.

Even during those years I was living in London I always came back to my home town. Either to see to a few cases, pay a visit to my old dentist or to call on my father but above all, to be here and clear my thoughts against the vast sky of Copenhagen.

That morning as I walked along that narrow piece of seafront, I found it different. Awesome. Breathtaking. I tried hard to record every detail in my mind so that the following day, and the day after, and the one after that, when I would lie here, in bed, and the footsteps and voices of nurses and doctors would stab the silence of the ward, I could close my eyes and see and smell and hear and breathe in my Copenhagen. Then I bumped into Kar.

'Hej'
'Hej, keeping all right?'.

Keeping alright. Those were the words Kar used whenever he asked about people's health or business or whatever people wanted to understand, but that day the words sounded full of meaning. Keeping alright. Surely, he can't know, I thought, but it was poignant nonetheless. Iwas very fond of Kar, in that demanding, almost conditional way in which Anna used to say I care for my friends, but at that moment I wished Kar had walked on instead of remaining there, standing next to me, trying to start a conversation on which I would not be able to concentrate.

'Been to the theatre lately?' I asked him, knowing that he could get carried away criticizing or praising without end some play he had just seen, so that I could pretend to be listening when in fact I would just dwell on my thoughts and enjoy the view unfolding in front of us. The three crowns above Christiansborg, the spires piercing the sky and in the air a waft of her perfume, which came from some other woman passing by, and yet it wasn't quite like hers.

'Not since last month. What a waste of time and money that was! Absolute rubbish, minimal décor, terrible lighting. And the leading actress was too old for her part and couldn't remember her lines. Pure crap it was. What's the title? The revenge of Mr Andersen. Have you heard of it? A postmodern take on the writer's private life. Hans Christian himself must've turned in his grave'.

'I've heard of it. Actually, Cecille went to see it and she also said it was shit', I said, immediately regretting to have mentioned her name.

'And you? What have you been up to? You've always preferred concerts to drama, haven't you?' A little skip in his voice betrayed his surprise on hearing Cecille's name, but I pretended not to notice it and concentrated on my steps and the scene around us. Then I gave in.

'I had lunch with her at *Piegare's,* the new Italian in Nyhavn, you must know of it. Good food, but disproportionate portions. It annoys me to see such a waste' I added, trying to divert from the question of Cecille.

Kar and I have shared secrets or half-secrets all our lives, and the only reason I hesitated about talking of Cecille was to keep my encounter with her to myself as the last joyful moment to take with me from this world in case everything went wrong at the hospital, yet once her name had slipped out of my tongue, sensing Kar's curiosity, I could no longer keep quiet, which was an extraordinary urgency. I'm not usually like that. I am a man. An old man. Reserved, in control, discreet, but I suddenly felt the need to tell Kar about her even if those were my last words. Or perhaps because they could have been.

'It wasn't exactly a joyful lunch we had. For the first time, we found we had to break the ice before we relaxed and felt at ease with each other. Then it got intense, it always does with Cecille, but not exactly bubbly and lively like it used to. There was no reproach or sadness or any crap like that, but it wasn't that joyous. You could tell that her happiness is elsewhere now... Grette was away' I added, as if I had to justify myself. Not that Grette's absence would justify meeting Cecille a deux.

'I see', Kar said. 'How is she?' he finally asked and I liked him for giving me the opportunity to indulge in the evocation of that fragile, pure, bitter-sweet piece of poetry in my life.

'She said she's going through an exceptionally happy time, and it showed. She was... very calm'. I was trying to find the exact adjective there because Cecille had always been too complex, too difficult to describe in a few words. The story, or lack of it, wasn't worth telling unless I conveyed every detail with complete accuracy. I wanted Kar to comprehend exactly how I felt and in order to achieve that I needed to tell the truth. I wanted to stick to the truth.

'She looked very self-possessed. *Comblée* as she would say. She looked better than ever. Bit subdued at first but happy, in an absolute, serene way, and God knows she deserves some happiness in this life'

'She must be...?'

'Forty-four..., forty-five'.

I took a deep breath and closed my eyes for a second in order to picture Cecille in my mind. Forty-five years of age sounds like early youth to me now. Besides, Cecille looks younger. Not like she looked when she really was younger, but a different kind of young. Fresher, more relaxed, definitely happier than I remember her being at twenty-one. When I said to her that she was still the same, only improved, she chuckled rather confidently.

I suggested to Kar that we stopped for a cup coffee and he agreed. We turned back to the café where we used to go for Sunday brunch during the light seasons. It has solid wood tables and a shabby cozy feeling. I don't like modern cafes in chrome and glass and abstract paintings. We found a table on the pavement, facing the boats and the crowds and the sun. Kar sat down slowly to give his knee time to flex without hurting and then he took off his jacket. I worried that I was going to look too thin if I did the same and regretted not putting on a pullover so that my bony shoulders would not be as obvious as they would surely look under a light shirt, especially compared with Kar's, who had put on weight as he got older. I decided to keep my jacket on and felt irritated by the number of silly details like these to which this cancer has made me pay attention.

Kar ordered for both of us. A cup of white creamy coffee for him, a black one for me and a Wienerbrød each. We were familiar with those details about each other and Kar also knew that I have always been fussy about food and drink. I don't drink without eating, I don't eat without drinking. Not point in doing it otherwise.

By the time I finished my first cup of coffee, I had told Kar everything about my conversation with Cecille. It had been just an hour, too short a time for old acquaintances who haven't seen each other for many years to catch up with their personal news, and it felt even shorter for someone who was probably seeing an old acquaintance for the last time, except that Cecille didn't have that piece of information. Acquaintance. I am not satisfied with that word, but we are not friends either and I would not know what other word to use to describe our old relationship.

'Why do you think you feel like this about her?' Kar asked. 'I mean, I never thought you cared so very much. Not in this kind of way. We've talked about her at times but you never seemed to feel like this. I remember you saying that she wasn't a good shag. Now you look tearful'

Kar's sudden interest, though kept under his usual control, picked me somewhat. Asking me why did I think that I was feeling so moved by her memory or so touched by her furtive presence in town was not only unusual, but almost indiscreet of him.

'No idea' I lied. 'I've always been very fond of her. Have known her since she was a baby, as you know. I used to pick her up when she was a child... she grew up together with my boys... she was funny and sharp and used to boss my boys about like most girls do... Then one day, she was a young woman, hurting and madly in love with someone else when she came up to me for help, I guess, although I misread the message, of course. Trust Ole to make a mess of relationships!'

'I remember the occasion outside Rosenborg', I continued as if I were dictating my memoirs to Kar. 'Until then she had felt like a part of my life because she belonged in my time, my space, my family even. She grew up alongside Anders, kept in touch with him all the time we were in London... In fact, at some point we all thought that they were going to become more than just friends. Her parents said once that she would end up being the mother of my grandchildren... then I saw her that day coming out of Rosenborg Castle. She saw me drive past and when I turned to wave, she ran up to the traffic lights and there jumped into my car in what must have been a fraction of a second'.

I played that scene in my mind's eye again and again. I watched it in slow motion so that I could look at her and see her the way she really looked. The way perhaps she never looked.

'She kissed my cheek and put her hand over mine as I changed gears' I can see us clearly again: It was the end of Winter and there was continuous birdsong in the chestnut-trees as the sun was setting, but the temperature was still quite low. She'd been to see the Blue Exhibition at the castle. Her eyes were bright. She said she felt exhilarated by the cold breeze.

'After a year of seeing each other in secret, like a criminal who runs for his life, instinctively and breathlessly in a last attempt to save himself knowing that he is about to be caught, Cecille announced that she would be my mistress or my secretary or my slave, anything, as long as I allowed her to stay with me. But I knew better, I wriggled out of it, of course, except I didn't do it soon enough. She thought she needed me because she needed to be needed, wanted, loved, and she just wanted to speed up her life: Grow old before her time beside me so that life could become shorter and lighter. She would've died with me, if necessary, she told me and yes, she felt that way, but only because that would've been easier, more accessible, less frightening, less hurtful than staying alive. She was in a very dark place at the time. Totally crazy, as she said over lunch, laughing at herself now'.

I could hear myself telling Kar all of this without haste, as if I had been presenting a case to a judge, or like one of those actors who read plays on the radio in the middle of the afternoon. I spared Kar redundant or private snippets, naturally, but I allowed my mind to indulge in every image of that distant year when I used to stand by the window and wait for Cecille to walk up the driveway, determined, grave, always in white like a bride *manquée.* She would throw herself into my arms as I opened the door. I said that she would throw herself into my arms because that was exactly how her embrace used to feel. That was evidently how she felt in those days: like a broken flower, like a wounded bird, as if her life depended entirely on my holding her, but I understood that later. All I knew at the time was that when she pretended to be so happy waking up by my side, she was in fact buying herself some time, replacing the one she truly loved and never cared for her with someone whom she thought would never turn her down. A horror of being rejected one more time, a horror of loneliness and lovelessness had been her reasons to be mine. And I too rejected her.

'The summer turned into autumn and the autumn into winter and by the time we had gone full circle Cecille started saying all those self-convincing lies. "I need you because I love you. Would you marry me?" Those were her words. In that order, I remember them well. "I need you because I love you"' I struggled to suppress all feeling in my tone on saying this.

'That's tremendous. I'd no idea. Although you two did have some kind of special affinity after all. I remember that'

'We did indeed, but it was all a bit mad. Don't even know if the attraction was sexual, in fact I think it wasn't. It was all too fragile to sustain something as complicated and solid as a long-lasting relationship: Mainly, we both needed to escape from the threat of oblivion. I was divorced from Anna, hadn't met Grette yet. The rest of our affinity lay on a few superficial factors: some similar tastes, some intellectual affinity... and a generation gap between us. How long could we last?'

What if Cecille had remained here, nearby, instead of packing up her suitcases and bidding farewell to everything that she had wanted, longed for and needed with a desperation bordering on insanity when I didn't return her feelings? It was a thought not worth considering. Instead, I felt sick of myself on telling Kar how I had left her when she had begged me to hold her tightly, to keep her in my life forever. "'Don't leave me"', she said one day. "Don't leave me". She wasn't being melodramatic, I knew. She really needed help and I did leave her nonetheless. I lied to her in order to set her free when all she wanted was to be captive... and to save myself the trouble of facing up to the facts, of course. I let her down. I realized that the other day, sitting in front of her at the restaurant. She didn't put it into words and I recognized some real affection for me. Her eyes, the colour of blue water when she smiles, the colour of blue velvet when she is sad, have always been the most expressive ones I have seen in man or woman, and I could hear that in her silence, in all those words she never uttered, there was the certainty that I too had betrayed her. She thrust her youth into my hands and I threw it away.

By accepting my invitation, she was now telling me that she had chosen to forget about those days. She has chosen to overlook my egotism; she had opted for dismissing the memory of my betrayal and along with it all memory of our naked bodies under the willow in the soothing siesta or between the coolness of my sheets. She is past that. She is beyond and above a stage in her life that has been full of lies. She has forgiven me because she has forgiven herself her own mistakes. Her magnanimity has become my punishment. I didn't tell Kar what she and I have chosen to forget, and when he asked me whether I felt guilty or remorseful I lied that I did not. I was light years older than her, what else was I to do?

'Seeing her after so many years had triggered a lot of memories, stirred some old feelings, that's all' I said, 'I'm still fond of her, we have met on other occasions since those days but it felt different this last time because she has changed so much. She needs nobody now. She's found herself, and it felt slightly poignant to be so absolutely and inexorably cut out of her life' How selfish is that? I didn't confess my unabated sense of guilt nor my determination to put the records straight if it is the last thing I do before I die. Cecille deserves it.

Kar was baffled by my pathetic outpour of sentiment, so I brought the subject to an end. It has always amused me to find that a man of his intelligence, or perhaps because of it, could not understand ambiguity, nor follow a simple joke, especially when they were made –innocently- at his expense. He would take every word, every gesture at face value and, without getting offended, he would simply not see what was it that other people found so funny. Good old Kar. Subtlety wasn't an attribute by which he could've been defined and yet he could deal with the most obscure and intricate facts. The mind of a scientist, no doubt. Curious to a fault, but literal.

We chatted on until it was time for him to go and meet an old colleague with whom he had arranged to have lunch. I remained seated and read the paper. Kar walked out of the café and disappeared from my view but then, perhaps thinking that I was in a melancholy state of mind, or because he got suddenly possessed by an imperceptible warning, he stepped back to where I could see him again and waved briefly, somewhat meaningfully at me. I waved back.

More than half an hour went by while I tried to make sense of this world I was reading about and then called the waiter, but instead of settling our bill, I ordered some lunch. Salmon in a dill and ginger sauce and a sprinkle of chili and baby potatoes. I was allowed to eat large or rich meals if I felt like it, but they might trigger vomits again, which would have been the most unfortunate thing to happen to me at this age, especially since that was, is, a very peculiar type of vomiting. With no nausea, no queasy warning, one finds oneself puking all over the place. It´s been pure luck that every time it's happened, I was on my own. At home, in the living room, yes, but alone. And on two occasions at the club's gents. It's funny how you can get away even with something as disgusting as vomiting in public if you are still young, but you do so when you are old and the whole world around you run up to see if you are about to die, making the event all the more conspicuous and embarrassing. So, too much food as well as very rich dishes were now pleasures of the past. I do not mind that very much, but what I do miss, is a glass of good red wine with supper.

I enjoyed my lunch observing everybody around me and thinking of all the people who have shaped, complemented and enriched my life. I thought of my first wife, Ulla, and the miserable, anachronistic way in which she died after giving birth to our second son. And I thought of them, my sons. Anders, following in my steps; Torben, living abroad. And William, of course. I still wonder whether he will retrieve his filial love from the bottom of his heart and make peace with Anna when I'm gone. It happened to my brother when Mother died. He made it up with our father as if they had never fallen out with each other.

I can just about respect William's decision not to discuss his relationship with his mother with me, but he's old enough and should know that neither Anna nor I will be here forever… Regardless of how wearing her outbursts of rage may have been, Anna gave him his life and have always adored him in her way. Such a talented woman, so beautiful and yet so little tenderness in her life! (At seventy-five years of age, a barrister by profession, who has seen endless couples tear at each other throats over the years, the lack of justice in this life never ceases to amaze me). I also thought of Julie and her unconditional availability whenever I had an afternoon free for sex in her own bedroom; of Petra, bringing up a daughter who, according to her, was also mine until DNA finally proved that she wasn't; and of Lilla, and of Ralph and his loyalty throughout years of clandestine sex, clandestine love. He had shown me a side of myself which I had never dared to see or challenge until he grabbed my hand at the Petersens' party and drew it to his crotch. Darling Ralph. His wife took his children away with her and left him when she found us in bed. Their bed. Yet Ralph kept our secret from my family, my friends, and above all, my sons. I thought of him while I enjoyed my dessert and of what he must be doing in America these days and then my thoughts drew back in circle as I remembered Cecille mentioning my relationship with Ralph, or her suspicions about it, in a five-page letter she sent me from Sweden years ago. She has always been remarkably intuitive and dangerously accurate in her observations, but she would never mention it to anyone else.

I remained there, sitting alone, brooding and thinking of her until at some point, when the waiter came to bring me the bill, I refocused on my present and my improbable future and realized that if I were to allocate a day to think only about the closest members of my family and my closest friends -and lovers- I might still run out of time. It was a pointless, bittersweet conclusion, but I felt blessed by whichever god has been watching over me. I dwelt on it as I walked home, full of years, full of the past and full of gratitude, feeling the smooth pavement under my soles, raising my eyes to the sky, which was now swathed in a fine haze. I found it all too beautiful one minute, and suffocating the next.

A little bit after eleven that night, when I had already done my packing for the hospital: pyjamas, dressing gown, toothbrush, flannel, toiletries, plenty of books and paper and pens and ink, -I have always preferred fountain pens to ballpoint pens-, the telephone rang.

Chapter 2

Anders

Anders came last night as he had promised. He looked exhausted, gaunt, older than his age. His new lady does that to him. She is too demanding, too ambitious, too spoilt. She wants everything and she wants it now. She forgets that he has child maintenance to pay for and lots of other contributions to his child's education and his ex-wife's roof and all that kind of money for all that kind of reasons that make divorce a profitable business to set up. I really think that his present partner is being unreasonable, but who am I to say anything?

I went through equally acrimonious times when Anna divorced me. Besides, Nja is undeniably striking in a bold, in your face sort of way. I bet she is equally demanding in bed. I know her type. I have seen her go and embrace men or put an arm around them. Briefly, innocently, perhaps, but it makes me uncomfortable. In Italy or France that would not mean a thing, but we are Danes and I have noticed that when she kisses men, including me, she leaves her cheek, wholly, heavily, against mine a bit longer than it is necessary. Anders would think I am being sick but I've been around a while and know that for some men it might come across as an invitation, as sending a message: Look how hot I could be.

Besides, Anders himself has said as much about her, right at the beginning when they were meeting behind his then wife's back. Silly Anders. Why would he have to do what I did? What is so attractive about my disgraceful, rotten habits that he has to go and do the same all over again, especially after being so critical and judgmental of my own antics? Can't he see the wrong I've done? It pains me seeing my eldest son so uncompromising and selfish, but if I make any comment on his behaviour, he always replies "Look who's talking" and there the conversation ends.

His daughter came with him last night. It was lovely to see her so grown up. She is a very vivacious, clever girl. Clementina's eyes are sapphire blue, like Anders' and like Ulla's, her glossy wavy hair already reaches below her waist.

'I once saw a girl who looked just like you' I told her. 'Long time ago. In the sixties, it was. Her hair was longer than her skirt, can you imagine? She was walking along the Strøget, with other friends and I tried to catch up with her and see her face, too, but I lost track of her hair and her high-booted legs as she merged into the crowd or disappeared into some building. I was quite young then'.

Clementina listened amused. Although my comment made her look at my own head, subtle as she is, she didn't mention my sudden baldness. I've probably scared her, what with my bandages and hollowed eyes. I teased her saying that she is my favourite grandchild, and she laughed. It is our silly little joke, since she is my only grandchild. Then I added that she looked absolutely beautiful and she blushed, all feminine shyness and delight spreading over her face.

'I brought you a car's magazine in case you get bored. It's quite good, Dad thinks' she said, and I thought that for all I am worth, it would be a shame to deprive her of her grandfather at such an early age. It's good for children to have us around. Her other grandparents moved to some small town or other in the Italian Riviera before she was born and she only sees them once a year.

As for Grette... well, Clementina feels inhibited by her and Grette isn't naturally good in her role of step-grandma, which makes any attempt at the happy family-game quite awkward, if not impossible. Preposterous, as William used to say when he was a little boy copying his mother. He used the word whenever he remembered, regardless of whether it fitted the context or not. He was such fun!

'When are you going home?' Clementina asked me 'Then you can take me to Tivoli again.' I nearly cried. At my age, men become terribly sensitive whereas women seem to have cooled down, got rid of all their hormonal turmoil and cope better with widowhood, solitude and even illness.

'Come on now, Clem, farfar's getting tired. Why don't you go to the cafeteria and get yourself a drink? I'll join you in a minute'.

I had to take a deep breath and hardly avoided being sick at the mere mention of drinks, as I pictured coffee and cakes.

'Dad!'

'That's fine. It's the coffee. I can smell it, I swear'

Poor Anders. All this nonsense about diseases, tubes and syringes must stir up old memories for him. He had a hard time when Ulla died. He was only six. Old enough to be aware of the facts but too young to process an incident of such magnitude. Seeing your mother die. Losing her forever, finding yourself half-orphaned... Nothing compares to that. Besides, I probably didn't do enough to help him. I was too distressed myself to know what to do with two young boys. Worse than young: Torben was a newborn baby and for weeks and weeks I could not bring myself to hold him because buried deeply at the back of my mind, was a feeling of resentment. I blamed him for his mother's death. I knew it was brutal and irrational, but I could not help the feeling. In that respect, Anders did better than me. He embraced his little brother with such tenderness and determination to protect him that it was almost too poignant to witness.

He would not go and stay at a friend's or a cousin's unless baby Torben was also invited. He used to say that that was what their Mummy would've wanted. That Torben would've felt even lonelier if on top of being separated from his Mummy he was also separated from us. Anders used to come back from school and tell the nanny to have a rest just like Ulla had done when he himself was younger.

Then he would do his homework or play with his soldiers in the baby's room and keep an eye on him. In acknowledgement of his care, or in compensation for it, baby Torben gurgled away, chubby and rosy against the white embroidered covers.

Terrible thing to be robbed of one's childhood, but I could see later on that playing the role of a grown-up big brother had been Anders' way of coping. He believed that doing something altruistic and precocious would make his mother proud of him. His sense of responsibility kept him sane, despite the nights when he used to cry himself to sleep.

I made a point in those days and for years afterwards, of going and seeing them both several times during the night, but only on very few occasions did Anders curl up into my arms and sob. Otherwise, he would just weep quietly, like a man, after I left the room. It was heart breaking and there was nothing I could do. Whenever my sister could have them, I would send the three of them, -the boys and their nanny- to stay with her for a long weekend so Anders would run free in the fields, go fishing with Harald, feed the pigs and get covered in mud or sand or wet grass without being told off for getting dirty. Elba and Harald's farm was Paradise to my boys in those days, and if Elba was an angel, Harald was the hero who could achieve everything, from helping a sow to give birth, to making a wigwam with an old blanket and a couple of sticks.

In their absence, I would drink myself stupid until the eve of their return. Kar's unfailing call on Sunday afternoon was my time reference. After his call, I knew it was time to stop and sober up. I've been lucky enough not to have succumbed to chronic alcoholism. Throughout my seventy-five years of age, I have been both blessed with astonishing good fortune and blighted with tragedy in equal measures.

'I bumped into Erika this afternoon. She and Jensen will pop in to see you one of these days' Anders said, and by the over casual tone in which he said it, I guessed he had been phoning people around in order to inform them of my condition.

'There's no need to go telling everyone, you know. People start speculating about all sorts of outcomes. I'll be all right'

'Erika is like a sister to you, Dad! I phoned Anna, too. She's got a right to know and would be upset if we didn't let her know. Let's be honest, Dad, you might not pull through this one. Would it not be healthier if we all got prepared for any eventuality? Say farewell, give one another a hug, tell each other what we need to tell...?'

I almost laughed at his candour. You can trust Anders for a reality check, I thought, but at that moment an iron bar hit me in the skull, right where the tumour had been, I presume. I sometimes feel like one of those amputees who claim that they can feel the missing limb. Along with the blow there was a warm, almost burning sensation inside the back of my head as if hot blood had been gushing out of a broken artery. When it was over, I could've described that as a brain haemorrhage, although, obviously it was not.

'Dad! Dad! Nurse!' I heard Anders quite clearly but was paralyzed by the pain. The nurse rushed in and injected me straight away. Anders held my hand and I pressed his tightly until the effect of the drug started to kick in. It was my fault. I had decided I could do without it during the day and sure enough the pain, as if it were a self-willing entity, seized the opportunity to hit me. Stupid old me.

'There, there' said the nurse, holding my other hand.

'He'll be alright, but you should go now' she told Anders.

I managed to mumble that I was sorry about it and eventually, saw the expression of relief on my son's weary face. I forgot what he was saying before I succumbed to the pain, but remembered what he'd told me a few minutes earlier. It was evident that he had phoned friends and family who will probably come in a crowd to see me off and kiss my forehead and pat my hand. I couldn't think of a more depressing, futile, selfish way to go, could he? I liked my friends to shake my hands, I liked my women kissing me, not the nauseating, patronizing token in the decrepitude of death. Anders apologized.

'Det er Ok. You meant well. You've always meant well. Please don't go yet. Tell me something nice, something funny' I heard myself slurring the words by now, my speech getting more slow, less clear.

Anders can be hilarious. He developed his sense of humour when he reached his teens. We were living in

London in those days. Torben was seven, fair-haired and beautiful, and little William was three. Anders was the skinny teenager who, instead of driving us mad with rebellious moods, made us laugh out loud with his spontaneous remarks and his well-known jokes that he managed to retell as new ones. He may have found humour a way of attracting attention and holding it, Anna said. She was good at observing and interpreting his moods.

Anders made up some songs in those days, heavy metal, he said that was, and she would play them on the piano, bashing the keys and pulling aggressive faces and singing together. His songs were Anders' way of touching Anna and Anna's tuneless racket was her way of wrapping her arms around the motherless boy he was. They both looked happy then and I believe they were.

In any case, I was glad that Anders attended to my wish and stayed on with his beautiful daughter, against the nurses's instructions. He probably stayed moved by the same feeling one experiences next to someone dying before our eyes, but his company was comforting, nonetheless. I struggled to keep my eyes open but was fully conscious and pleaded with Anders to keep talking.

'Has Clementina told you of her award?' he asked me as she walked back into my room. Her voice reached me before I could turn my head and see her approaching my bed, a hot chocolate in one hand, a paper bag in the other.

'These are for you, Grandad. I asked a doctor who was having a break at the café and he said that if what you have is a brain tumour, you have no problem in eating any kind of stuff', she announced as she left a brown bag on my bed, as proud of her initiative as I felt proud of her spontaneity.

The bag was full of liquorice and cinnamon sticks and I couldn't bring myself to tell her that some flavours, like some scents, make me desperately sick. I managed to roll the edges of the bag in order to keep the smells tightly locked inside and said that I would have them all for pudding. She smiled in between generous sips of hot chocolate.

For once, just for that once since I've been diagnosed, I wished I were a child again and all of a sudden, I found myself yearning for my mother and her tender care, longing for those days when my father was at home, Ernst, my dear brother, hadn't yet gone away, and Elba was so full of life and carefree, dreaming of growing up and marrying her prince on a white horse.

I could feel all that at the same time I listened to Anders telling me about Clementina's achievements: a winning poem and a swimming prize. I congratulated her and said that she would be the next most famous little mermaid in Denmark. She reached over my bed and gave me a kiss, leaving a warm, sticky, chocolatey trace on my cheek. I closed my eyes to enjoy the sensation for a little longer, -ah, the joy of having a grandchild-, but Anders noticed that I was tired.

'C'mon, elsker, now we must let Farfar rest' he whispered to Clementina and they tiptoed out of the room.

After that, I must have fallen asleep because I cannot recall anything else. I wish I could stay awake day and night in case these actually are the last hours I will be with my children. Mr Henriksen said this morning that this falling asleep all of a sudden is only drugs induced, but I'm not sure. I used to have the same symptoms for some time before the diagnosis. On the other hand, I've read masses of papers about these things in the last few months and no information is conclusive.

Chapter 3

Elba

'There's a series of symptoms that are typical and inevitable, but many others vary from patient to patient', Mr Henriksen explained this morning.

'Like love'.

A hint of smile crossed over his face while he checked my reflexes, pushed my eyes open and checked my temperature and everything else he considered necessary to gather some clue on my progress. Or my decay.

'You haven't become aggressive or forgetful or depressed... Your sense of taste is back, your sense of smell, too...'

It was exciting listening to such observations, who would not feel hopeful? I could see myself walking out of here, wandering along Nyhavn, stopping at Brød's for mid-morning coffee, losing track of time at bookshops, finding a gift for Grette at some chic little shop, marshmallows for Clementina... I was already out and about.

'And you're quite sharp'. Mr Henriksen added I immediately hated him for his patronizing tone. Quite sharp. Of course, I am bloody sharp. Perhaps I am not so well balanced after all. This swift change of mood from appreciation to ire might be a symptom too. I turned my head and stopped listening to this Henriksen, and then recalled that many of my women, (wives, girl-friends, mistresses), have all spotted that feature of my character throughout my whole life. How can you love and hate the same person with such passion? You don't just get irritated, you fly into a pure wrath! You are a horrid, immature, selfish pig! Anna used to shout at me. Clever Anna. Immature pig, Lilla also shouted at me once, as she threw a bunch of flowers with vase included, at my head. Maybe it's just that, then. A Viking temper, unsuitable for a barrister, that's why I never became a judge. Sheer immaturity. Pig... pigotry. Ha, that's a good one. I will mention it to Anders next time. Pigotry. Your father is given to pigotry. I'd better write it down, lest I forget.

'You mustn't!' an imposing, tall nurse came straight away, throwing her arms about exaggeratedly and pushing me back onto my pillows, which had already been plumped and slipped into fresh pillowcases by an older, heavier, gloomier nurse.

I protested and warned her that I had such a revolutionary idea in my mind that if I didn't put it in black and white the world would be deprived of my contribution and she would be responsible. She giggled, a throaty, sexy giggle. Then I saw through the open door that the consultant was checking on the other patients and wondered whether she was just trying to impress him with her efficiency. In any case, ten minutes later, making a big fuss of how she was risking being told off for disobedience, she came back and handed me the pad and the fountain pen I brought from home. Another smile like that and I will get seriously better, I thought with amusement, but failed to find enough strength in my voice to tell her.

She answered my mobile and passed it on. She tucked it neatly between my shoulder and my ear and as soon as I heard my sister's voice, I was riddled with guilt.

Elba is only a couple of years older than me but she always sounds so maternal, so protective and endearing that one feels guilty for not seeing her more often, for not calling her, for not sending a line every now and then. I think that it is her raw sensitivity, which comes out so transparent, almost tangible, that moves me almost to tears every time we contact each other.

'Why didn't you say?' 'Do you think I would've let you go into hospital on your own?'

'Jeg er ikke et barn, my dear'

'No, you just behave like one sometimes'

I was sure that Elba disapproved of Grette being away while I was unwell so I explained that Grette didn't know anything about it at that stage. The conciliatory lawyer in me has always kept making excuses for our loved ones' misdeeds for the sake of maintaining harmony, regardless of our age. A pig and a peacemaker at the same time... ought to ponder on that!

We chatted on for longer than I was allowed to, but the nurses were busy somewhere else and I was feeling calmer and livelier all the time.

Our conversations always go back to the same things. Once we have fed each other updated news about our children and grandchildren, we both go back to those days when life was easy. Elba married when she was only eighteen, looking more angelical than ever on the day of her wedding, and moved with her husband to a farm about ten kilometres away from us. Every evening, while her husband finished up some work in the fields or stopped at the pub for a drink and a game of cards, she would call for tea. She used to bring a churn full of butter from her farm saying that it tasted much better than the one mass processed by machines. We would then spread a fat layer of that creamy treat onto freshly baked bread and sprinkle it with sugar or with salt, depending on our preferences. It was heavenly!

'Do you still sing from dawn to dusk?' I asked her.
'Why change a habit of a lifetime?'

Elba's got a powerful voice, knows every song under the sun and sings with such feeling! If only she had tried to do something about it, she would've certainly made it onto the big stages, Anna observed more than once, but instead, Elba chose farm work and bringing up her daughters as her main commitment, that is, assuming that one chooses what we do with our lives, which only now I am starting to doubt.

On one occasion, when she was about to give birth to her first daughter, she came to see us on foot, staggering all the way along the lane which was covered in a metre of snow. Mother and I rushed out to meet her as soon as we saw her silhouette, heavy with pregnancy and a bag on her shoulder, walking into our driveway. Mother panicked about her condition and said it was the most idiotic thing she had ever seen a human being do, but Elba laughed it off and explained that she preferred to be closer to town in case the baby decided to arrive during the night. Her husband's car had broken down that very morning and she had lent their truck to Søren, who needed to take his children to school. Madness, Dad said. Sheer madness.

At half past two in the morning, without waiting for the midwife, the baby was born. Elba called her Lara, after Pasternak's heroine.

'Do you see much of Søren these days?' I asked. 'I dreamt of him the other night. We were such good friends once'

'Søren died three years ago. I told you about it, remember? You were in Rome or somewhere. The eleventh of May it was. I called you on the very day'

I did not remember and that frightened me. I could remember any other comment that Elba had at times made about Søren (her brother-in-law and a common friend in our youth) except the news of his death. I wondered whether I should carry on asking her about other people, other events, to check whether I had forgotten other things, but I didn't have the courage to do so. I may have forgotten everything I've heard in the last year, or the last two years, or the last week, for that matter. But no, no, I'm fine. I remember Kar, for example. Kar is dead too, as Birgit told me that night after I'd been with him at the café only hours earlier.

'Kar's dead too'.

'I read about him on the paper. Another thing you didn't tell me!' Elba reproached me.

'You're right, I should've... it was a great shock to me. Birgit phoned me that evening and said that Kar had collapsed, fallen over and died. He was probably dead by the time he hit the floor. She had been in the kitchen making a cup of coffee when she heard a thumping noise like that of a pile of cushions tumbling onto the carpet, or something like that, she told me. Massive heart-attack. Birgit had to make arrangements and I wasn't able to help and Grette was still abroad at that moment'.

'Easy departure for him, but how sad for Birgit'

'And everyone else'.

I still cannot grasp the concept of life juxtaposing death in a period of time so ridiculously short. How a man with whom I had been having coffee in the morning could be dead by the evening? When you think about how death in our family has always come after long phases of illness, agony, unconsciousness, decrepitude... Kar's sudden death is beyond my tolerance.

'Don't distress yourself now. Just think how blessed he was to leave this world like that'

If I believed in an afterlife, I could console myself with the idea of seeing Kar soon, but I do not believe in fairy tales. Besides, Kar wouldn't like that.

Elba sent me a hug, as usual. She has always been one of those people who never misses a birthday, a wedding anniversary, a funeral. She knows everybody within a ten kilometres radio and beyond. She has kept in touch with people we used to know in our childhood. She would rather neglect herself, her home, whatever, than not going to help someone who is ill, or lonely or miserable. A heart of gold under a flaming hair, father used to tease her, and she would always reply that her heart was not in her head, and Dad would add that surely hers was, because he couldn't remember a single day when she hadn't made a decision based on her heart's desire rather than on reason. They laughed. They resembled each other. We were happy.

'Listen, Elba' I said, and she listened when I promised to go and stay with her and her husband for a whole weekend if I ever come out alive of this damn hospital. If that was alright with her and Harald, of course.

'Of course, it's alright. Since when do you have to ask if we're willing to welcome you? We shall make all the arrangements tomorrow'

I made to tell her that she needn't come to see me, but I knew it was a waste of time because she would not be persuaded otherwise. To her, I will forever be her little brother, the one whose school uniform she used to iron and starch every weekend. The one who would borrow money from her to go out on a Saturday when she was already Mrs. Persson. She and her husband became the most supportive part of my family. Harald had a great sense of humour. He was totally unflappable, quiet, kind. He still is. I loved staying with them. It took away the pain of losing Mother and then Ernst. Elba wept in silence, through her songs. I can still see her in her apron, stubborn curls falling over her forehead while she peeled, cored, chopped and boiled potatoes over the dark green range they had installed in their kitchen when it was still a commonplace cooker, long before it became fashionable the second time around.

She used to make the most delicious pear jam I've ever tasted, and would give most of it away. A jar for father, a jar for Mrs such and such, a jar for old Mr such... Just the sound of her voice brought back so many memories! Then, as if reading my silence across the line, she said:

'I'll see you tomorrow, then. I'll bring you some jam. And be a good boy'

A good boy who turned into a mad man and a foolish old sod. I felt exhausted. Talking to my sister is always emotionally charged, because of all the things that she makes me see about myself: The simple happiness of my childhood, my acquired sophistication and detachment, my irretrievable innocence... Paradise lost.

I managed to turn to one side by myself without feeling any hammering onto my head and put the mobile down. I made myself as comfortable as I could and tried to relax in my position, wishing I could get rid of one pillow and lie back without feeling pain, but it would be unwise at this stage. Two hours later, I was still awake in the same position, worn out and confused.

When Anders came again this evening, I recognized his voice, I knew it was him, but I could not talk to him. I only mumbled that I didn't like the Venetian mask he was wearing and he said he wasn't wearing any Venetian mask. Then I saw someone dressed in white from head-to-toe walking across the room, waving at me and I waved back assuming he was a nurse, but Anders told me there was nobody there. Odd. Very odd. And frightening. It's two minutes past midnight now and I can't remember anything else about this evening of post operation consciousness. I have only these two pictures in my mind: Elba's phone call and Anders' visit. The rest of the time has been totally erased from my mind. This is what I dread the most: being unable to remember what happened five minutes ago, repeating things or worse still, not being able to understand what's being said or done around me. And what if Elba never phoned and Anders never came?

Chapter 4

Confidential

It looks bright and clear out there. Eventually, I fell asleep last night, deeply and till very late this morning, so I woke up feeling fresh and free from pain. A quarter past eleven it was when I opened my eyes and saw the clock in front of me and then Grette to my right side. We wished each other a very God morgen, as we always do, half joking, half meaningfully, then exchanged the usual questions, answers and compliments about each other's health (mainly mine) and businesses (mainly hers).

I told her she had lost weight, because it was true and because it makes her happy. She held my hand and as if in exchange for my kind comment, told me about the outside world and what a lovely summer we are having. Sunny, warm, dry. Then she let go of my hand and searched into her handbag. I followed her movements thinking of how she has always looked impeccably turned out in a rather formal, severe sort of way. It's a pity that she wears her hair so short. It makes her face look less angular, her chin less sharp. Less chiselled. That's the way a sculptor would describe it.

'Here's a letter for you', Grette said and I found it quite honest of her, considering that the stamp and the hand written envelope must have given her the clue. She left it on my bed, as if she didn't care, but she did. I know a few women rather well and by now I am knowledgeable enough to see that Grette was niggled by my receiving such a letter; her tone of voice was too casual to be natural; her feigned indifference too obvious to be true.

I hesitated between reading it in front of her with equally feigned indifference or to leave it aside until she left. I opted for the latter, knowing that both options were wrong.

'Tell me a bit more about the world out there' I asked as I lay in my bed and she obliged, which was lucky since all I had intended was to divert her attention from Cecille's existence. She mentioned all those events which by taking place repeatedly, one day here, next day there, have lost their inherent capacity to shock us and disturb us: floods, bombs, fraud, violence, wildfires... One would think that there is no point in struggling to stay alive, but there you are.

As soon as she left, I ripped open the envelope. I would've recognized the handwriting in black ink on heavy paper even if it hadn't been signed. The text was fairly innocent whereas the sender was not, or I should say, the intention was not. For all her magnanimous attitude, I guess Cecille would be pleased to cause a minor unease between Grette and me, if only for old times' sake, or simply, out of vanity or feminine sense of honour or whatever it may be called. Women are like that.

Her letter started with her usual politeness, the one that she possesses naturally and puts to best use to convey formality whenever she judges any other tone would be inappropriate. She had been so glad to see me well, (she didn't say again but well), she hoped that I was keeping fine and sent her warmest wishes to my sons, whenever I happen to see them and, by the way, she could've sworn that she had seen Torben in town the afternoon before she left, so much did the blond resemble him. She asked her taxi to stop, but the man had soon disappeared amongst the crowd.

She added a couple of irrelevant comments so as to confirm a sense of lasting friendship and finally, signed her name and her husband's as if to make clear that there is no other special link between us other than a very open, honest, even solemn kind of affection. Not a mention of our last conversation. Just a page, a bread-and-butter note confirming that she had been glad to see me, in the same way one sends thank you notes to the hosts of a dinner party we have attended, not like the interminable letters she used to write. Sly as a woman.

Obviously, she was mistaken about Torben because it is ages since he has been to Copenhagen, but her comment reinforced my already desperate longing for his visit and I wished that instead of phoning me as he promised Grette he will do, he could fly over soon. Perhaps I should have told everybody about my condition earlier on, no sooner I started losing my balance and getting those splitting headaches. I kept quiet about it, telling myself I was being selfless.

Instead, it seems that I have created more chaos in this way than if I had told them with plenty of time ahead so that they could plan visits and such things. I have always had a knack for thinking things through, very carefully, very thoroughly and getting them wrong nonetheless.

You wouldn't think I made the good lawyer I did. Better close your eyes, Ole, I told myself, take a deep breath and relax. Take a deep breath and relax. The nurses' mantra was getting infectious.

'There you are, my darling!' Elba said, throwing her arms around me the best she could, negotiating drips and wires, her green eyes glazed with tears like every time we meet. I was glad that Grette had already left. Elba looked older, not much, but the flesh on her cheeks has shrunk slightly in the last couple of years. Her back, however, is still as upright as a candle, as it has ever been. Mother used to praise her poise when she was a teenager, carrying herself as if her head was pulled by an invisible wire from above. Dignified. The kind of effortless elegance some people have and others have not. Like Cecille. I said that aloud and Elba looked stunned.

'Cecille? Cecille Bossen?'

'I need a favour' I said. 'I've just received a letter from her. She was in town two weeks ago. We met for lunch. She asked me for a notebook she had once sent to me with... hundreds of poems. Not big deal, but there were a few other letters and papers inside the notebook. Highly personal, private, confidential papers. They're in my safe'

'Cecille has asked me to give her back the whole lot many times in the past, but I have always refused -cannot think why- and reassured her that they were safer than my own life, so she agreed on my safekeeping. She trusted me, but I'm ill now and Cecille doesn't know about it. I need the folder. Now. I want you to go and get them. Now. Now. Please! Will you go?' I threw off my bedcover and sat up in bed.

The room turned around like a spinning top as if I were its plunger. I held my head in my hands, covering my eyes, while Elba reached out and held me. She was taken aback.

After the room stopped spinning and I managed to reset myself, Elba asked what the hell did I want Cecille's notes for?

'You're not allowed to read yet. You need to get better first, don't you?'

'Please. You don't have to understand but you're the only one who can go and get them for me. Would you mind? They're in my safe. In a folder tied up with a faded purple ribbon. I brought the key with me' I pointed out to the second drawer and wondered why I hadn't thought of those papers before...

Elba looked worried. Cecille Bossen's letters? The keys to my safe in my hospital's wardrobe? She must have hesitated about my sanity and I tried to reassure her by explaining things a bit more carefully. I struggled with some words, which I could hear myself slurring them again until I regained some calm. Elba remained silent, stroking my hand, waiting for me to recover my balance.

'Cecille and I were lovers a lifetime ago'

Had I not been her beloved brother, Elba would've walked out of the room. She is very principled. Yet she stayed with me, listening to my vacuous justifications.

The anxiety and the urge to get those papers back to me, safe from strangers' hands, made me feel very tired. The pain was in crescendo by now. I administered myself some more painkillers into my veins and could soon feel the tension leaving my limbs and the back of my neck. My body felt relaxed at once, sinking heavily onto the bed and my mind dived deeply into a cushion of images and sounds.

With my eyes shut, feeling my sister's presence next to me, I was transported to Elba's farm and then to an image of Anna and the boys in our apartment in London all those years ago and then again, Elba coming to visit my parents, laying baby Lara on the bed that had belonged to Ernst until he joined the Navy. I remembered that too. One memory incoherently slipping onto the next, but every image was so clear that it made me think that my brain, at least a part of it, was still working properly.

'Please, do get Cecille's notebook for me. Any sensible person in my shoes would've destroyed before coming here, don't ask...'

I didn't think I'd fallen asleep, but when I opened my eyes again more than five hours had gone by. I felt much better and Elba was still there, smiling, looking less worried and wiping my forehead. We finally agreed that she would go and stay in my house, have a girlie chat with Grette and sneak into my bureau tomorrow morning, no sooner Grette is out. 'Sherlock Holmes style' Elba joked, and I thanked her in advance for not reading the notes, which was why I trusted her and no one else. I could cope with further recriminations, I have hardly anything else to lose now, but I cannot contemplate the idea of putting other people through more heartache, which is exactly what would happen if Grette were to find out the whole story.

'Aftensmad tid' the nurse announced, and the room filled with such a powerful aroma of vegetable soup that I was sick straight away. I have never been very keen on soups and now they have become simply intolerable. The poor nurse apologized profusely as if my illness were her fault, and walked out taking the tray back with her.

A few minutes later, another nurse came. A man, this time. Very few words, measured smile, sheer efficiency. He brought some pasta tossed in cream and a few roasted, plain vegetables. My retching had stopped and the soft, innocent scent of creamy hotness made me feel hungry at once.

Elba was asked to leave, so she ran her fingers gently over my bandages, smiled and left, acquiescent and happy to be on a mission to save me and a few more people from disaster, while the nurse tucked a napkin under my chin. I ate the whole plate of pasta with a glass of apple juice –not an ideal combination, I must admit- and then, a summer fruits pudding with a thick, delicious syrup, the only way I can eat it.

I don´t know who is in charge of organizing the menu in this hospital, but it reads like one at a smart restaurant. I still have some intolerances, but I am told it is normal. Take desserts, for example, or sauces. I can eat apples and bananas and pears and peaches, plain or cooked, but no citrus and no berries, unless they are cooked or exceedingly sweet like in the pudding I've just had. I cannot stomach tomato sauce, or tomatoes in any way for that matter. Dairy products and cheeses, I can. Any kind, any time. Odd. I remember reading about human's palate changing preferences every three years approximately, so now that I have had my brain in this sort of mess, I wonder what I will end up enjoying and what I will dislike. I mentioned this to the nurse and she said that everything will settle within a few weeks, especially once I come off radiotherapy.

He made my recovery sound so imminent and promising! Just like after Mr Henriksen's comments before, the nurse's words made me long for strolls in the park and swimming in the sea and friends and children and wine and roses. Pure delusion, possibly, but who would want to live deprived of all those things? I can see myself out there, looking and feeling younger than my age as I used to do. Active again. Positive. In control. Eager. For the time being, though, all minute indulgences such as newspapers, magazines, books of any sort, TV... beautiful girls, are out of my reach. Not recommended, they say.

Chapter 5

The Madonna of the box

Sølvbirk farm, 1981

Everybody goes to bed early at the Perssons. Cecille knows she mustn't cause too much trouble because Elba and Harald get up very early, her parents said. They work hard, Elba and Harald, so Cecille behaves herself. It is easy to be a good girl at the Perssons.

In the next bedroom Anders is still awake, she is sure. She has seen him hiding a torch under his duvet and playing battles with his toy soldiers, but she will keep her word not to tell anyone. In a day or two, Anders will have a baby brother or a baby sister. Neither he nor she can wait to see what it will look like.

This afternoon, when she rode with Harald to the neighbouring farm, she asked whether she could ride on her own. No, she couldn't, but there will be a pony ready for her and Anders next time they come to visit. And no, the baby won't ride until it is a big boy like Anders. Or a big girl like her. Of course.

When they got back, they all had cups of tea and cake or pastries, while Harald favoured toast and that glorious butter so efficiently obtained by Elba and their daughters rocking the milk churn up and down, up and down on their laps until the cream curdles and turn into butter.

Elba says it is still the best method. It's probably her only concession to bygone days. Once the butter is ready, she shakes it all out into a bowl and everybody spreads it on fresh bread with home-made jam of varying flavours according to the season. In September there are pear jams; orange, lemon or grapefruit ones in January and February, and apple or berries during the Summer. Cecille dislikes the smell of fruits being cooked but the process fascinates her. A huge saucepan is what she will buy when she grows up. Then she will make kilos and kilos of jam in it and store them in dozens of jars like Elba does.

In the meantime, she observes and learns and longs for those occasions when Elba asks her to help prepare a blueberry pie, while Lara and Julia do their homework. It is difficult to sleep when you are thinking of cakes and jams... They have all been sent to bed earlier than usual because the night is bitterly cold. Cecille gathers that unlike her parents, Elba and Harald are happy to snuggle up in bed and read or listen to that music Elba told her is called Liszt. She can hear them talk. Softly. Friendly. She is still restless, still a bit too alert, too lucid for this time of the evening. Her mother is always saying how her body clock is forever wrong and Cecille is starting to think that her mother is right after all.

No amount of work or studies or obligations later on in life will change this involuntary habit of thinking, creating, drawing, doing things, reading, long after everybody else has gone to sleep.

She would like to go down and knock on the Perssons' door and ask Elba for something. She doesn't know what. She would like to talk about how much she wishes she had a baby brother. Not a sister. No. But she remains in her bedroom. The one with the slopping ceiling and the thick, printed curtains. The whole attic belongs to her and Anders. She finds it almost magical, except when Anders is silly and wakes her up because he is scared.

The footsteps stop right on the other side of her door. Someone's hand, still invisible, is quietly turning the brass doorknob. Cecille hides beneath the quilt, then changes her mind and sits up. The door opens.

'You ought to be asleep, my fairy' Elba says feigning impatience.

Cecille likes being called my fairy. 'May I see the prints first? Please?'

'Well, have a quick look and then you must sleep' Elba says, gently stroking the child's cheek and secretly delighted at this distinctive interest. Before she can go and fetch the prints, Cecille jumps out of her bed and tiptoes to the large white wardrobe where she knows the box is kept. Inside it she finds souvenir cards from old Christmases and children's Christenings or Confirmations with reproductions of Madonna and child, cherubs and saints, all draped in beautiful robes.

Cecille looks at them one by one, tracing the contours of the faces with a soft finger. Sometimes, she leaves a kiss on the most beautiful baby Jesus she finds, not because she finds Jesus familiar, yet, but because he is a baby. She is as intoxicated with the beauty of the smiles and the vibrancy of the deep burgundies and cobalt blues as she is shocked by the blood spurting out of a crucified Christ on a card that somebody has sent from Spain.

The effect of this nightly treat at the Perssons' will lie dormant in some corner of her mind for many years. She will remain affected by colours the way some men get affected by a football match results, but she is not fully aware of their impact until one afternoon at the National Gallery of London when she is twenty-two. She shuffles along the great paintings of the Renaissance, stops to look at them, to observe them, critically, studiously, standing face to face with Raphael's perfect Madonnas and in no time, she is back in the maroon attic, in the Perssons's old farm, sitting up in bed, asking the kind, fun loving woman who isn't her mother, to let her have one more look at those prints. Closing her eyes for a few seconds, she can see Anders again coming back from the pigsty, mud up to his hair, striding across the green yard, as Harald called the mowed piece of land at the back of the house. In two or three days, Ole would pick them up and take them to see the new baby.

Chapter 6

Ulla

It may sound pessimistic to say *for the time being,* but there are brief, clear-cut moments when I feel so well that I can hardly believe I am here, tucked in a hospital bed with my skull sewn up and all my senses and movements and reactions carefully monitored, in case something stops working as it should. In case the green line on the screen comes to a halt.

At other times, I feel absolutely convinced that I will die, and get terrified. Once a coward... Not like Ulla. Poor Ulla.

When she felt herself passing away, she said to me, You're still young. Do marry again. Have a family. I will be watching over you. I love you.

She died so peacefully, not a shadow of fear upon her face.

I fell in love with her as soon as I set my eyes on her the day I walked into her classroom. I had decided to improve my French by attending one of the courses that the University used to run in those days as optional complements to other courses.

When I entered the room, the lesson had already started. It was a rather sombre, rectangular room, with narrow vertical windows through which the sun threw shafts of light that divided the students into sunny and gloomy groups, like a Caravaggio. Ulla gave me a disapproving look for being late and continued with her lesson, ignoring me for the rest of the morning. And for the rest of the week.

It was my last year at University and I had been with not a few girls by then, but I had never seen one like her.

The second week, we bumped into each other along the corridor and she could not ignore me when I asked her for some papers I hadn't yet been given. I should have turned up on time, should I not? She could not stand unpunctuality.

'I'm sorry. It won't happen again. Promise'

She dug up some papers from the overflowing satchel she carried wherever she went and handed them to me, with the same air of efficient indifference with which she had treated me since the first day.

Towards the end of the term, I had found out enough about her to feel hopeful, if not confident, of winning some acknowledgment from her. She came from a town in the south of the country, but had been living in the capital for over eight years. She shared a house with two other girls, one of whom turned out to be the sister of a good friend of mine. She had many friends, men and women, as she would say later, but didn't seem to have a special man in her life.

On the last day of the term, I summoned up some courage, like I used to do in my teens, before approaching some pretty girl on the last day of summer holidays, and turned back to speak to her. The rest of the students had left the room after thanking her politely for her dedication and patience. She had her coat on and the elastic blue bow with which she held her hair in a pony tail, caught between her teeth, while she brushed her honey- coloured hair.

She didn't show surprise or irritation when I invited her for a drink to say thanks properly, but replied that she could not see what was improper about saying thanks the way everybody had said it there, a couple of minutes earlier. I ignored her rhetorical question and mentioned the festival of French movies on show at almost every cinema for that week. A sparkle of surprise crossed her eyes, but she let it pass.

'I'm afraid I'm quite busy this week but I would like a drink, then'. I liked the way she accepted one invitation in order to turn down the other, without being rude.

I took her to lunch at the harbour, which is never original yet always irresistible. Despite a fine drizzle, or because of it, the place looked its most charming. She made conversation awkward for the first few minutes, until I told her we were not in the classroom anymore and that she needn't patronize me for everything I said. She was taken aback and apologized, putting me on a more favourable position than I had been until then.

I told her about my plans for the future, because she asked about them. I was twenty-six years old and was finishing my training to be a barrister. She started telling me about her hobbies in an attempt to avoid personal details. She went to the theatre occasionally and to the cinema whenever she could. She would've spent her life there if she had had the time and the money. It was her weakness, her passion. She even bought a specialized magazine in film making and everything else related to it. It was a monthly publication from France, that was why her language lessons were sprinkled with articles and debates about moviemakers, movie actors and moviegoers. She could not resist that world.

When I asked her about her background, she shrugged her shoulders as if there wasn't anything worth mentioning.

'I don't have any siblings. My parents still live in the same house where I was born, in Honning. They have always seemed to be so old. They're rather uneducated people who took pride in working hard and getting me properly educated, as they used to say'.

Nothing had made her mother prouder than walking her to school. When it rained heavily it was her father who came to pick her up in his old bicycle. She hadn't disappointed them. She was no Einstein, she said, solemnly, but she succeeded in what she had started. She taught Scandinavian Literature and Mythology at the University of Copenhagen. And she could sew, knit and embroider, like in the children's rhyme her grandmother sang for her.

'And where does the French come in?

'Oh, teaching French for adults is only an aside and it gives me a bit of extra pocket money, but I'm not doing it next term'.

Instead, she was going to accept a teaching post in Oslo. For six months. It would be fun. She had never been to Norway. She had never been anywhere other than a year in Rouen where she lived with a French family who could never pronounce her name correctly. The man of the house had given up trying and used to make jokes of it, calling her *oh la la*, while he ran his hand along her thigh if she was unfortunate enough to be told by madame to sit next to monsieur. She could not wait to be home, but made the most of her experience and imbibed everything she was able to learn and apprehend about the Gallic culture, history, language and literature. Above all, its Literature.

'You couldn't beat the French novel for its development of the genre and its influence upon the Literature of the rest of the world during the nineteenth century. Have you ever read Flaubert?'

I didn't blink for fear of losing sight of her, as if she were a vision that would vanish if I dared close my eyes. I paid for the meal when she pointed out that it was almost time for mid-afternoon coffee.

'May I buy you a coffee? It'll have to be somewhere cheaper than this'. We walked back from the harbour and she led me into a quaint little café, with bleached oak tables and crocheted rugs.

An hour later, we parted on her doorstep. She needed to catch up with her notes, mark some essays, read so much. I ignored her stretched hand and kissed her on both cheeks. She giggled. I could not tell whether it was joy or embarrassment, nor could I tell whether she was flattered, happy or niggled when I called her the next day.

Only after being married, she told me how much she had wished I would call her. She chose to come and pick me up, it was easier for her, she said, although I didn't see how or why, given that she had no car and lived in a side street off the Amager Boulevard, but I was happy with any arrangement.

She turned up in a black coat which hardened her features and emphasized the formality about her, but her hair hung loose over her shoulders and she was wearing perfume. We went to see *Hiroshima, mon amour*, although like a lustful teenager, I could only pay attention to the love scenes. I held her hand. It was soft and small, almost too small for her proportions. I looked at her, following the line of her nose, which would've qualified for Hollywood screens, but she didn't move and her eyes remained fixed on the Japanese man and the French woman.

When she eventually turned, I kissed her. Avidly, I kissed her. For longer than the lovers on the screen, better than every other couple in the room, I kissed her. Ten months later, on her twenty- eighth birthday, when I was already a barrister and she was back from Norway, I married her.

It took me years to go back to the beach after her death. There was nothing Ulla enjoyed more than swimming in the sea or simply being in the water. Floating, playing. During the first years of our marriage, we used to rent a cottage by the seaside and she would prepare picnics to take with us and spend the day on the beach.

Sometimes, we would stay there well into the evening, watching the sunset and eating bacon sandwiches under the stars. Anders would run and run around, squealing and giggling until he would fall asleep, dead with exhaustion after a day in the sun, the cool breeze and the sea.

Ulla's face never looked more radiant than on those occasions and I felt the happiest man alive, grown up and secure in her love, the husband of a clever, beautiful woman, the father of a gorgeous, healthy child. In general, women are the ones who tend to be admired, or praised or even envied for their progeny, but I think that few other things, if any at all, make a man prouder than parading himself with his family, overwhelmed by an almost defiant sense of joy. It is a primal instinct that has not abandoned us and out we go into the world showing off our conquest and our descendants, the ones who walk like us, or have eyes of the same colour as ours, and who will inherit our hut, our weapons and our land.

The last summer Ulla was with us we went to the south of France. She was pregnant and had accepted engaging a local au-pair to look after Anders. It was a perfect time. Her skin looked golden and healthy. Her eyes looked bluer and her figure, bulky with Torben inside, looked toned and agile nevertheless. Some days we got up late and had breakfast on the terrace overlooking the sea in the distance. At other times, we would get up and go for breakfast in one of the cafes on the seafront, while we watched other early risers make their way to the beach, mostly new arrivals, still pale and ready to blister under the already unforgiving sun. We ate, we drank -I drank-, we talked, we took siestas, we made love. Ulla used to go swimming after five, saying that the Mediterranean afternoon heat was too much for two cold weather loving Vikings, pointing at her expanded belly.

I can still see her in my mind's eye, coming out of the water, tanned, smiling, her nose in the air like a teenager with not one care in the world. Yes, I can see her: her dainty footsteps on the sand, her lips tasting of cacao, her breath smelling of oranges. She had a craving for oranges, she said, as she indulged into yet one more juicy giant one from the village market.

When we returned to Denmark, she threw herself into the nesting routine so natural in pregnant women. She transformed her studio into the new baby's little bedroom saying that she wouldn't need a studio any longer because there would be no time for her to do anything else other than looking after our two children. Her friend Manu found her decision a betrayal to feminism, but she took the accusation with a mix of humour and pride and simply carried on with the decoration. She didn't see much of Manu afterwards.

By the time the baby was born and brought home, he had a cozy room in red and white, with ladybirds and strawberries embroidered on the sheets. Being the days before it was possible to find out the sex of the foetus, Ulla had avoided using blue or pink. As for pale yellow, which was so practical according to other mothers, she wasn't going to use a colour that look so dreadful on Scandinavian skin, she said. Besides, strawberries and ladybirds would mean using the national red and white without being twee.

She was thirty-nine. I was thirty-eight. I remember her and the day of her death very clearly and now that I am approaching my own departure, cannot help wondering whether there is such thing as being able to meet her again.

I try. I do try to look forward. I am an optimist. I am, by nature, a happy person, but all I seem to be thinking these days is of the past. Memories, memories, memories. Mainly pleasant ones. Vivid ones, true, but memories. A way of accepting death, I suppose. A fast forward journey towards closing the circle. I must insist on seeing Torben. Soon. And Cecille's notes. The simplest way would be to destroy them, that is probably what I will do unless I decide to send them back to her by private courier. I feel myself getting confused at times and must clear up the mess before I lose the plot.

Chapter 7

Talking brothers, missing notes

Torben is here this morning. And Anders. I cannot talk to them, or see them. *An opiate*, the nurse said and I can see now that she was right after all: morphine really did it for me this time. They have thought of other analgesics but, for what I heard them saying, I was in need of morphine last night. I can't remember.

The church clock strikes ten. The light outside is brighter and brighter. I know this because instead of a purple haze I can feel an orange one behind my closed eyelids. The registrar has just been and will be back in a couple of hours, so all is not well. He sounded less relaxed, I could tell.

My sons keep chatting, although I do not know at what time they started or what time they arrived. Unless they are not here and this is only a dream. I might be hallucinating. I so much want to talk to them, but I can't and it is a horrible sensation. Worse than being dumb, or deaf or blind, although I have never been any of these and wouldn't know.

I hear Anders call Torben's name with joyful delight and that surge of genuine love that transpires their words when they see and talk to each other. It is great to see him after such a long time, Anders says. Torben replies with equal joy, and asks about Lena and Clementina. Anders explains that he is now with Nja, that Lena is doing alright, probably wealthier these days, and taking care of Clementina, who is growing up so pretty and sharp...

It can't be just a dream, can it? Torben says he is sorry to hear about Lena and then asks how Daddy is. He means it. Seriously. How am I?

He hasn't called me Daddy since his teens, when he became rebellious and difficult to live with. Now that every affectionate gesture and word has acquired a greater value, hearing him refer to me as Daddy is touching. How needy can one get?

His voice sounds deeper. His Danish is sloppy in a cultivated, deliberate way, like the one used by tweedy intellectuals and artists, not the one a doctor normally uses. I don't like that, but I guess it's inevitable after ten years of living in the States. Even Ralph mentioned in his emails that after a couple of months in Chicago he is already speaking through his nose.

'He had a tumour the size of an orange. Right between the two hemispheres. It could've damaged his vision, or his movements, even his speech, apparently. He had seizures, headaches and what the doctor identified as auras.

'Olfactory hallucinations', Torben calls them. 'Pungent smells that are not there and that only the patient can smell', he adds.

'He never mentioned any of his symptoms to us' Anders says and I detect a shade of admiration in his voice. 'He may have suffered all of these things, or one of them or a hint of each... oh well, you know about all this better than me, surely'. He goes on about my stoicism and all the rest. 'Can you imagine Dad ever suffering from any of this...? Inconceivable. Ninety per cent of the tumour was removed but he needs radiotherapy and so on'

I'm touched by the care and concern with which my sons refer to me and my tumour, not knowing that I can hear them. I feel as if I am eavesdropping on a conversation that I should not hear but there is nothing I can do about it. In a lower voice, Torben says that there isn't such thing as catching the cancer in time, if it is a GBM of such characteristics. 'Glioblastoma multiforme', he explains, 'is a type of a primary brain tumour, so it arises from the brain itself rather than travelling or metastasizing from another part in the body'

'Which means...'

'It means that although some are benign, the malignant ones like Dad's, tend to grow rapidly and spread into the surrounding brain tissue. Surgery might grant the patient a few more months but despite all treatments the outcome is still quite poor because it's often impossible to remove the entire tumour surgically. The survival rate is low, Anders. Don't go kidding yourself. Father must have had plenty of symptoms.

I can hear their breathing, heavy and troubled during a long pause which must give both of them the time to assimilate what one has just said and the other one heard.

'Hardly a year, at the most' Torben adds, his voice trailing off, if I understand rightly. 'Do you think he has personality changes, for example?'

'Not that I noticed, no' 'Severe pain?'

Anders explains how the pain has not subsided at all and how it needs keeping under control by varying doses of morphine, and how I seem to be overexcited. He is right. When I'm awake I'm over alert, over anxious about things, about everything. The consultant thinks I ought to have chemotherapy as well, but I refuse to. He will make me get up and walk soon and see how I evolve.

'I guess he's not well, really' Anders concludes.

'I guess not', Torben adds.

They are both right, of course, but can feel in them a lingering sense of denial. Poor boys, they are kidding themselves. So hopelessly full of hope. Torben says that being over alert is quite natural in these cases. Excitement, heightened self-awareness, even euphoria in this type of patients, namely me, are quite common. A kind of reaction to the proximity of death, perhaps. A combination of a psychological aspect and a physiological one. Then he asks for the surgeon's name and says he will speak to him as soon as possible.

'Mr Henriksen. Please, man, do find out as much as possible. Anyway, how is life in the States? When did you arrive? Don't you think that so much morphine is wrong? Isn't it addictive?'.

If Anders has so far tried to appear cool, calm and collected, he certainly is not bothering now. 'I'm sure he will recover, so isn't there a risk of becoming dependent on the stuff?

Torben reassures him, defending the inevitability of morphine in cases like mine. Then I hear a gentle tapping which is probably Torben tapping his brother's shoulder.

'This morning. I arrived this morning. Still prefer Denmark but one thing led to another and I haven't been able to disentangle myself from the American system. It's what I wanted some years ago, you know, but now I'm not so sure'.

I am hearing all this. I couldn't bear to think that this is a mere hallucination. I can tell that Torben isn't happy in America. His voice betrays unease, doubt. Things are not going as smoothly or as happily as he has been trying to make us believe every time he phones.

Something has vanished from him. The joy he felt on seeing Anders again soon becomes a dull, flat note. Like going from yellow to grey in a few seconds. That is the way the consultant asks me to describe things, God knows why. To rate things or events in different hues. Well, Torben certainly sounds grey (light grey). I wonder what exactly has changed in him. Why. When. How.

Their conversation continues. I remain unable to participate, to open my eyes and look at them. My sons.

I hear Anders say that I've been such a caring father and so indulgent, especially towards their youngest brother.

'You're rewriting history, Andy. He's never been a caring father. He's been such a pig at times'.

Anders says something in my defence, according to his tone, but I cannot make it out.

'You're just like him', Torben cuts in. 'There's never a problem with you'. Torben's voice gets louder and deeper, like elephant grey. Does Anders remember the day I broke the news that they were going to boarding school? I had enrolled them without telling them, months before they found out. Suddenly, it was the end of August again and Anna rushed them both to Peter Jones to try new shoes and new blazers and new everything because they were being sent to the country for a better education. Just like that. No warning, no goodbye to their friends from previous schools, no explanation. Out of sight. I couldn't wait to get rid of them. Have you forgotten about it?'

He hasn't, but it had all happened such a long time ago. Of what use will it be to go back to that now? It would be unfair to me and it is immature.

'See? You're just like him' Torben almost screams. 'You never find fault with yourself. You've always defended the indefensible. It's one of the flaws in your character, one I have tried very hard not to imitate, even at the time when I looked up to you because you were this cool, older brother who excelled at any sport he played. Look around, Anders! Look at what happened to mother. And Anna. And... Cecille Bossen. Do you know what that poor girl's gone through?'

Anders tells Torben to shut up and double check the facts before saying any more.

'Anna was already an alcoholic when Dad met her. It was only luck that she stopped drinking for a while. And Cecille? Cecille Bossen? What the hell are you talking about? And what about our mother? Mum died of natural causes. She died when'...

'I know perfectly well when Mor died, tak!', Torben says, his voice trembling with anger or hurt. Or both. 'I was born. She died. You can't improve such symmetry. I've lived with the guilt of having caused her death all my fucking life... filled with envy for those years you had her with you, but I'm not a docile, insecure, melancholic child any more' he protests, and angrily, very angrily, he adds that it is Anders who should grow up and start checking the facts, for once.

I don't know what else they said, and dosed up as I was, I am not sure if I actually heard their steps as they left the room. It might all be imagination, unwellness, madness. Perhaps I am not even awake as I think I am now.

A nurse is asking the chap in the next room whether he would like the lights off. He would. I cannot hear his voice but his lights are out and the immediacy of this reality brings me back to the lonely, clinical paleness of my hospital room where probably it's only thanks to my sons' exchange about my condition that I remember the first station of my via Crucis.

It was the middle of the afternoon, on my way back from Kronborg where I had gone for lunch with one of my ex-colleagues. I had to pull up at a lay-by and fainted over the steering wheel where I remained unconscious until just by chance, or by some god's command, a police car going past, saw me and stopped. I had experienced other anomalies before then, the red spots in front of my eyes, the flitting but repeated bouts of confusion which I could identify as such, but was unable to control or shake off the splitting headaches which spread right up to the bones in my nose, but the incident on the motorway was the first time I acknowledged my helplessness, my need for medical assistance and above all, for human company, although I was determined not to alarm anybody unnecessarily.

It feels like a whole era has gone by since the moment I was taken in an ambulance, frightened and lonely, to a hospital from which I might never come out again. I am still scared. Every day I am scared, even though I have put my life in the best doctors' hands.

When the oncologist told me about the result of my MRI, I asked him how long would I have? His expression, undoubtedly repeated on a monthly, weekly, perhaps daily basis, had the same impact on me as the Raphael's Velata the first time I stood in front of her, a hand over my mouth gaping in ecstasy, my eyes hardly blinking. I thought I was self-possessed, well informed, intellectually and

emotionally equipped to stand there and face it, but I was not. I knew that was the end of me, Hr Ole Morgensen, control freak, obsessive perfectionist, god of independence, reduced to this shameful invalidity.
I think it's this loss of control what hurts me more than my disease, but how can I regain control of myself when it feels as though my life has been snatched away from me by some stranger in a white coat who says that I only have a few months to live?

At that point, the only way I could take back control of my life was to seize my illness and undergo its process as stoically as possible. I now wish I could look in the mirror and tell myself that I was brave enough to find the way forward, but like most patients, I panicked as soon as I heard the devastating news. Instead, I've been telling myself again and again that the hospital is great, the doctors are competent; the nurses, a vision in blue and green and that I have plenty of friends who would care for me if, succumbing to cowardice and self-pity, I were to call every one of them and tell them about my death sentence.

I cannot get used to being dependent on others. So shameful it is, so irritating and demeaning. Even when I try to put the world, -my own narrow world-, to rights, I cannot do it without Elba's help.

She was supposed to bring me the notebook today. I've been doped all this time. She must have come and gone. What happened to the notebook?

Has she left it with me, here? If Torben arrived before Anders and the notebook was already here, he may have read it and that is why he talked of what I did to Cecille…

I can't see them here, but Elba would not leave the damn notes lying around, would she? She knows they are top secret. She can't have… I am sure she would've stayed a little longer until I woke up. Unless she was told to go. Or maybe she had to. What if she wasn't able to rescue them? In that case they are still in my safe… or are they? *For pokker*, where the fuck are they?

'Nurse! Nurse! Where's the bloody nurse?'

The nurse, an old dragon this time, asks me to apologize for my rude manners first, and then, like a conciliatory mother, she opens the drawers and the cupboard and takes everything out as I ask her to do.

There are two sets of pyjamas, carefully folded by me or by one of her colleagues, I don't know. There are the books I brought and cannot read yet, the pack of sweets given to me by Clementina, my wash bag, my talcum powder, the Bois de Portugal Grette bought duty-free at some airport, my socks and the clothes I was wearing when I came in. I am taken aback by the existence of these items, especially by the clothes and shoes the nurse has pulled out of their hiding place. I feel as if I have been here all my life. As if I have never known any other life but this. Or worse still, I don't feel myself capable of putting shoes on and walking out of here ever again.

When I ask the nurse to pass over my keys, I check that the key to my safe is back in the key ring where Elba found it yesterday. It is not. I check twice, three times. I ask the nurse to count the number of keys for me. There are five. Not six. The key isn't here. The notebook and envelope are not here. My only fear is that I may die and everybody will find out but then, if I die, what's the problem? For the last forty-eight hours I've been trying to convince myself of the futility of my concern and yet, I can't help agonizing about papers that belong to someone so dear to me. It would mean betraying Cecille's trust one more time.

My only consolation, -in health terms-, is that not recalling what happened to the key might not necessarily be a consequence of my cancer, but a recurring failure in my life. A chronic obsession for organization that makes me produce the very same mistakes I so much try to avoid and detest. A gaffe. One after the other. I wonder what will happen once everybody discovers it, given that most of my friends believe that my organizational skills are second to none. It's all quite funny, really, but where is the missing key? Did Elba keep it? What if she did mean to keep it apart and then lost it? I need to know. This feels like being robbed of one's passport in a foreign country, where one doesn't speak the language, the consul is on holidays and the solicitors work for their government.

'Hi!' A tall, blond man with the bluest eyes enters the room. There is a beaming smile upon his lips but his forehead remains tense, taut. There are sparks of a nervous electricity, (or is it anger?) in his pupils, which I recognize at once.

'My dear Torben! It's so marvellous to see you, son. So bloody marvellous!' I am genuinely delighted to see him back at this time. I do not say that I've heard him here earlier on. I cannot help wondering whether he did want me to hear him. He is a doctor. He knows that many patients can hear every sound around them despite being in a coma. Especially, when we are in a coma. I stretch my arm towards him and he steps forward.

'Hey, I just wanted to check that you're ok. God nat, far. You must sleep now or they'll throw me out' he says, jerking his head in the direction of the corridor and promises me that we shall talk tomorrow. He grabs my hand and holds it in his. I want to protest and say that tomorrow might be too late, that I want to hear his news and catch up with his stories right now, but the nurse injects the horrid stuff into my veins and I am off, feeling a damp palm upon my forehead.

Chapter 8

Torben

Never in my life have I been so aware of what time of day it is when I say something, when I think of something, when someone comes in, when someone goes out. As if every thought, every feeling, every action were planned to the second. Perhaps they are, but that is a philosophical, different matter altogether. I find myself paying constant attention to what time it is when I open my eyes, when the surgeon comes to see me, when the telephone rings. Does this endeavour to know exactly where I am result from a fear of dying, an eagerness to capture every second while it is still possible, or is it just one of many alterations my character is undergoing?

It is three minutes past five, for example. The surgeon jokes about my precision and says that brain tumour sufferers can become so creative and intellectually active that he worries about his future, lest some of us decide to graduate as a surgeon and end up increasing the competition. He is a nice man, Mr Henriksen. His hands are so big and clumsy-looking that one would never guess his routine consists of dealing with grey matters and nerves, I such a nano millimetrical precise fashion. I stumble upon the word in my head and decide to say it aloud in order to test my speech. Micromillim... Nano millimetrical. There.

When I woke up, at eight minutes to one, the registrar was beside me and told me that he wasn't surprised by my late start given the emotionally draining day I had yesterday. I didn't know what he was talking about until he told me I had become very agitated and worked up about a notebook and some keys. A notebook and some keys. He mentioned these items as if they were crucial evidence of my deterioration, surreal objects in a madman's mind, but I didn't bother to explain that such two objects, if nothing else, relate to a very real and honest person in my life, whom I want to protect and therefore, it is perfectly sensible and indispensable to try to recover them at once. Never mind.

Then he added that my son had sat by me all night. He had just sent him to get some lunch. *Your son sat by you all night.* I asked him to repeat those words to make sure I had understood correctly and when I was sure that I had, my eyes filled with tears. For a moment, I even thought that it must have been Anders, but soon Torben came back into the room, looking like someone who has not had any sleep for many hours, which was obviously the case after all those hours watching over me in addition to his jet-lag. He must be worrying sick about me, I thought.

Torben is the most handsome of my three boys. Always has been. When he was just a boy, he was a picture, but I could never tell him so. One just does not say things like that to a son, so I used to comment only on his academic or sporty achievements.

Otherwise, I have never known what else to talk about with him. I am more conscious of it now, after hearing him complain to Anders about my selfishness. There has always been a barrier between himself and me, but I could not tell whose fault it was. I could tell that he was fragile, that the tough image he so much struggled to project was only a mask, a protective shield. Yet, I was unable to break through it.

He used to feel very awkward if we were left on our own in the same room. The silence became solid, like a piece of nothingness obliterating our efforts to reach for each other emotionally, affectionately. Our eyes wandered away from each other, avoiding each other, searching in our heads for some trivial reason to make our excuses and walk out of the room.

Sometimes, if Anna rushed upstairs to get changed while we were still having breakfast, Torben would get up and say that he had to phone one of his friends there and then or else his friend would be out for the day and he would miss him. He was tactful, but all the time I knew that he could not stand my presence there. Not that he hated me, I know he didn't, he simply didn't consider me close enough to him. He once said to Anna that he was scared of me, frightened of me, and I could never understand why.
I have made lots of mistakes as a father, surely, and as a husband and in any other role I may have played, but I don't think I have ever frightened anybody. Perhaps I did. What do I know? I threw a party when Torben graduated as a doctor and he told Anders how touched he was, surely expecting Anders to pass his message to me. To me, he only said *Tak, far.* It was enough to me but not for him, I knew it. We never bonded and it was my fault. I never did with, for

and to baby Torben all those caring things I later did with, for and to baby William.

'Have you had a good lunch?' I ask. He has. A very good one. How do I feel now? A cold tone. Dark blue. Not like one who sits by his father's bed all night, but I am used to his moods. I say I felt quite well, considering the alternative, and that he shouldn't have stayed the night here. Hospitals are especially depressing at night.

'You are telling me. I'm fine. Read a bit, fell asleep, had a chat with a nurse as a matter of habit, I suppose... read a bit more... daylight came quickly. The sun rises so early here. Went out for a few minutes. Nothing beats a Danish summer dawn'

'A Norwegian one does', I said, but he didn't agree.

'We have everything here. Light, temperature, shades. And trees, and birdsong and flowers. It's very... idyllic. Like the drizzle in England, always present, never too much, remember? I used to like that'

'Thanks, son, for coming. It's been a while. I'm sure your patients need you more than I do, but it's great to see you!'

Not long ago, searching through the net about brain tumours and other equally cheerful topics, I came across a site which dealt mainly with the psyche. With the mind rather than with the brain as an organ. I wasn't particularly interested in such aspect, but one of the titles on the right of the screen caught my eye and I swiftly read through the report. After years of thorough research, a professor somebody or other arrived to the conclusion that what a baby experiences within the first six weeks of his life leaves such a powerful imprint in his psyche that it will affect and condition absolutely everything he does or does not do for the rest of his life. It was much more complex than that, but it stuck on my mind because I could immediately find some analogies with my boys and their respective experiences in the early days of their lives. The professor held that such effect was inevitable and I found such inevitability perplexing and worrying. I wouldn't have thought that all could be decided at such an early stage!

'You ought to go and have some sleep... freshen up... or go for a good stroll around town. We're having the most amazing summer this year, you'll love it. Make the most of it. I am fine... you mustn't worry about me'. Always in the same cautious tone, I add that he might find that seeing it all again might help him make up his mind one way or the other, who knows?

'I walked through Kongen Have the other day and after a morning drizzle, the scent of roses was inebriating under the warm sun, you should've seen it...' Torben does not listen to my comment about the parks and the roses.

'Who knows, indeed?' he says. 'Do you remember when...? Oh, never mind. What I miss the most is the European feeling to everything: The traditions, the presence of a past... if I can put it that way'.

He explains that he thinks of himself as a product of the old world, so he could go and live in England, France or

Sweden or Belgium or Italy or... anywhere in Europe, for that matter, do I understand?

'I do. I used to love going away, moving house, country, the lot, but I had to stop at some point. I was forty already'.

'I'm thirty-four myself', he interrupts, the muscles in his face tensing up again. 'I loved living in England. We lived very well there'

'Don't you live well in the United States?'

He keeps quiet, looks away, crosses his legs this way, that way. I close my eyes wondering whether I have asked too much too directly, trying to find a clue, a lead, and then an answer, and all the time, I am aware -and glad- of my present mental agility. When you have a brain tumour, you become obsessed with your own mental development, so Mr Henriksen said.

Then, to my astonishment, Torben works himself up into such an outburst of tears that he frightens me. I want to call for the nurse, but that would make things worse, so I desist. Besides, I am dumbfounded by how deeply upset he is. Or is he playing on it in order to make a point? Or not, surely not. He swears and curses and utters his words through his teeth, a mix of anger and pain and frustration, accusing me of annihilating his inner freedom, undermining his confidence, of never being available...

I never heard this voice he is using now. It is distressing to see an adult, a man like him, of great composure and introversion, breaking down in this fashion, in front of me, because of me, and surely hating himself for feeling unable to stop. I let him cry, and he does. I do not say anything, not that I would know what to say. Questions or justifications are out of place. I keep silent, secretly hoping that he will relax instead of tensing up as he has always done if I attempt the slightest touch.

When the breeze blowing through the open window sweeps the bitterness away, Torben gazes long and hard into my eyes, from a distance, sitting upright now. Neither his damp eyelashes, nor the hurt in his eyes are any different from those of years ago when he used to cry, full of indignation, over what he believed to be an injustice.

'I'm so sorry' he says, at last. 'Sorry, father' His chest is still jumpy, heavy with suppressed sighs and sobs. I ask him what should he be sorry for and I mean it. He carries on with his apologies for bursting into tears and disrupting a time when I ought to be relaxing as much as possible and...

Once again, he does not finish the sentence. He does sound like a child now. A vulnerable child. I try to make it easier for him and embark on my own pompous, but frank justifications.

'When your mother was dying', I say, 'she held you in her arms and said to you "They will tell you loads about me but the only important thing you must know is that in the nine months I carried you inside me, and in these two blissful hours looking at you, I have loved you like I've never loved anyone else”. I have always been jealous of that love. Insecure, immature, a pig that I am at times.

I tell him all this as if by admitting my own meanness and retelling him about his mother’s devotion I could palliate or excuse the absence, the solid void, the sense of loss he experienced in his childhood. There were occasions when I would spoil both my boys them rotten with too much; at other times, I neglected those areas in which I should have been more generous because those were the things that mattered: time, attention, advice, conversations... Every parent is condemned to fail in his role, one way or another.

‘I’ve always cared for the three of you, generally and individually’ I add. ‘As much as your mother would’ve done. In different ways, yes, but in equal measure’.

Torben lowers his eyes and without looking at me, stretches an arm over my bed and pats my hand. No more words are needed. He rubs his eyes, strokes his own sleeves, twitches in his chair. I can tell he is cringing at the pathos of the situation but if I do not say it all before I die, he will end up blaming himself for never telling me what he thinks, what he feels, what exactly distresses him so much. He does not reply.

I peep at him through my half-closed eyes. So tall, so strong, so mighty from the outside. He is wearing a trendy navy cardigan, one of those with round collars and front zips that I’ve seen displayed through the windows of every young man’s boutique in a defiant salute to old men pocketed, vee-necked cardigans. From underneath it, a white linen shirt looking slightly tired peeps out casually every time he stretches out or straightens his back. I can see what women must see in him and wish Ulla were here to see what a handsome son we have produced.

'I told you I was in America, with this girl, Susan... but I wasn't', he starts telling me in English, which is the language he uses to discuss feelings or emotions. 'I came back from New York two years ago and since then, I've been living in Christiania'. He swallows hard, his voice trembling, presumably wondering which of these pieces of information will send me up the wall, either the fact that he has been in town for two years without bothering to come and see us or that he is living like an outcast. A hippy or whatever they call themselves these days. Living in Christiania. Land of peace, love and happiness, with its open-air hash market! God almighty! Torben holds my gaze and tries to explain. He can bore right into your soul, with those eyes.

'You know? Christiania is actually...'

Oh, yes. Yes, I do know that its residents have succeeded in developing an enviable sense of community and organizing themselves in ways that nobody, except themselves, would have believed to be possible. I also know that they are a group of people with a very peculiar approach to life, not to say, people with wasted minds, and occasionally violent, but how am I to digest that a son of mine, a PHYSICIAN graduated with honours, may have made such choice. A doctor, for Heaven's sake! What is he doing in Christiania, surrounded by rebels and dreamers?

'Well, it's fine by me if you're happy' I don't know how I manage to tell him. 'Honestly. What's the problem?'. I do not say that if I hadn't felt so poorly, I would have probably asked him to leave. I do not say that it is humiliating and insulting. How could he live less than an hour from me and not call on us, on me, from time to time? Being there all this time without popping round for lunch on a Sunday? To meet somewhere and have a drink together? Why on earth would he concoct such a perverse story about feeling nostalgic and wanting to come back?

I keep my cool though and the gods in hell know what an effort this is, until it dawns on me. He is back. Back to us. That is why he was praising our culture, our dawns, the light, the roses... How did we not bump into each other in all this time?

'There's no Susan, as you must've gathered. There's Samuel though'.

Samuel. Samuel! I should have known. It was all there. Anna was right. She tried to tell me about him once, but I shut her up. Now there is Samuel...

I grab the bottle of water and drank eagerly from it, without bothering to pour some into a glass while I wonder how am I going to process all this information without having a fit. He used to have girlfriends in the past. One after the other and a few more hanging around, queueing up to grab the first chance to catch him. Is he bisexual then? Like me?

'Samuel runs his own business... he designs, makes and sells furniture. All cutting-edge stuff, high end, nothing cheap. He is a designer-cum-carpenter-cum-woodcarver. Impeccable taste. Smashing manners. You should see his work. He makes masses of money and we're about to buy a plush apartment in town'

I have to stifle a chuckle on hearing this, thinking of the oh so deeply socialist convictions of these middle-class dropouts.

'And you? What do you do?'

'Work in a hospital in Odense. Four or five days a week. Some nights. It depends. I commute, but a colleague has just told me of a post in London... I'm considering it'.

In Christiania, he is sometimes called to heal and deal with the troubles of everyone else in the community who suffers from allergy to hospitals, convention or common sense. My words, not his, of course. *Torben the god*, they call him and he is proud of being useful, needed, well thought of (loved, I guessed), but the god is now in tears and I cannot make out what else he is saying. (I am still asking myself how on earth could I make amends to my past faults). Even his homosexuality seems to me an act of defiance rather than a genuine inclination, although I would've never judged him for that, so why escape? Why?

'Can't understand why you didn't tell me. It's not as if I cared about you being... It doesn't make any difference to my feelings. None at all, so why?'

'"Sexual inclinations are like religious beliefs. Inner convictions, personal choices, complex, sometimes dogmatic, but above all, private and individual. Untransferable"'. He quotes me to the letter.

We spend some time winnowing the truth from what has been an unnecessary series of fibs, like one separates sober days from drunken nights in order to find out what really happened at the scene of the crime, as it were.

Torben says he now sees how not cutting the umbilical cord before leaving, whoever or whatever it was that he meant to leave behind, became stronger in his mind, following him around, tugging at his sleeve, sitting upon his shoulders. I could've told him as much. The farther he went, the heavier the baggage. The farther he went, the deeper the yearning to be back, but what can I say? If he has not been strong enough to tell the truth it's because somehow, I have managed to undermine his confidence, to make him feel inadequate, undeserving of my understanding or my respect.

In my turbulent head, it all sounds as embarrassing as it is painful, but we have crossed the bridge and the water beneath us can now run freely and wash our sins away. We shake hands, my son and I.

For the time being, we content ourselves with the initial progress, however minor. I then persuade him to go and have a rest. He needs it and so do I, so I take a deep breath, close my eyes and try to sleep, but cannot help hearing his words again and again in my mind, until I am able to process them calmly and compassionately.

What I keep wondering is whether Anders knew about his brother being around. If he did, that would mean that he condoned Torben's decision and never told me because I was the real bastard he now makes me see I have been. Fuck. Fuck. Fuck.

In fact, judging by the words they exchanged while I was asleep...

It doesn't matter. After more than seven decades in this world and forty-five as a lawyer I have come to agree with that old cliché that says that the truth lies somewhere in the middle of the opposing arguments.

A nurse comes into the room, draws the curtains closed and tells me to rest. The reddish, yellowish glare I could see with my eyes shut turns to a peaceful blue and in the serenity of this dim light another flood of memories comes clear. England. Late eighties. Those years seem to have left such an imprint on Torben's mind. I guess that notwithstanding the fact that my marriage to Anna was a highly mercurial one, life felt cozy and homely and the overall atmosphere was warm.

Torben told me more than once that he has never forgiven me for walking out on Anna, for not thinking of them, for putting my own interests first. "Why on earth, he shouted at me once, did I get rid of the woman who was like a mother to them?" It is really ironic how he accuses me of the same charges that William accuses Anna:

depriving them of a home. A home that used to be full of those gloomy musicians who never seemed to talk to one another because they had their mouths full of salmon nibbles washed with copious quantities of my aquavit. I used to wonder then how they were able to rehearse. My sons loved all that. Neither Bach nor Bartok put them off. They'd rather have Anna's friends pouring into the house than the Sunday lunches in country pubs or trendy restaurants that followed our divorce. Neither the trendy clothes, or the ready cash, nor the expensive trainers which became too numerous and insignificant in my foolish effort to overcompensate, made up for the home they had lost, a home where Anna waited for them at weekends, with plenty of treats and cakes that tasted strangely home-made.

I feel myself drifting away and hate it because I am terrified of dying in my sleep. Images of Torben merge with the vision of a river flowing smoothly, steadily, between the greenest of banks, now he is sitting by my side in this room, now in my own room at home, and now there is Anders and Anna with a bright green scarf around her neck, swatting mosquitoes and then Anna becomes Grette frying eggs in a pan over a barbecue on the river bank from the boat sailing upstream I point out some highlights along the way to a group of strangers and the Queen of England I am sitting behind her while I explain to the other passengers that those elaborated posts standing on the lawn carved and ornated like the spires of the Colleges act as meeting points for blackbirds it must be Cambridge and then the water is high and washes away the frying pan with the eggs in it and a colossal star crushes onto the roof without any sound just shining...

Chapter 9

Trinitatis, October 1990

'Oh, darling, that powder pink's perfect on you. Pity that your hair can't stay wavy'. Her mother announces as she breezes into the room. Cecille spins around to look at herself in the mirror and feels happy with what she sees. Ilse and Eleanor can now come into the room.

'Doesn't she look beautiful? her mother states rather than asks before her friends have time to make any comment. Ilse agrees. Eleanor looks speechless and then she agrees and adds that Cecille looks perfect, like a bride. She's almost moved to tears. Typically, Eleanor.

Both her friends had their Confirmation last month and Cecille thought they looked terrific! They chose to have a huge party together, with their respective families and friends, but when her mother asked her what kind of party she wished for, Cecille said she wanted something simple or no party at all. It suited her. Only it didn't. Of course, not. She wanted a big party, with a gorgeous dress and hordes of people. Be a star for the day. It's not as if her parents couldn't afford it. Her mother took her answer to the letter though and didn't mention it again, except for hinting at some possible presents at different times. Her father was in Stockholm. Some work there keeps him coming and going every other week. Too busy to think of his daughter's Confirmation.

The dress she is wearing is classy rather than beautiful and it is the one she wore last year for her cousin's wedding. She does not mind too much. In fact, she likes the colour and how it fits her, but she is sure that her mother has told Ilse and Eleanor to make a fuss of it because at the last minute, she realized that she hadn't taken her only daughter to get a new one. Cecille never asked for it and it was never discussed.

Somebody is ringing the doorbell. Through the window she sees there is a car parked outside.

'Better to go by taxi, girls. I didn't have time to get my car washed' her mother says.

They arrive at Trinitatis in time and Cecille walks in solemnly, a lump in her throat.

'Walk upright, darling. Shame the dress got a bit creased'

Most of her friends, aunts, cousins are already here. The church looks amazing with so much light and candles! Cecille has always loved the altarpiece, baroque and dramatic! Eleanor gets her violin and plays Bach.

Cecille knows exactly what her Confirmation involves and has prepared well for this day, but now she is too emotional and cannot grasp the priest's words. The more she tells herself to relax, the more self-conscious she feels. The priest reads her well and smiles warmly. Cecille likes her. Her cousin Sinnah offered to host her party and has done a good job of laying tables, organizing the catering and arranging flowers to Cecille's tastes. Sinnah knows that she likes scented flowers and does not care very much for those without aroma. Her mother ordered a fine cake that everyone enjoys. Her godmother gave her a silver bracelet of chained roses carved in relief. Quite romantic and feminine. Her Art teacher gave her an Anna Ancher print and Cecille cannot believe her teacher got it for her! Kasper and Anna gave her a camera. Cecille is delighted, she's always coveted one of her own. Her father phones sometime during the evening.

Her friends sit next to her at the top of the table. Ilse on her left, Eleanor on her right. The boys, dressed up and feeling awkward, look out of place. Not much to say to one another in the presence of adults. Torben, neither young enough to play with Sinnah's kids, nor grown up enough to join the teenagers, goes and sits next to his Dad.

Eventually, they play music and some dancing and timid groping takes place. Ilse, happy with her Matthias; Eleanor, with Anders and so on. Pity that Patrick didn't turn up. He is never there to see her when she looks at her best, Cecille thinks. Yet, this is her party. She'll make the most of it.

Chapter 10

A love story in a few seconds

Twenty-two minutes past eleven. I've just opened my eyes. My mouth feels so dry and it's so noisy in here. I thought it was due to early morning activity, but a nurse came to check my temperature and said it is night time. Half-past eleven in the evening. Nearly midnight, in fact. I've been asleep for over twenty-four hours and still feel exhausted. Old. Worn out. Very ill. Instead of waking up fresh and sharp as in the last few days, I find I could hardly speak.

First, my tongue stuck to my palate and when I finally manage to utter some words, the nurse cannot make out what I am trying to say. I cannot ask whether she does not understand me because my speech is awkward or because I am not making sense. Either alternative is worrying and degrading. Not being able to make myself understood. I, who have always been told how clear my diction was, how pedantically accurate my use of language was... Speaking was my skill and language, my tool. I'm a barrister, for God's sake!

Yesterday, or the day before, Mr Henriksen suggested I should start walking by myself, but now I think he is likely to decide otherwise. What's more, I feel that he might suggest chemotherapy again, which is exactly what I've been dreading all along, much more than the resection itself. People get so run down by it, and if what Torben told Anders the other day about the life expectancy of a Glioblastoma multiforme sufferer is true, then what is the point of so much agony? I would rather let myself go, check myself out of the hospital and die peacefully at home. Or perhaps I'm too ill to be moved at all. Fandens også!

The night is blue and cool. Someone has changed my blankets for a light quilt, presumably in response to my complaint about the sheets being too taut over my feet. The window has been left slightly open and the curtains drawn back because they know I like to get a glimpse of the city beneath and beyond.

In a building opposite this one, I can see a man standing on his balcony. If he could see me, I would think he was looking at me, but he can't because from his side, my window is at an angle and my head is far from it. He is naked, stretching up his arms as if he had just got up. Perhaps he has. He might be one of those guys who works shifts and will soon have to drive into the night, towards a factory, or a lab or a sorting office... I can tell he is strong from over a hundred metres apart. Young, short legged and stocky. Unless I am dreaming or hallucinating or simply cracking up. Now a girl joins him. Her hair in a pony tail and one head taller than him. She stands next to him, looking at the night sky, dressed in a very light, baggy pair of white trousers, possibly pyjamas, because her slim legs show against the light of the lamp behind them, and another lamp above them paints a lunar landscape on her bare breasts.

They do not seem to be talking, but they look at ease in each other's company. Now she folds her arms and starts swaying sideways until her hips gently hit his, probably to the rhythm of some song I cannot hear from here. The man rocks back, making sure he sways to left and right as the same time as the girl so that their bodies can't touch. They play the game for a few seconds until he alters the rhythm and when their hips finally touch, he wraps his arms around her and they move away from the window. A love story in a few seconds. No sounds, no words, no special effects, no plot. Just a man and a woman taking the air in a clear night on a balcony of an old city. Perfect.

'You did have a siesta, Dad' Anders says, bursting into the room. He smiles and holds my hand and I have to repeat three or four times that he shouldn't have come at this time of night, before he understands what I'm saying. It seems that my speech is really altered. Have I had a stroke? I won't know unless they tell me. I could communicate in writing, I suppose, but they won't let me have pen and paper either, unless I beg them.

Despite the concern in his grey eyes, Anders tells me I am fine. Funny how one has to let them believe that you believe them. He has only called on his way home. Nja and he went out for dinner at the Hansens, he says, as if I should know who the bloody Hansens are, but I don't. I would like to tell him about the visions, the dreams and the nightmares I've been having in the last couple of days, if only to get rid of them, to stop them coming back, but I can't.

When I try to tell the nurse about them after Anders is gone, she dismisses my unease as a minor one and tells me not to worry, failing to spot the difference between mild concern and sheer terror. If only I could restrain the horse and dismount here!

Chapter 10

God dag

Bright, transparent day out there. I woke up when Mr Henriksen was about to leave the room. He turned back to wish me God morgen and explained that I have had a seizure. Odd. I can always tell when they are about to happen and always remember them afterwards, but there you are. He said that I was given a stronger dose of painkillers and carbamazepine and that these, in turn, produced some side-effects such as vomits three or four times in one hour. I had to be hydrated and fed via a drip. How utterly depressing.

'Despite all that, your heartbeat is perfect now', Mr Henriksen said. And your blood pressure too. Would you rather I came back later?

'Nej, tak. Do what needs doing, please'

I had the greatest relief to hear my own voice coming out clearly and see that he understood exactly what I said without any need to repeat. I felt completely pain-free. That is what I call good news after what seemed to have been a worsening of my condition.

'Fancy something to eat now?

'How about bacon and scrambled eggs?'

Mr Henriksen replied it was good to see I hadn't lost my sense of humour.

'Why should it be funny? I might not be here tomorrow. Besides, if you've ever breakfasted on eggs and bacon, you would know I'm not kidding, sir'.

'I'd rather stick to salmon and caviar' he joked. 'Or bread and butter, come to that'. His forehead looked serious but there was a tease in his voice and a smile in his eyes.

'Bread and butter it is, then'

Instead, Mr Henriksen suggested some yoghurt, muesli, honey... but I protested that all those things would make me sick. Bored sick, not vomit sick, so he settled for my choice and in a gesture completely at odds with his character, Mr Henriksen patted my arm with his big hand, before leaving the room. He would have some apples sent to me as well. Could I manage apples now? I nodded and he smiled back.

This apparent progress after yesterday seizure is not a miraculous one for him to be so pleased about it. Was he being ultra kind just because he knows the end is near? This is the worst bit of this condition: you spend every minute wondering what next? When? How?

I sat up as upright as I could and shouted, feebly, but I shouted, as soon as Mr Henriksen left the room. A nurse was beside me straight away, 'what a service', I told her, and when I asked, she answered that nobody called Elba had left a message, nobody called Elba had come to see me while I was sedated, nobody called Elba had telephoned. Nothing. I asked her again, but she was adamant. 'Messages and phone calls are religiously jotted down and never lost', she assured me.

Good old Ted and Sonja and Erika, they have all called at different times when I was asleep, or spoken to Grette or my sons. Only Elba has not materialized or texted anyone at any time. I explained to the nurse that Elba, the lady I was asking about, had promised to come back the day after her first visit, and she was one to keep her promises, only I could not remember when exactly had been her first visit.

'Either way', the nurse insisted, 'Elba hasn't come yesterday or this morning or ever. *Aldrig*. 'Listen' she said. 'If you behave yourself, calm down, and are a good boy, I might get a wheel chair and take you for a ride, how about that? Mr Henriksen said it's time we started taking you out of these four walls'

I could've kissed her if it hadn't been for her condescending tone, the one she surely uses to talk to an old man well into his second childhood. If you behave yourself and are a good boy. Stupid woman. I said that if she kept talking down to me, I would denounce her for sexual harassment and she laughed, which was really lucky because although I had tried to make the point light heartedly, my tone had come out brusque and emotional. I can't see why I care to be polite, really. After all, I am a brain-tumoured patient. A sick-brained patient. A dying patient.

I could make the most of my condition and be an absolute pain in the backside, but I don't have it in me. I do not have it in me. The expression is laughable. If I were to say it aloud, I would sound like an idiot, like a bad actor in a pathetic role, but I realize now where I've heard it often: at Court, where I worked for over three decades. Some of the women who wanted to take their husbands to the cleaners, were told by some sensible judge or other that there wasn't a hope in hell of getting all they claimed to be their fair share of their assets, so they gave up and changed their argument for something like Oh, I never really meant to run away with the house, the car, the savings, the cat and the dog. I just don't have it in me, they said, adopting a saintly expression. Too saintly. Much too late. I should have written a book about the personalities of all the couples I have divorced. They would've made Freud proud. Or crazy.

Anyway, after much rage controlling, both the nurse, (Leila is her name. She is Filippino), and myself embarked into this new adventure. She sorted out the drip and I sat myself comfortably on the wheel chair, one second feeling strong enough to run a marathon and the next second, relieved to sit down again no sooner I stood up. Edges and silhouettes got blurred for a second or two, but at least the room didn't spin around us. It has to be a good sign.

We had not reached the door when Grette arrived, slightly flushed, a trace of sweat on her upper lip and make-up free. She's one of those women who needs some on her lips to brighten up her complexion. I prefer her with some lipstick on.

'Is anything the matter?' I said before greeting her and she replied that nothing was the matter, tak. Finding me ready to go and visit the gardens in my new vehicle made her day. She did look moved but her tone was tight and brittle. As she made to push my chair, the nurse obliged, and I realized how genuinely pleased I was to see someone I love, someone with whom to share a transcendental moment, because after all these days here, being able to catch a glimpse of what goes on outside the four walls of my room was a major achievement for me. I am sure that children must feel as elated when they find they can walk by themselves, a few steps at a time before falling over and trying again, until they manage to stay up for the whole day and be physically independent for the rest of their lives.

'Imagine having your life ahead of you...'
'I'd rather not' Grette said.

No more was needed to wipe out the joy I felt on seeing her and instead, felt troubled by her edginess. It wasn't mere disappointment, but sheer irritation. Poor Grette. I could not live without her, but she has always been a woman for the present and future, never one given to much introspection. She finds my interest in the past dispiriting and futile. I can't blame her, but if you meet and marry in your fifties, it's impossible not to be carrying a vast amount of luggage, which you feel like revisiting every now and then. I rather relish the fact that I have always had a good memory and indulge in reminiscing about those moments which have been complete, rounded, happy. I think everybody does. It's human nature. It doesn't mean that one wallows in melancholy or nostalgia, as Grette observes as soon as I say "on one occasion..." or something like that. I understand her, though. If your parents barely survived the Holocaust and your grandparents perished there, then you are not likely to be encouraged to look backwards and revisit your past.

'Where's Elba?' I said, as we advanced down the blue corridor.

'At her home, I suppose'

'I told her to stay in our house, surely you saw her'

'She stayed for dinner, slept over and left the following morning. She grabbed some papers from your safe, -thank you for trusting me- and took them home. She said they were some of your parents' documents and that you had asked her to take them with her. None of my business, surely'

Grette's tone now was plainly sarcastic and although I could not see her face as she walked behind me along corridors and out of them towards some French doors on the ground floor, I could picture her arched eyebrows and her eyes, wide open with chagrin. I sympathized with her. If I were her, I would also feel excluded, except that by playing behind her back, as she said, I am in fact protecting her from heartbreak, but there you are. Life is so full of intricacies, misunderstandings, secrets, scandals, offences, intrigues, hurt...

After some seconds of solid silence between us, pushing amongst the crowds of visitors and staff, Grette says she is sorry and her apology moves me while we finally go through the double doors onto the garden, filled with dahlias, red roses and the scent of linden trees.

'It's I who is sorry, elsker', I said, and I meant it.

Grette smiled through tearful eyes and I could not help feeling relieved to be aware enough of my need to apologize and by the knowledge that Cecille's files were now in good hands. What I could not and still cannot understand is why the hell has Elba never phoned.
I apologized to Grette one more time.

We walked by a group of patients and their visitors, who turned to smile and wish us God dag. Then we stopped by a wooden bench, beneath a silver birch, next to a cluster of lavender shrubs, where Grette sat after fixing my chair at an angle so that we could face each other. I felt so exhilarated, so indescribably exultant taking in the beauty of all those shades of green, blue, pink, yellow in what to me, after weeks of boredom, looked like the most beautiful place in the world, that I closed my eyes in order to record them again, into the grooves of my ailing brain. One never knows when a recollection might come in handy. Grette said something I feigned to acknowledge but ignored it, only because I wanted to resist any violation of my moment of bliss.

She thought that I was getting tired and suggested going back to my room. I refused. The air felt fresh. Life was good. I felt happy.

Eventually, Grette also sat back and turned her face up to the sun. I was certainly in love with the world again.

Chapter 11

Erika

'There you are! How are you, Ole, darling?', a woman calls out as she walks hurriedly towards us. It is Erika. She strides along ahead of Jensen, a hand to her summer hat to stop the breeze blowing it away. She has looked the same for the last forty years: light in her step, slim, smartly dressed and day-dreaming. She herself has admitted on more than one occasion that living in a world of her own is a skill she has developed to perfection. I don't know anyone else who can be so up to date with what is happening in the world but remain oblivious to what goes under her own nose.

Grette does not like her very much, -Anna could not stand her-, but they brush each other's cheek and kiss in the civilized way they both can handle. Jensen, on the contrary, looks like he's always looked: short, vain, ill at ease with himself and the rest of the human race. If it weren't for Erika, we would've ceased to be friends long time ago.

After exchanging the usual greetings and comments about my health there is a slight pause, minimal, hardly noticeable, in which Erika seems anxious. I look at her, but she averts her eyes, something she has never done before. For years and years, we have guessed each other's thoughts without the need to speak them, but at the moment, she is acting as if she knows something she doesn't want me to find out.

Erika is the youngest of the Konig girls. They used to live opposite us when we were children. Mrs Konig became a war widow at twenty-seven, bringing up three daughters with a dignity and a strength of spirit I have only found in my own father, Grandad and a few other people of their generation.

The girls used to make a fuss of me while I was a child and they, adolescents. We had Christmas dinners and Sunday's tea together, the Konig ladies, as Dad used to call them, and us. On summer evenings, Mother and Mrs Konig used to go for endless walks, engaged in animated conversation, giggling gleefully like girls. I guess they must have looked forward to those Sundays. If I close my eyes, I can still hear their cheery laughter, their joy, their uncomplicated contentedness. I can see their silhouettes ahead of us, turning to blue and then to purple and then to black in the dying light, and the six of us trickling down the road behind them.

The girls liked to sing and Elba and Erika made an enviable duet (both of them still sing those old songs). Erika used to jot down the lyrics straight from the radio, sometimes engaging me to help her grasp all the words in time. Ernst and I, bored with silly women's chitchat, or tired after a whole day of football and tree-climbing, kicked pebbles or threw them ahead in the hope that any of the Konig girls would bend to pick up one or two and offer us a glimpse of her thighs, knickers or other intimacies. It never happened. We were too slow to realize that pebbles, as opposed to jewels or flowers, tend not to make a girl bother to collect them.

Years went by and by the time Mrs Konig moved to a small house in town, the girls had found jobs and were only seen at weekends. Margrethe, the eldest, married young and went to live in Århus. Later, Renathe followed in her steps. Erika was the last one to leave the warmth of her maternal home. She exchanged financial insecurity for a life of luxury next to Jensen, an old school friend who had moved away in his childhood and who, after bumping into her twenty years later, clung to her like to his saviour only to humiliate her ever since for being stronger than he's ever been.

Erika will never admit to herself, let alone to anybody else, that Jensen is a bully whom she has spoilt like an enfant terrible for the last forty odd years, but the tension and the lack of warmth between them has always been palpable. Their unhappiness transpires their carefully chosen words, cautious glances and polished manners. Parallel lives, never touching.

The details and frequency and intensity of their arguments I have only found out through their daughter who, caught up in their turbulent household, came up to me expecting to find salvation in my arms, blind to the fact that I could not save her, and indifferent to my rejection.

'So, when are you going home?' Jensen asks. Grette hastens to answer for me, saying that it will be very soon and that once the radiotherapy is over, she'll take me to the Italian Riviera and we shall relax, eat, drink and enjoy the promenades along the Mediterranean, the way I like it.

I notice Erika listening attentively to Grette's enthusiasm and I wonder whether she, like me, is trying to fathom whether Grette's outburst of optimism has the intention of distracting us all from a reality which only now, notwithstanding my apparent, current progress, is starting to sink in. Perhaps I am wrong. Perhaps Erika half-closes her eyes as Grette speaks only because she is thinking of another summer. I don't know.

It was such a long time ago. Erika had cycled into town to do some shopping, when she saw me across the street and stopped to say hello. I suggested some coffee and she pulled her bicycle over the curb onto the cobblestoned pavement. I held one of the handlebars and told her to make a dash for the only available table in the dappled shade of a chestnut tree while I sorted out the bike.

She was wearing a pair of blue linen bermuda shorts that emphasized her long legs and from the corner of my eyes I could see other men leering at her as she walked past. We sipped our coffee, talked about nothing in particular, but always understanding our silences as much as our words, in the same way I understand my sister. Then we parted. She still had to go and cook some lunch and it was getting late.

'Fancy dropping by for a drink? Six thirty?' she asked, and rode away without waiting for me reply. It wasn't necessary.

I had to ring the bell twice and was about to leave when she opened the door. She wasn't ready yet. I followed her onto the balcony, where I would get inebriated with the scent of the wistaria my father had given her a few years earlier, and which grew vigorously from a substantial terracotta pot and spread over the whole south facing wall. I remember Erika making some comment on the beauty of the evening.

Jensen was out. I could tell he had gone out in a huff, spoiling Erika's plans for my imminent call, but I didn't mention it. I knew he was having a passionate affair with a German woman who lived opposite his parents' villa further out north. I had seen them at the Club, sunbathing by the swimming pool, rubbing suntan lotion on each other's chests. He didn't try too hard to hide it. Erika knew. All our friends knew, but nobody discussed it. She would be right back, Erika said.

The light was still sharp and the streets were already quiet with that lull that falls upon them once everybody has gone home from offices and banks and factories and before anybody goes out again to dine out, see a play or watch a film. I felt uncomfortable on the balcony, something was amiss and got up to leave. I told Erika I was leaving loudly enough for her to hear from her bedroom, but she didn't answer. I went a bit nearer.

Sex was disappointing despite her eagerness, which I was lucid enough to interpret as revenge on her husband rather than desire for me, but we carried on for the whole season, meeting in hotels and rented cottages, pretending that the affection we felt for each other was enough to quench our thirst for adventure, passion and lust. At times, we pretended it was true love; others, that it wasn't there.

When the Autumn came, we went back to our normal lives and undamaged friendship. Neither of us had said a word about finishing our illicit, unsatisfactory love affair. It simply died away along with the warm summer nights and the leaves on the trees.

By the next summer, she had Cecille in her arms and Ulla and I had Anders. If Erika or myself had ever felt guilty of our betrayals, life seemed to have forgiven us. Perhaps she is revisiting those days now that she knows that my journey is coming to an end.

More visitors arrive and others are leaving but we stay outdoors a little longer while the sky gets steadily greyer and the vibrancy of the garden softens beneath the clouds.

Jensen talks about Queen Margrethe, the EU and the American president. Grette argues a few points on the matter and Erika tells us about the latest exhibition at Louisiana's where she went last Saturday with her good friend, Amelie.

'Shall we move to the Café… unless I look too scary to make an appearance?

'Nonsense. Let's go' Erika replies already up from her chair. Both she and Grette add that I look very well, indeed.

'Won't the smell of coffee make you sick? Grette worries, but I insist that I still fancy having a cinnamon whirl there because it will surely taste better than in my room, so we all head for the cafeteria, Grette always behind, pushing my chair, Jensen always ahead, shuffling his Italian loafers cool-man style.

Dr Sorensen, one of the day doctors, who was skimming the chocolate powder off his cappuccino with great concentration, immediately puts his spoon back on the saucer, walks towards us and tells me how good it is to see me making progress. So polite. Not like Dr Dubois, who pretended not to understand my French when I addressed him in his mother tongue assuming it would be a kind gesture. Never mind. Dr Sorensen's manners make up for others' rudeness, and I'm grateful for his concern.

Then, like the spoilt man everybody says I have become since I've been in hospital, I am allowed to order pastries and black coffee with a good blob of whipped cream floating on it like a tiny ice floe on a dark lake. I said this to the girl and she grins warmly, probably thinking I sound like her grandfather. God!

Jensen orders the same and Grette and Erika have strawberry tart and plain black coffee. I feel so thrilled by the normality of the experience that I can hardly bear it until Jensen mentions what earlier on, Erika and I, with just a look, had tacitly agreed not to discuss.

'Did Erika tell you about Cecille's visit? She came to see us last month' he says, his eyes filled with pride.

Grette, who had by now relaxed and forgotten about my supposedly lack of trust in her, shrinks and tenses up again the way she always does when something or someone from my past, distant or recent, resurfaces. Erika starts swinging her foot, her toes curling up inside her shoe. It is a habit of hers. She does it unconsciously whenever she feels ill at ease. She is an insecure woman. Too much embarrassment could kill her. I, the tacitly discussed culprit, so to speak, opts for the truth, although I must say that the words come up to me spontaneously, almost accidentally, rather than as the result of careful consideration. It was a silent wings moment, as I call it. You can't see any bird but you know its wings have flapped.

'She called me. We had lunch together. She is very well, isn't she?' I notice my tone sounds slightly defiant, almost provocative. Grette's cup jars against the saucer. Jensen blinks, not knowing what to make of it.

On one occasion, not long ago, he was furious about something Cecille had said to him and after moaning and swearing while he was telling me of their argument, he added "Forgive me if she's your friend, but she's impossible sometimes", as if Cecille being my friend was more important to him than her being his daughter. I didn't bother to correct him because I knew then, as well as I know now, that Jensen is one of those people who will forever miss the point.

'She's very well, indeed' Erika picks up my words and blushing slightly, her skin matching the hues of her scarf, she emphasizes how fulfilled Cecille feels with her antique dealer husband and her cultural, enriching life in Paris.

Although not a single shadow passes over her eyes, I detect the tiniest change in tone I have noticed before. Whenever she speaks of her daughter, there is something not quite defined, not clear, a mix of something that I have never been able to ascertain. Is it a certain jealousy of Cecille's youth? Is it a kind of hidden resentment, some unacknowledged feeling gnawing at her heart since Cecille grew up? Their mother-daughter bond has always intrigued me because they have always been such a part of my life.

While observing her sitting at the hospital café, I guess that it isn't the mere longing for her own lost youth on seeing her daughter's unlined face and glossy hair that troubles her. It is a feeling much stronger and far more complex than her maternal love, which wriggles its way out of her heart in the microseconds of silence squeezed between her words every time somebody mentions Cecille. It is the same kind of feeling that I have spotted on one or two occasions in women whose husbands were granted custody of their children. They would come to my office and turn up at Court distressed and dismayed by the outcome of their trial, yet, all along, their eyes would betray a sense of relief, which they had probably not recognized within themselves. One knows so little about oneself that the mere idea that it is possible to know someone else is an utter fallacy. An illusion.

'Does she have any child by now?' Grette asks, and I immediately dread that she may have read any of Cecille's letters. I am still wondering whether she has and if so, whether she is simply and deliberately being bitchy the way women can be in circumstances like these.

'Sadly, no' Erika replies, and that "sadly" puts an end to the subject. I am sure that Cecille would've simply said No, without humiliating herself any further, and for a second, and on her behalf, I despise Erika for saying sadly, and Grette for digging into a raw wound, when Cecille is not here to defend herself.

Soon afterwards, the Bossens stand up to leave. Jensen and I shake hands, Erika kisses my cheek, leaving a faint waft of expensive perfume whirling around behind her and we all exit the café together; two of us towards the safety of a secluded, organized, tentative survival bubble, and the other two towards the world, full of misery, eagerness, indifference, darkness and hope. Or is it the other way round?

As Grette takes me back along the corridors, I keep thinking about Erika. I am still not sure of how much she knows about Cecille's pregnancy. She knew nothing at the time of the accident but after so many years, Cecille may have told her. The affair continues to affect me, to rule my life, my relationship with my wife and with these old friends of mine, Cecille's parents. My concepts of guilt, indulgence and forgiving have forever been altered after what I choose, selfishly, to call the accident. I wish I could phone or write to Cecille and say 'Look, let's be open about it, let the people who want to know, know' but that would only be to ease my torment and increase hers. The ultimate egotistical deed, since its consequences in my life would be irrelevant at this stage, –or at any stage, actually-, compared with the consequences the whole thing has had on her past, present and future.

If only she decided to tell the truth, leave the past behind her, adopt a child... We could all be redeemed. We would be granted some peace over the matter. Instead, she is an infertile, barren woman who has endeavoured to forgive me and in doing so, reminds me constantly, continuously, of my cruelty. If only. If only Cecille had never seen me walking past Rosenborg Castle as she came out that cold, cold afternoon. I hinted at something like that over lunch at Piegare's the other day and she laughed it off, throwing her head backwards, saying that regrets are cheap ways of justifying oneself.,

'Besides, *«Si j'avais» ... n'existe pas' »,* she said.

It is twenty-past six now and I cannot stop thinking about a story that developed over twenty years ago, of which the consequences altered forever the rest of our lives. Hers, mine and all the people attached to us by blood, marriage or friendship. Life is not for the faint-hearted.

Grette stays with me until I am taken to the torture chamber also known as radiotherapy room.

'So, you've been busy while I was away' she says no sooner we get onto the lift, glaring deeply into my eyes through the mirror. 'Did you tell her you're ill?'

'Of course, not' I reply in all honesty, but I would deny it even I had indeed told Cecille about the cancer. Telling Cecille before her or anybody else, would've hurt Grette no end and I am not that cruel.

Now it is the first time, I think, that I am glad to be on my own in this room with plenty of time to think things through once I finish with the evening routine. Anybody would think that I have had more than enough time to think in the last few days, but one cannot truly reflect on anything when there are sons visiting and coming up with the strangest confessions, and seizures and pain and drowsiness inducing pills interrupting our chain of thoughts at any moment, not to mention the discomfort caused by the radiotherapy. I will have my supper, (I have ordered chicken in champignon and bechamel sauce with roast potatoes and carrots) and then will go for a short expedition along the corridors, holding onto my good nurse's arm. If I feel strong enough, I might have a shower by myself tomorrow, she promises, instead of being given a bath by the dragon- looking one. I wonder whether it's deliberate, something carefully calculated to annoy or disappoint sad men like me, but it is a fact that bed baths are given by dragons, not mermaids. Fantasies, not encouraged. It must be one of the hospital rules.

Chapter 12

Anna

I am hardly awake when the telephone rings. The bloody thing seems to ring inside my head. It does not hurt, but it sounds loud and sharp, like an amplified, splitting ringing. The nurse comes in to check that I am able to pick up the receiver myself. Of course, I am.

'Dad' he nearly screams, and it takes me a few seconds to overcome my shock before I can ask him how he is. He is fine, how about me? He has only heard a couple of days ago, after he returned from Hong Kong. Couldn't phone sooner. He's in London now. 'I phoned Anna and she told me at once...'

'It's Mummy, not Anna' I interrupt

'God, you must be ok if you're still nagging at me. Anna doesn't mind me calling by her name'. William sounds half amused, half irritated.

'She's not well either, please go and see her', I tell him, and then change the subject so that he can reflect on it later. 'This IS a surprise. Are you well? How's work?'

Yes. He is good. (Not well, but *good*, for God's sake!) I almost ask him whether that is the Grammar he was taught for a fortune, but manage to stop myself in time. He will be coming over "a.s.a.p.", he assures me. Can't wait to see me.

'What happened, exactly? Did you say "brain tumour"? Is Anders there? And Grette? Torben should know what to do. Is he also there?'

He's full of questions and concern. I explain that most of the tumour has been removed and as he can hear, I am all right. I'm on my way to a full recovery so there is no need to take time off and make changes to his diary when we all know he has been so busy out there.

'Nonsense. I'll catch the first flight to CPH, don't worry about me. I'll be there at eight a.m. Danish time'

'Ok. Look forward to seeing you, Will. Please take care. Go and get some sleep and don't smoke too much'.

He hangs up and I am left with the sound of my three sons' conversations in my mind, all of them about me and my prospects of surviving this odyssey. I feel so egocentric and guilty for inflicting such degree of concern on everyone around. We haven't had a family gathering for some time and it will be overwhelmingly poignant in the circumstances. Feels like an approaching farewell and I don't like it. Find it rather frightening.

Still... It'll be lovely to see William. I know I can't help being irritating and overprotective with him even though he's a man now. Thirty years old, already. It seems only yesterday when he was born in the middle of a chilly November afternoon. Even Anna admitted afterwards that the timing was another one of her eccentricities. Most babies are born at night or in the early hours, apparently. She had such a healthy pregnancy, though. Really glowing and cuddly and delighted, but her labour was a long one and she would not let me comfort her before or after the birth. I wasn't present at the birth, but no sooner the nurse called me in and handed out the baby to me, I was hooked. Happy, awkward, moved and every other feeling in between, all at the same time. A father again.

Anna was sent home that very day. She wanted to be back in our room, on her own, and I drove back from the hospital ever so slowly in order to avoid causing her any more pain, annoying everybody else on the Fulham Road. Luckily, a friend of hers had suggested that I should take an inflatable rubber ring so she could sit on it all the way home. Drowsy and exhausted, she kept stretching her arm to touch our little William who was lying in his cot on the back seat, indifferent to the rain on the windscreen, the other drivers, and our joyful tears.

Since that first night, it was up to me to get up in the middle of the night, heat up milk, feed William and change his nappies. When he started teething, I rubbed soothing cream on his gums and later on, if I got a phone call, he would sit on my lap, poke my ears or tug at the ridiculous beard I had grown in those days. Always smiling. Always happy.

Meanwhile, Anna grew more and more distant, more detached. She started seeing counsellors and changed one after another, claiming they were a bunch of cranks. One of them told her she had the soul of an artist and she burst out laughing in his face. 'You have to be very stupid to go on paying money to those people', she concluded.

Poor Anna. She had it all. During the six years we were married, I wasn't able to take my eyes off her. She had the looks of a femme fatale and sharp brains to go with them. She was irresistible, in a challenging, intimidating sort of way. She wasn't a woman for weak men like the one I proved to be in the end, but I was grateful to her since day one because despite her eccentric ways, she was always kind to my children and they got on marvellously with her. I could not work out then why William, her own flesh and blood, had not stolen her heart. Only her music kept her sane, but she wasn't getting as many contracts as she had done a few years earlier and that was smothering all energy and creativity in her.

There was no incentive for her to go on and there was nothing I could do to help her out of her depression, her self-destruction. When she was sober, she played the piano with my older sons, took them out shopping, helped them with their homework and told them crazy stories that even Anders at thirteen found gripping. She never did as much with William, and by then, I had somehow taken over her place. William felt rejected. I tried to talk to her about it, to contain her sadness, tried to understand the reasons for it, but she would not let me. She had had a ghastly experience long before we met, was all she said. I tried to help. We had both gone through tragedy in our lives, I could've understood her, God knows I tried, but she refused being helped and we argued day and night in those months which were to be our last together.

One autumn evening, I came home from work to find her sitting in our bed, waiting for me, brandishing her great-grandfather's sword, swearing she would kill me if I didn't leave the house at once. She was drunk. That night I left. For good.

I wandered about all evening, first turning onto the small back streets, then following the straight lines of the King's Road, Sloane Street and Knightsbridge right up to Piccadilly and on through Soho and China town, that little town within the town, crowded with tourists, suburban visitors and staunch Londoners. I needed the noise, the anonymity, the indifference. I let myself be led by the crowds in one direction, then in another. I felt myself going adrift into the night until I anchored my newly acquired homelessness at a Latin bar crammed with shoals of people of all sexes and heady smell and cheap music. That was life. All else was a mirage. The life I had experienced up to that evening, with a striking pianist, in a Chelsea town house, with children coming at weekends from boarding schools and little William asleep beside his teddy bear had been an illusion, something that belonged to someone else. I was forced to be free again and didn't recognize the feeling.

I must have cut a sorry figure sitting at the bar, elbows on the counter, unable to enjoy the fire that the whisky produced in my veins. The music never stopped. A girl or two rubbed their breasts against my back as they squeezed their way to and from the Ladies. I had nowhere to go, but made myself stagger out of the bar and find my way back to my illusion. Was I still hoping to erase Anna's alcoholism, her virulent, vitriolic outbursts? Who could tell? Several taxis drove past slowly along Regent Street, but I just walked on. When I let myself into the house after hours of sitting on my own threshold like a beggar, the nanny was already up. If she was surprised to see me there, bleary eyed and drunk, she didn't say.

I told her she could have the morning off, but she kindly replied that she would rather catch up with the ironing and tidying up Willo's room. Besides, she said, Anna might need her. I realized then that she already knew that I had no place in my home any longer. She had immediately placed her loyalties with Anna. She was looking after her job. Who could blame her? She tried to stop me going upstairs, but I pushed her aside and climbed the steps two at a time despite my state. My suitcases had already been packed and were waiting for me outside our bedroom.

I stood there wondering how was it possible that a mere wooden door could actually have turned into a definite, insurmountable barrier between two people who had lived together and loved each other until a few hours earlier. I believed then that that love was still there, alive and kicking inside us in spite of burning words and furious rows. Only much later did I discover that such love was gone. The love that required compromise and altruism and understanding of each other's ways had vanished and turned into a selfish, individualistic, mean feeling adulterated by routine. It could only be rescued and purified if we were to stay apart.

I knocked on the door. I tried the knob, but it was

locked. Sleepless and in turmoil as I was, I saw the situation unfold itself before my eyes as if until that moment I had been watching a film, not my own life. I would've kicked the door open in the best Hollywood fashion had it not been for William coming out of his bedroom, in his soft pyjamas, shouting Daddy, Daddy, as he jumped into my arms. He asked me why I was crying and I lied that soap had got into my eyes. That was all. But I had not shaven yet, he observed, already noticing the alteration in my routine, which was also his routine and which would never be the same again. Anna's sword had finally pierced my heart and stuck in my chest, it turned one way and the other as the pain became actually physical. I held William tightly in my arms, hiding my face against his little shoulder and slowly walked downstairs until the nanny lured him out of my arms and took him to his breakfast. I turned back to get my suitcases and left.

Anders and Torben were at school. William stayed at home with his mother and his nanny until I could prove I was the right parent to take care of him, but during that time Anna sobered up and she was granted custody of a child who was, to her, little less than a stranger. A couple of months later, William was sent to live with her parents in Surrey and she went back to her music, and worst of all, to her gins and her whiskies. I booked a flight to Copenhagen and moved back straight away. Erika and Jensen put me up for a few weeks. That was the end of my second marriage.

Since that morning when he was baffled by my crumpled collar and my undone tie below my still unshaven face, William and I only met during his school holidays which later became University holidays, work holidays and the few occasions when I could take myself to England. I have probably seen him as little or as much as I have seen my other sons since they went to boarding school, but William has always felt left out and never got over our divorce. He blamed his mother for it then and still does, in the same way that Torben blames me for his loveless schooldays.

For two or three summers they came together to visit, Anna and William. She and I became good friends again, after our lives were legally and definitely split apart. We used to arrange those visits thinking that it was a happy time for William, but I could tell that he remained anxious throughout their entire visit, hoping against hope that we were going to live together again. He anxiously followed every gesture, every expression, every word his mother and I exchanged and the fact that we did get on well during those days must have given him false expectations. On the day of their return to England he would hardly talk to his mother. It was heartbreaking to see two human beings I loved so much hurting each other, unable to make it up, unable to make contact other than through resentment.

'Would you like all lights off, Herr Lundgren?' a nurse asks the poor sod in the next room and her voice and the immediacy of this reality brings me back to the sterile, clinical whiteness of my hospital room. I am now aware that I've only been awake for Willo's phone call in the whole day, and my eyes are almost closing again. Bloody dosed up, I must be.

Chapter 13

Madame Aleyeva

Paris. April 2006

'So, what will you wear on my big day?'

'A stunning frock I found at Posh's. It's vintage, in the most striking "Dior pink", the girl told me. Eleanor replied.

'Bravo! You always manage to look stunning for next to nothing. Fancy finding a dress like that... and the colour will offset your dark hair so well!

'... and the girl even threw in a matching nail varnish into the bargain, but I think it might be too much. Might go for nude'

'Or be bold and go for red nails. Red and pink. Very eighties. Go for it'

'You know what, my dear friend? I haven't seen you this happy for a long time! Even when we're all so excited about your wedding, you seem to be both excited AND cool at the same time. It's great to see you this well. I mean it'

'I know. I AM very well. Been for a long time, actually, but cool? Well, apart from fretting about the catering, the lights, the music and the seventy-two guests...Yes, I suppose I am'

They both laughed.

'Well, seriously, I know you kept saying how happy you were in your texts and so on, but I was a bit wary that you might be marrying for...'

'Money? Vlad is far from being rich'

'No, no, not for money, but just not to be alone, or bored, or... don't know. It doesn't matter. I can see you're over the moon and that's what counts'

'Venya is the most amazing guy I've ever met, believe me. He's... Can't describe him well. He's just... Veniamin. I adore him'

'Have you told him about...? He has the right to know, you know...'

'I told him I can't have children, if that's what you're wondering. Explained as much as it was necessary and that's it. I'm not lying to him, it's just my secret in my past. We all carry some baggage'

'Precisely, it's in the past. Surely, he'd understand'

'Drop it, Eleanor. What d'you want me to confess? What does it matter, now, anyway?'

'So, if it doesn't matter, why not tell him? You'd feel better for it, I'm sure'

Cecille could see why Eleanor insisted in making her tell Veniamin the whole truth before she married him, but she couldn't do it. It was not about protecting others or herself.

'What if he leaves me?', she said

'Why would he leave you? Oh, sweety, this is the twenty-first century. Veniamin wouldn't mind. Don't cry.

I'm so sorry, please, don't cry', Eleanor leant over the table and held Cecille's hand tightly. 'Are you really that scared?'

At last, Cecille put on her sunglasses, not minding that the day had turned cloudy and the light through the windows was dim and grey. She couldn't bring to tell herself, let alone anyone else, how much she dreaded being rejected.

'Thank you for this. I've always wanted to see the Rodins. I'm not that big on Art, as you know, but I got hooked on his works since I saw that Danae back home, when we went to the gallery with the school' Eleanor said, changing the subject.

'At the Glyptoteket. I love that one, too. He must've sculpted it at the height of their relationship'

'Do you think he used Camille Claudel?'

'Who knows? He fell for her beauty and her unparalleled talent, but then... God knows'

The two friends had enjoyed their visit to the museum and a lunch snack at its café. Eleanor had tucked into a classic croque-monsieur, but Cecille had a wedding dress to fit in, so she had taken an endive and pear salad.

'Anyway, let's go back to my wedding. Indulge me. What did Erika really said when she called you?'

'Oh, she wasn't amused. She couldn't understand why you didn't choose Trinitatis, where you were baptized and confirmed. I must say it would've been nice, too, but I told her that marrying in Paris was the ultimate chic. "The ultimate snub", your mother said. In the end I managed to persuade her that it was your big day and only yours, that only your choice mattered, all that sort of things... She muttered something and grumbled, but I'm sure she's fine, now'

'Dad told me that he'd done his best to convince her, too. In fact, he seemed really moved when I told them. It's always been so difficult to know how he feels about things, but he seems to have mellowed a bit'.

'They will be fine and happy for you on the day, you'll see'. Eleanor reassured her.

'Skal' Cecille said, raising her glass of lemonade.

'Skal. To you, to Venya, to us, to happiness', Eleanor added.

'And friendship'

They finished their drinks, giggling and reminiscing about old, innocent mischiefs. Cecille insisted on paying the bill and having done so, they both walked out of the Museum's café and towards Invalides in order to catch the RER to the apartment Cecille and Veniamin had bought two months earlier in the sixteenth arrondissement. It had cost them an arm and a leg, but it meant realizing a dream they had both entertained for so long. It only had what they called a bedroom and a half, but the building was from the turn of the twentieth century and the salon and their own room were large, with high ceilings and tall windows opening onto small balconies. It had been decorated by the previous owner and instead of painting the main wall blue in their bedroom, as she had anticipated, Cecille changed her mind and kept its original white, bought a four by two metres abstract mural off one of her artists and hung it above the bedstead. It occupied the whole width of the room and the effect was dramatic and bold. Even Erika, averse to Modern Art, had found it "beautiful" on the photos Cecille had sent her. Eleanor had also commented on the kitchen, where Cecille had ripped off the doors of the cupboard and chosen to have all crockery and crystal on display. It made the kitchen look smaller, but it added coziness and she liked the effect of the light on the glasses.

'Are you sure you'll be comfortable in this half room?'

'Stop fussing. It's absolutely fine. I wouldn't miss the chance of helping you get ready for the world. I'm intrigued by your choice of colour, though. I know you've always loved blue, but...'

'Well, I'm not marrying in church, plus, I've always worn quite a lot of white so it would've felt kind of non-special, plus... my hair is so fair that if the lighting is not right, I could look like a ghost'

'You wouldn't! But you're right. This shade of blue is just sublime. Very regal. I hope Veniamin hasn't seen it?'

'Of course not! He went to stay at his sister's the morning before the dress was delivered'

Cecille hugged Eleanor once more. She was happy to have her closest friend staying over and helping with the last details. In two days' time, she will be Madame Aleyeva. She will keep her maiden name for business, or probably double barrel, but she will forever be someone's wife. Veniamin's woman. Her lover's love. Her husband's mistress. She'll never admit how fulfilled that makes her feel.

Chapter 14

The beach

'You must destroy the whole lot if you want to avoid causing more damage. I can't see why you haven't chucked all these papers away yet. What d'you want them for? I can't see why it could be such an issue for her, but if she asked you to get rid of them, then bloody do so'

Darling, practical Elba. She turned up this morning when I was having breakfast, apologizing profusely for not coming sooner. She had got a call from her daughter who is eight months pregnant and had to rush and see to her, but it was all false alarm and here she was, as she put it. Reassuringly. Determinedly.

'Thank Heavens you're here! I couldn't tell you how relieved I am... and grateful'

'Look' Elba carried on 'It was an accident. It could've happened in the twelfth century and will continue to happen in the twenty-fifth century, but if this wretched girl has asked you to keep quiet and doesn't want anybody to know about your involvement, then burn the evidence, the poems, everything, for God's sake! I told you; I can't understand why you haven't done it yet! It's only a question of common sense'

I did not like her referring to Cecille as "wretched", but I let it drop or else Elba will go on and on telling me off.

'Have you opened the red envelope, too?' She looked offended. Of course, she hadn't.

'Shall I burn everything?'

'Not the envelope. She sent it to me sealed before she set off on a hiking trip to Peru after graduating. She was going on her own and thought I should know whatever it is that she enclosed in that envelope, in case something happened to her. Not the way a young person thinks, but Cecille was like that. I never read it, never opened it. Burn it all off, please, but not that, nor the poems. I'd like to read them' I begged.

When Elba is in an authoritative, justice- making sort of mood, she can be callous; so, fearing that she would refuse, I played my helpless-man- about-to-die card. She obliged, naturally. In fact, she had brought the folder neatly squared inside her bag and produced the notebook straight away, holding on to the other papers. I opened the notebook and read aloud:

The beach

They walk along the beach,
far from the multitude, far from the pain.
They've run away, they've broken free
from the dark cell, where unloved ones do remain.
They reach the edge beneath the shifting sky
and in their self-deceiving hearts
they feel there is no tide, no abyss, no black night
that could swallow up their hope,

their blinding faith set in the newly conquered,
tempting light.
Regrets crash hard against the rocks.
They wander by, believing in their dream,
their forward, straight path is all they see,
but lurking in their shadows,
reality will take away their hope,
their blinding faith.

September, 1996

'She's not Shakespeare, but her soul is in those lines: The hope, the faith, the disappointment, the frustration she could not overcome... "Regrets crash hard" Heavens above, Ole!'

I remain silent. I need to speak to Cecille. I will make a fool of myself, or worse, but I need to call her. Does Elba think I'm going mad?

'You're seventy-five years old, for fanden! Don't you think it's high time you took some responsibility for your acts?'

Cecille's telephone number is in my diary. I ask Elba to pass it on to me, but she's about to walk out of the room in protest or in defence of Cecille out of solidarity with her gender, I guess, so I put down the telephone and ask her back.

'You're right. Best not to call', but I secretly decide to call in the evening, when I will be alone again.

'At least she was an adult, wasn't she?'

'Sure'.

I manage to change the subject and the morning goes by, planning and enthusing about my -according to Elba- imminent visit to her and Harald in the country. I mention Torben's tantrums and reproaches in order to get some advice, -a feminine point of view on these matters is always the wisest- and she says that in family affairs and feelings there is no absolute truth, that both Torben and I are right, and both of us are wrong. For a moment, I think that she ought to have been the barrister in the family. She could've become a judge. All Torben and I have to do is forgive and forget.

'Easy, really. It only takes a lifetime', she adds, and we end up laughing out of despair.

At lunchtime, she squeezes my shoulder and leaves, promising to burn the folder as soon as she gets home and to phone and let me know when it's all over, "for your peace of mind", she adds, with fine sarcasm.

'Can't wait to hear of the bonfire'. I think that burning is better than shredding, it is more meaningful, perhaps for that atavistic idea that fire purifies everything.

I close my eyes and sleep for a few minutes until a young man comes up with my lunch. It's William.

'Well, well, well, how is the old patient?'

I choke on my words. So lovely to see him, he looks broader round his shoulders and quite tanned.

'You haven't been cooking yourself in the sun, have you?'

'Don't start, Dad. Are you well? I spoke to Grette. She said you've been out and about since yesterday. We could go out now if you want?'

So, we do. The garden looks duller today as the sky remains overcast, but there is a humming bird hovering around the pear tree and it cheers me up. Mother used to say that they are a good omen, a sign of coming joy.

William talks endlessly, as he always does. Avid for news from this end, eager to tell me everything that has gone on in his life from the exact moment we last saw each other until now. He doesn't spare me any detail and his enthusiasm amuses me. There is a lot of Englishness in his accent, (plum in the mouth type) and his Danish vowels are quite rusty, but he's such good company. This boy could ask me to do anything for him and I would gladly oblige. He could lure me into hiking across the desert with him and I would believe that it is the best invitation I could've possibly received in my whole life, and he knows it. Funny –and dangerous- what charm can do for you. As he carries on with his tales of bankers, hedge funds, investments and stocks, grand hotels and expensive meals, I think of myself at his age.

Every now and then during the course of his chat, I interrupt him with a banal question just to buy myself some time to get a bit of mental rest. Eventually, he stands up and goes to get himself another beer and I make the most of this brief pause to revise what he has been telling me.

Everything in his life is so clear, so straightforward, so defined. I enjoy looking at him as he strides up to the bar: taller, older, handsome. He does not resemble me in the least although at times some expressions in his eyes, or the way he rubs his forehead when he is considering some idea reminds me of Anders and Anders is the only one who has taken after me. Otherwise, with his dark hair and his greeny eyes that seem to take over half his face, William is like a male photocopy of Anna in the same remarkable way that Torben is a male copy of Ulla.

'Skål' he says, still a few steps afar and gulps down a good amount of his beer before sitting down next to me. 'Mother sends her love. She didn't want to phone you 'cos she doesn't want to bother you too much... She said you had both loved each other madly, but the timing was wrong. Oh, Dad, why are you crying? Please, Dad, don't distress yourself. I just thought you'd like to hear what she said'

'Stop it. Now. Stop it, please!'

'She wanted me to tell you all this... It was the truth... Please, don't cry'

'Take me back to my room, please. Please' I need to lean on him on the way back much more heavily than our way down but my fragility is more emotional than physical.

We walk back in silence. A poignant silence, but a very individual one, even though the gloom is overwhelming to both of us.

The way back seems interminable. First, the yellow corridor with the bright pictures on the wall, right onto the long red one, left once and right again onto the green one with the children's drawings on both sides, and finally, the longest, most familiar blue one, with eighteenth century marines on one wall and large windows along the other wall.

At last, comfortable and safe in my bed, I ask William if he has been kind to his mother and talked easily with her instead of their usual minimum dialogue. He says he did. He told her about his posting, his friends, his possible transfer back home... He did because after so many years of arguments over the way she chucked me out, the way she left him with his Grandad and his Grandma in the country, the way he would spend so many nights praying that I and his brothers would get back home... he eventually found that after months abroad, far from all of us, everything that he had considered to be terrible injustices became clearer and much less mean. He said that the anger and the resentment were gone, that he had tried to find the old grudges in his heart but they were not there anymore. Instead, he found that he only feels tenderness and compassion and forgiveness towards this woman whom he barely knows and who barely knows him, even though they are mother and son.

'It's odd how only the fun memories, the amusing ones emerge, don't you think? The way she's always had of saying some things, both when she swears or when she jokes. She can be so witty' he tells me.

Do I remember on one of those occasions when I went to see him at his Grandad's? I took him to Guildford because I had promised to buy him a pair of trainers. It was a drizzly Saturday morning and the place was busy with shoppers. It was me who spotted a poster advertising Anna's concert at the Royal Albert Hall that very evening. Then another one, and another one. Anna had told him about it, but he had forgotten and on seeing the posters, he immediately thought that I was in England because of her concert, that I was going to see her play live again like she wanted, and that surely both of us were going to reconcile and set up a home again where the five of us would live happily ever after.

'I remember you kept talking about trainers while we scurried under the drizzle, in and out of shops, but all I could think of was that unless you had a reunion, perhaps a remarriage in mind, you wouldn't have bothered to fly from Copenhagen just to see me and buy me a present'.

There was nothing he wanted as badly as my return to them. He so needed me, he missed his brothers... and he needed Anna, he now realizes. He never admitted to it in those days. Instead, he ended up turning that love into disdain and set out to hurt her with his words whenever he could. There were times in his adolescence when he genuinely despised her and the harder she tried to understand him, the more he pushed her away.

She would turn up at his Grandad's all loving and sweet and so full of presents, and take him shopping and to

Museums, but all he could do was to push her away with some acid remark. She never said much in return, never slapped him in the face as he would've deserved on more than one occasion, he is sure. She behaved as if she believed to be deserving of his rage and took his insolent comments on her chin.

'Poor Mummy'

I let him speak. His eyes are full of tears. I feel we are all having a lifetime of psychotherapy sessions in a week, and despite my despair, I could almost laugh at the pathos of this situation. What we can laugh at we can face; what we can face, we can conquer, says Rabbi Sacks in one of his books. I see that now.

The moment, so precious to us after months of not seeing each other is inevitably interrupted by a nurse who comes to take me for another session. Willo gives me a hug and leaves, relieved to be out of the hospital, I guess. Feeling slightly rested, I insist on shuffling along up to the radiation room, and despite the pain in my throat and my neck after the ordeal, I manage all right all the way to and from there. It must be about a hundred yards away, although it is difficult to estimate distances indoors. When I get back to my room, I lay down and fall instantly asleep, only to dream of Anna in that disjointed, messy way most dreams occur, but every fragment in itself is like a real, compact one. She even treats me to a piece of her music, sitting at her piano, looking happy, radiant, healthy, in the middle of a stage. The audience, made of unknown but complete faces, is silent, enraptured by her interpretation.

In another scene, we are in a house which is not like the one she lived but it is hers in the dream. The room is rather large and daylight is poor but there are lamps everywhere. Too many, in fact, and they have fancy shades, all different. The walls are painted in terracotta and there are huge interior plants tucked in one corner, leaning towards the light coming through a Georgian window. Anna is smoking non-stop, which she never did, but that must be a symbol of her drinking habit, both tobacco and alcohol being equally destructive. We are sitting on a sofa and there are numerous rugs on the oak floor and as many throws draped over chairs and stools. I have come up to see her in order to discuss accommodation for our children, which are four, not three as in real life, as if we were sending them away. I am asking her to do her best to find a good family who could lease a room for Torben so that he can live there better than in an unwelcoming hotel or a draughty camping. Those are the exact adjectives I use in the dream. As far as I can tell, anyway. Unwelcoming. Draughty. A hotel or a camping. Two extremes. Does it mean something? I suppose I can interpret that as the hotel being my present house –Torben would not stay with Grette and me in a million years-, and the camping being Christiania, although people live there in very good comfort. Who knows?

In any case, Anna promises to take care of it, saying that a friend of hers has a house full of rooms near the hospital where Torben has chosen to work. Her eyes are full of life and silver verdigris reflections flicker in them. Then I woke up.

I take her words in the dream as a promise of regeneration. Perhaps she was telling me not to worry about Torben. Perhaps telepathy is possible. Or premonitions. William, however, never features in my surreal meeting with his mother, but it might just be that his future is pretty well planned and there isn't much reason for concern in that respect. His job, his new home, his friends... all seems to be on the right tracks, notwithstanding the vertiginous level of activity he appears to maintain.

I turn again to the other side, feeling my body comfortably stretched and relaxed after a healthy kind of tiredness caused by my walk along the corridors and by the intense emotions. The freshly made bed in crisp sheets and the pillow smelling of the lavender pouch Grette brought me make me feel better, less negative. I've had enough of doom and gloom.

It's half past seven before I close my eyes and twelve past ten when I open them again. Supper is still on the bedside table, but it does not matter because I ordered chicken salad. I am hungry and thirsty and eat and drink it all up a bit too quickly. I get hiccups. I have to get up and pace up and down the corridor in search of something or somebody to scare me. That is what we were told when we were children: If you get a fright, your hiccups stops. Charming little nonsense. But I'm not scared. I'm elated. Being up, out of my room, on my own, walking cautiously and feeling bloody well. I stop at one of the windows to get a different look from the one I see from my room and half of the view is black and golden around the chestnut trees submerged in the shadows of the last twilight and the street lights. The other half is purple, iridescent, bleeding inky purple as if some giant had spilt a fancy cocktail over the sky.

I remain here for a few minutes, contemplating the world and our lives in a fruitless effort to find a formula for redemption here and now, without the need to learn the lesson in a future incarnation, a belief with which Elba has been trying to poison my mind. Reincarnation. I hate the idea, thank you very much. Once we are gone, it's all over. No soul, no hell, no heaven. Only ashes. Finito. What's done is done. No chance to make amends. The only time is now. And thank the gods for that!

On the way back, noticing that his door is slightly ajar, I put my head round the door intending to say good night to the patient, whoever it might be, but the poor old sod is asleep, his cheeks hollow with illness, his body tucked flat under the covers. It's a depressing sight, a reminder of what we are here for: get better or die, and suddenly I feel like laughing. What we can laugh at, we can face...

I'd better go back to my room and laugh out heartily in peace.

Chapter 15

One match missing in the box

Quarter past three. Still awake. Cold one minute, hot the next. Might have a temperature but hope the nurse won't come and check until six or seven. If she does, she'll give me some tablet which will send me to sleep when all I want is to stay conscious. This is the only time when I can concentrate and ponder on unresolved issues and try to find some answers without any interruption. I've made a list of things to ask Torben when he comes, lest I forget, and another one of comments and observations to make to different people. To Grette, for example: Every time she's here I forget to ask her to get me some honey next time she goes to the Torvehallerne Market, where she buys her favourite rosewater and gardenia scented soaps. The honey from there is the only one that tastes like the one we used to have when I was a child.

Mother used to slice the bread with that knife of hers with which she cut so dexterously, and we would spread a spoon full of honey on a slice or two and relish such treat, in the cold winter evenings. I loved it. Mainly because I have always had a sweet tooth, but also because since those days, honey's become a sort of comfort food, so now that I have more of an appetite, I have a good enough reason to indulge myself ("...and is there honey still for tea?").

I must also tell Grette to fetch a suit from the dry-cleaners and to replace the batteries in the smoke alarms. I meant to do that before coming but alas, there must be so many other things I meant to do and then forgot or simply dismissed as trivia. I certainly was in a cloud of terror and self-pity. Unless I have done them, of course.

I'm still not sure whether my memory is intact or whether I have lost chunks of it without yet realizing, the way files get lost or go astray from drawers and cabinets, yet we only notice some months later when we need to refer back to them. My father used to have an odd expression to describe somebody who was slightly eccentric, a bit mad or rather brainless: there is a match missing in his box. I wonder whether I have also lost one match. Or several. What would Father say?

It would've been so nice to be like him. He had such integrity... was so jovial, so positive, so affable. There was never friction between us and even Ernst, who used to disagree passionately with both our parents, was never disrespectful to him. Dad commanded respect without being intimidating. He was just a fair man and everyone, including us, his children, found him honourable, incorruptible. Sadly, he expected as much from the rest of humanity. If someone deceived him or was disloyal to him, he simply moved on. There would be no grudges or rancour, but no reconciliation, either. He would feel hurt rather than angry, yet his optimism and his faith never faltered. How did he do it?

I have tried to achieve the same kind of balance, to inspire the same kind of respect in my sons, but alas, have I failed! They care for me, they are good friends when they are in a good mood, but they do not admire me and it's my fault. They do not look up to me because I have not succeeded in cultivating just one virtue by which to be admired in the same way I haven't cultivated a garden like Dad did throughout his whole life: I have a bigger one, a sophisticated one, if one can say that of a garden, but it's kept tidy by a gardener, not by my own hands. I inherited Dad's height, his blond hair and his joie de vivre against all adversity, but there the resemblance ends.

One morning when I had just married Ulla, a girl called Petra with whom I had some hot encounters, turned up at our doorstep with a baby in her arms. Ulla was upstairs doing her make up or something like that. I was preparing some sandwiches to take with us to the park and Dad was perusing the paper in the sitting-room, waiting for us. As my hands were greasy with salmon, I asked him to open the door. From the kitchen, I heard the conversation:

'And who, may I ask, needs him?' Father said.

Petra. I was beyond startled on hearing her voice pronounce my name with such familiarity in my own house. I would know who she was, she was saying. Dad smelt trouble and hastened to tell her that since I had got married, I seemed to have forgotten about lots of things, including some people. He had guessed right about her intentions, but it was the wrong move. His words only enraged Petra. She elbowed her way into the house and said that in such case, her presence would help bringing back some memories to my rotten mind. Such were her words.

By then, Ulla was coming downstairs. I tried to persuade Petra to stay calm and promised I would see her at work the following morning, since it was a business matter that she wanted to discuss, but she would have none of it. Dad looked dumbfounded, standing still at the threshold, listening carefully to our exchange, his eyes wide with astonishment and his chin tense and square.

Petra came that day because Sundays were days for family gatherings, weren't they? She thought I might like to have my paternal feelings awaken. Wasn't she lovely? She had called her Louise. She was two weeks old, and thus saying, Petra thrust the baby into my arms with such determination that I didn't have time to avoid holding little Louise, aghast and delighted at the same time.

It was a sweet, tiny thing, wrapped up in pink and as Ulla and I had been trying for a baby for some time, her little figure seemed to fit in our home to perfection. I never said this to Ulla, but at that moment, on a whim, I could've kept her.

However, after much insistence and persuasion, I managed to get rid of Petra, agreeing to see her in the company of a lawyer sometime during the week. Once under pressure, she soon dropped the case and admitted that Louise was not mine but her ex-boss's child. The man was also married, had four children, too much of a position to maintain and no intention of acknowledging his child. Petra had very little.

It was the mid-seventies and prejudice and finger pointing still existed in most parts of the country. She was desperately trying to save her baby-daughter the trauma of being illegitimate. I had nothing to worry about it in the end, neither did Ulla, who had thrown the salmon sandwiches in my face when Petra left, but Father said that it was just chance that the baby wasn't mine and in principle, I was as guilty as the real father for taking a woman to bed without the slightest shadow of responsibility, betraying both my wife and my lover's trust. After that, he refused to talk to me for a whole year, until Anders was born and his heart softened. He gave me a hug then.

Now I miss him. Round and round the tone of his voice echoes in my mind. Like mother's, like Ernst's, like Ulla's and Kar's. The structure of our life with all its pillars and underpinnings crumbles around us, leaving these enormous gaps through which the strong winds of desolation blow without mercy. Mr Henriksen says that I will be going home in a day or two and be able to carry on with an almost normal life and I can't help feeling enthusiastic about it until I feel that I have exceeded my welcome on this planet. I am now living on a stolen piece of time and space in which younger, nobler, more useful people than myself perish, when they should be still alive.

Chapter 17

Chopin's Concert Number 1 in Mi Minor

Erika and Jensen must have had some big row because Erika has spent the night sitting by my side. She tells me that after much insistence from her part, Grette accepted to let her watch over my sleep even though there is absolutely no need to do so. I guess that Grette must have been really exhausted to let Erika invade her territory. Erika is a night owl. She gets up late and goes to bed late. In fact, she seems to have enjoyed being here, away from home, as if this blue room and my company were her idea of a perfect vacation. There is no much time to chat, though.

Grette arrives when I'm finishing my breakfast. Erika jumps up from her chair, gives Grette a peck on her cheek, grabs her handbag and without finishing her coffee, she wishes us both a good day and leaves.

'I'll be back at nine this evening' she says, a foot already out in the corridor, before anybody can tell her not to bother. Grette turns to me, squeezing my hand as if she had to reassure me from Erika, whom she still finds threatening. Heavens knows why.

'I feel so anxious, elsker. I've forgotten a huge number of things. Must have. I'm sure I did' As I am explaining this to Grette, Mr Henriksen comes in and asks how would I know that I have forgotten anything if I have indeed forgotten? This is about to turn into a philosophical debate I am not fit to pursue.

I explain that during the night, while Erika dosed off in her chair, I pretended to be asleep but in fact went over conversations I held in the last few days, making a mental list of several facts or ideas which have taken me aback when I should have been familiar with them. The list was substantial, and I may have still failed to remember other episodes. I had forgotten, for instance, that the Bossens had their house up for sale. We had discussed the price, the probability of their buying an apartment, the expensive taxes, the lot, Erika told me, but I do not remember one iota of it. Neither did I remember that Anders and Nja were, -are-, expecting a child. They are planning to call him Ole if he is a boy. I had been very moved on hearing that, Anders said.

Had I? I haven't got the faintest recollection of being given such a piece of news. And I cannot recall the name of my street. I could find my way home if I had to go on foot from here. At least I think I can, but couldn't tell a taxi driver to take me home because I have forgotten my own address. Sommarksvej, Grette says, but I still do not recognize the name. Worse still, I forgot Grette's birthday three days ago. She meant to be delicate by not telling me, but I wish she had.

I point this out to Henriksen because despite this lapse, I've been thinking of buying Grette presents every time I've toyed with the idea of going out of here and strolling along the Strøget. I ask him whether there could be a subconscious association there, an attempt at remembering something, which gets interrupted half way through the brain before reaching its final destination, as it were. Could this be a kind of break in my chain of thought, a circuit cut in the wiring of my brain, some cable that doesn't quite connect, -in this case the one containing the information about Grette's birthday- which will remain forever missing? In other words, will I ever recover my memory in full? Or my thinking of presents and treats for Grette at this time of year is a mere coincidence?

'You should've been a neurologist or a psychiatrist, not a lawyer' Mr Henriksen says

'I'm considering becoming one'

He chuckles, before replying, thoughtfully, constantly pushing the bridge of his spectacles further up his nose that the three options are possible. How awfully reassuring. I wait for him to elaborate further. He doesn't.

'Perhaps I shouldn't worry too much, after all. I've remembered so many other things since I've been here. Don't worry about me'.

'I'm not worried at all', he says. 'In fact, I am sending you home this afternoon'

Elation and apprehension both fight over my heart. Being back home is above my serious expectations, but being out of reach of professional assistance makes me uneasy. One can very quickly get used to be cocooned in the tedious safety of a hospital. It feels solid and wraps around you like a womb. Coming out of it feels as traumatic as being born must feel. On the one hand, we grow limbs and fingers and hair and organs, get ready to go out, look forward to going out, can't wait to go out, but the actual moment must be so tremendously upsetting that as a phoetus, we try at times to postpone it, and as newborns, immediately to forget it.

Mr Henriksen reconsiders and compromises on tomorrow, after the radiotherapy session. 'And give your brain a rest, man' he says in jest.

Grette claps her hands in glee, almost jumping with excitement like a little girl. I've never seen her do that. Then she kisses my cheek. Like a sister. Almost.

'That's fantastic news, darling! I'm so pleased... Fancy being back home... It's the best news ever.

This bubbliness makes her look younger and livelier and my heart fills with love for her, for Mr Henriksen, for Mr Lundgren next door, for the nurses and the whole bloody world. Grette cannot stop smiling, sits up, pats my hand repeatedly, makes plans, chats incessantly for a few more minutes until finally, she gets up.

'Now, I ought to be going, darling. Work to do and then home to get things ready for tomorrow. I'll pick you up at 12.00 o'clock', she promises, already in the role she likes best: being the leader. The doer. The organizer. She does not seem too bothered that Erika will come again this evening. I get up after she goes and cautiously have a shower. Feel like skipping all the way home.

Invigorated and clean, I am fastening my belt to hold my trousers up when the boys turn up. William, looking solemn and older in a dark blue suit; Anders holding hands with his pregnant Nja and Clementina skipping ahead of them, a grin on her face, rushing to give me a toffee-flavoured hug. Torben, the tallest of them all, is dressed in black from head to toe, despite the summer warmth. When at some point, Nja says he looks cool and trendy, he blushes, like a kid. They all chat and act as if I should know why they are here and what exactly they have come for, but I let them speak, desperately trying to find some clue, without letting them see I have no idea of what the hell is going on.

We walk through a labyrinth of corridors, out onto the garden, and Clementina finds us what she thinks is the best corner to stop and then keeps silent. It seems that like me, she doesn't understand why we are all here. Anders puts a hand on her shoulder and explains that it's going to be only a prayer, said with respect but in an informal way, a few words to accompany Anna's soul on her way to Heaven. Anna is dead, then.

I'm supposed to have known about it and agreed to this farewell, but cannot remember and cannot feel her presence around us, or her absence. It is too big a loss to feel its emptiness yet. Clementina, who met Anna only once behaves so properly holding my hand, that one would think she is saying good bye to her own granny. William says a prayer in English and then the other boys indulge in a series of memories of their childhood in London. I have never been so aware of their love for Anna, nor as touched by it, and so proud of them as at this moment.

Elba tiptoes towards us, a handkerchief in her hand, and stands beside me as Anders turns on his mobile and plays one of Anna's own recordings of Chopin's Concert Number 1 in Mi minor, her favourite and major success. Torben blows his nose a couple of times, William bursts into tears and Anders also has to wipe his eyes repeatedly, but overall, it is a dignified, peaceful moment, considering that I couldn't do anything else.

Willo then fetches a bottle of champagne and a bottle of lemonade from the bar and we all toast Anna's eternal rest. Other patients taking the air near us look bemused by this ridiculous bunch of individuals standing in circle like druids, but I do not care. I am glad to bid farewell to Anna in a fashion that due to my circumstances, is as eccentric as she would've liked. In a few hours, William and Torben will be flying to England where tomorrow they will bid their last adieu to our Anna. Above the lavender, the humming bird hovers almost in silence.

I am immensely glad that they planned this in this way rather than via social media, which still leaves me cold and indifferent in situations of such emotional load. Seizing the moment, I announce my good news and more champagne is poured. Everyone claps and cheers and toast my health, including the patients around.

Everybody is gone now. Erika isn't coming after all. Grette phoned me to say that she is coming to have supper here with me. I have already done my packing, which wasn't much, and polished my shoes with a flannel I had in my toilet bag. My hair is a mess. I will ask to have it shaved again early tomorrow before going home so I can look more presentable. I look ridiculous, I've been so anxious and frightened that the last thing I could care about was my appearance.

My trousers also look odd, as if they belonged to someone one or two sizes bigger than me. Only the blue and the white in my eyes look somewhat deeper and brighter than they have been in the last few days and the rings under them look lighter and less deep. Perhaps it is the effect of the fresh air in the garden, the mix of emotions, the satisfaction of seeing my three sons reunited, especially Torben, after all these years in which he kept himself away. Or maybe I'm simply seeing on the mirror what I want to see.

Nevertheless, it has been a very good day if I add everything up. It feels like the last day of some holidays by the seaside when one finally gets to talk to the next table guests, kiss the girl who's been teasing you for a week. The weather turns brighter than ever and the sea is, for the first time since you've stayed there, turquoise blue like in the brochures. Bliss. But now you have to go home. Except that this time, home will be better than the holidays. The sky will look clearer; the air, sweeter; the house, more welcoming and life, much kinder. I don't care if I need to restart my routine a day at a time or if my legs will take time to recover balance and strength.

Everything will be different; some hopes have definitely died and many dreams will never become reality.

I know that my world has shrunk, that music has turned into silence and London, were I to visit it again, will never be the same without Anna there. That coffee by the harbour will never taste as good without Kar's company, but I promise myself to be more generous to myself and others, to forgive those flaws I haven't yet managed to forgive myself so that I can finally forgive everyone else. C'mon, Ole Morgensen, behave yourself.

I shall go now and say goodbye to my next-door neighbour, -a charming man of incredible intelligence, according to his son-in-law.

'You wouldn't believe it' this young son-in- law told me yesterday, 'but the old man has done every possible Master under the sun. Mind you, he's a nuclear physicist, worked for NASA for years and as soon as he retired and returned to his beloved Denmark... look in what state he is now... My mother-in-law's devastated. Mind you, she's the opposite of him, really. No much intellect, nothing too complicated for her. They've been married for nearly forty years. Very happy, too, I dare say. Mind you, not many people achieve that. Five children they had. Poor old Dad' he said and broke down.

I patted the man on his shoulder, baffled by his outburst of information and by his emotions. I assumed his urge to talk was mainly due to a nervous state of mind, but whatever the reason for this, it was touching to witness such respect and affection for his in-laws. I said so to him and then I asked if he and the physicist's daughter had any children and he said that they didn't, that she refused to have any child at all and that to make matters worse -for him, although possibly not for her- she was having a passionate affair with her best friend's husband and he, himself, didn't know what to do about it.

He said he was glad that her father wouldn't be around to hear about it, mind you, and he turned to look at the old man's door as if to make sure that our voices could not reach his ears.

On hearing about his marriage, the reason for his non-stop chat and his admiration for what his in-laws had managed to create over the years became clear. The poor chap was distraught for being unable to make with his own wife the peaceful, happy home he had envisaged.

He must have been in his early thirties, but sounded older and very mature. Old-fashioned even, like those people who seem to have been born middle-aged. He shook my hand when we parted, after telling him of Anna's death and commiserating for each other's sorrows. How pathetic is that?

Eventually, I went in and said goodbye to the poor physicist in case I have no time tomorrow and then sat down for a few minutes. I am being gnawed alive by trepidation and joy at the same time.

The breeze has picked up and is blowing the curtains further into the room one minute, sucking them out the next. I'd better close the window. The temperature has definitely gone down, I shall have to put on a pullover and a brave face when Grette comes. *After all, tomorrow is another day*. What a challenge!

Chapter 18

Home

Home, at last! Home! Home! Home with my books, my pens, my maps, my collection of ancient keys, my lamp, my desk, my photos, my notes... Home with our furniture, our prints and paintings and candleholders and rugs... our crockery, knives and forks, crystals, brushes, cushions... God! When did it all get so important? Important? No, that's not right. I could honestly get rid of all the stuff, I could move house without regrets, provided it was my choice, my decision... but not to be taken into hospital by the bloody GBM's.

I open drawers, cupboards, bookcases... only to reencounter my objects, my trivia, the series of illustrations by Erik Blegvad, which he so kindly signed for my children when we met him in London. I rediscover the scent of clean clothes inside my wardrobe, of cedar balls trapped in the chest of drawers... The exhilaration of being back in my nest is beyond what I could've ever imagined. Every room, every door, every window is a regained little haven. Talk of attachment. It's idiotic, but who cares? I walk up and down throughout the house, perhaps more than once, I cannot know, and only stop when my legs order me to.

It's ten past five in the evening and I find myself, -exactly so: find myself-, sitting on the sofa, looking at the magnolia tree in the front garden like I used to do when I first bought this house, waiting impatiently for Cecille twenty years ago. Post Ulla. Post Anna. Pre-Grette.

I don't remember resting in our bedroom, but Grette says she accompanied me there and helped me lie on our bed for a couple of hours. I try hard to recall going upstairs and seeing something in our bedroom as it must have looked when we arrived, but I fail. Were the windows shut? Open? How about the curtains? I struggle to remember some detail that could confirm or contradict Grette's words, but I can't and I wonder whether Grette is telling me the truth or whether she is making it all up in order to confuse me even further? Could she have planned to get rid of me by persuading me of my insanity? What if she's been planning to drive me out of my mind so that she can take me to an old people's home or to a psychiatric clinic and dump me there?

I agonize going about the possibilities until she reappears in the sitting room, bringing a cup of tea and a piece of my favourite cake and suddenly the domesticity of the scene returns my judgement and my sense of reality. Immediately, the idea of her betrayal becomes so ridiculous that I feel ashamed of myself and pleased that she is unable to read my thoughts. I hold her hand in mine for a second or two when she leaves the tray on the coffee table and I gaze gratefully, I hope, into her eyes. She smiles and lets go of my hand to pass me a napkin and my own cup. I take a sip with relish, only to find that after sixteen years of marriage Grette still serves my tea to her taste, not to mine.

Weak and milky. I like it strong and black. I could send the cup flying across the room, but I control myself.

My face burns with irritation and I wish Grette didn't notice it, but she looks at me, holds my gaze and, unusually for her, without knowing exactly why, she apologizes.

'I've felt so lonely while you were in hospital… your sons are very kind and respectful, but still distant. I mean… if you were to die, I don't think they'll bother to stay in touch. Anders, may be…' She tells me.

'They've made the place I occupy in their lives very clear', she adds. They have shown their unconditional love to me and to the memory of Anna, Grette was surprised to see, but there's no place for her in their hearts.

'I don't think that's the case at all, darling'

She hardly takes notice of my words and for the first time in my life, I see her feeling sorry for herself. She feels so miserable. She starts crying and I can hardly cope with such outpour of sentiment on my first afternoon out of hospital, but I summon up all the energy within me and with my irritation now gone, manage to utter some comforting words to my dear Grette. My third wife. My last wife.

Do we learn to love better as we get older or, contrary to so many interpretations, our capacity for love wears out like a commodity? Just by looking around, one would think that it persists, that it feeds on itself and grows and purifies itself like fire, but I'm not so sure that this is always the case. I move closer to Grette and put an arm round her shoulders long enough for her to relax and allow herself to weep against my chest. I kiss her hair, which smells of expensive shampoo, and close my eyes. Only a few months ago the intimacy of the moment, an intimacy that has been put on hold since she left for Napoli, and I for the hospital a month ago, would've been enough to push me on top of her and look into her dreamy eyes as her breathing got faster and louder under my caresses but not now. Not any longer. The thought depresses me. It does depress me because being made of vigour, passion and vitality as I was, now my bloody brain will no longer respond to any of that.

The fear of having to live with a damaged brain and a confused mind, lost in my own labyrinths has ironically led me to thinking so hard and examining my past so thoroughly, that I am turning into a hyper-responsible, sensible man. Utterly dull, in other words.

'Don't be upset, skat. You know what they're like. Anders makes us laugh; Torben makes us worry, feel guilty and dream all at the same time depending on his mood, and William can be a breath of fresh air, but none of them wear their heart on their sleeves'

'They did when Anna died'

'Yes, well, that was exceptional. "Wearing your heart on your sleeve" is a lovely expression, don't you think?'

'You can't help yourself, can you? Every word, every expression... all that accuracy! Grette teases me and she attempts a giggle.

Yet, I do give the matter about my sons a great consideration because I wouldn't like Grette to be forgotten by them when I pass away. I try to see what Grette sees, to approach the issue from the same angle. As she remains in my arms, I come to think that perhaps she is just using my children's indifference as a smoke screen to cover up some other sorrow, in that convoluted fashion women have of hiding or suppressing another issue. Women do not explain clearly what goes on in their heads. They say things are fine, when they are not, but we men need things spelled out.

Picking up a loose end of what I guess is a tangled skein of issues, and very subtly discussing it with her so that we can undo the knots without making her feel questioned, I go round and round in circles until she mentions almost unwittingly, that what she resents is the fact that I allocate time and care and attention to everybody else except her.

Nonsense. It's neither true nor fair but it is what she perceives and I have learnt to respect my wives' feelings instead of insisting on the fact that they are wrong. I am no saint and not wise either, but I know this much, if nothing else. This realization has helped me keep my relationships happier than they could've been otherwise.

'We all make the mistake of taking for granted the one we love the most, I know' I emphasize THE MOST for effect. 'It is a cliché, but like all clichés, it contains truth'. I do not try to justify my diverted attention but the explanation however simple, seems to hit home because the look in Grette's eyes softens and she stops biting her lips. She is at last persuaded of my loyal love and recovers some of her inner peace. Inner peace. I must be turning into a New Age man. Elba would be pleased.

Grette frees herself from my embrace and sits as upright as ever, following my words as if we were signing a contract, closing a business deal. It has always been her way of coping, giving and receiving. If we were arguing I would point out to her that she can do cold and reserve better than my sons or anyone else, but we are not. Besides, I am by now familiar with her fear of intimacy. Poor Grette.

When our love was more physical, she was the one who would wake me up in the middle of the night and lead me slowly but inevitably to our coupling. Once our roles were understood, then she could relax and acquiesce to other things, but she would've never gone further than a feigned orgasm if I had been the one to take the initiative.

On one occasion years ago, she invited a friend of hers, Ingrid, who had recently lost her husband, to spend the weekend with us. She went to pick her up from the station while I stayed at home, watching the end of a rugby match, enjoying the smell of burnt birch coming off the logs crackling in the fireplace. It was an autumnal evening and her friend was delighted to arrive at what she described as a 'warm home'. She said so very precisely, very deliberately because only someone who lost her other half could make a remark like that.

I poured some drinks and then Grette showed Ingrid her room while I went to the kitchen to see to the lobsters. I was halving a lemon when Grette appeared behind me and put her arms round my waist, whispering in my ear that while upstairs she had taken off her knickers. Then she got hold of the knife in my hand, left it aside and ran my hand up her skirt right to her moist groin. She gasped as I touched her. We swiftly turned round and leaning and balancing against the table, she had a most violent orgasm as I entered her, worried and excited at the idea of being caught by her visiting friend.

Throughout dinner, she remained dreamy and languorous in such an obvious way that, she later told me, Ingrid had guessed the reason for her detachment. Being in control has always been Grette's most powerful shield.

This evening though, as I evoke that odd occasion and Grette cooks her trademark salmon risotto, the mere idea of having sex makes me feel tired. Instead, I compliment her cooking, drink only mineral water, read the newspaper and come to bed, eager to relax and sleep like a baby in the comfort of our own bed, but the shock drives me out of my mind.

'Green walls and... two beds! Grette! Grette!' What possessed her to change our superking-size bed for two single ones without consulting me is beyond me and my tolerance?.

'What the fuck have you done? What did you think you were doing? This is my home. I'm not dead yet. You've gone too far. I could throw you out of our bedroom. Out of our house. Out. Out of my sight'.

How could I not notice the change when I was here this afternoon, if I really was here as she assures me? Perhaps I got confused and disorientated precisely because it wasn't our room as I knew it. I swallow a second tablet or else my wrath will kill me. The nerve of the woman.

This morning when she arrived at hospital, punctually at 12.00 o'clock, I was ready, waiting for her, full of excitement and fear. I had my hair shaven off by a bloke with a hunchback who was doing the rounds at seven o'clock, tidying up heads and beards of long staying patients, he said. I could not decide whether he was being just pragmatic or slightly morbid. In any case, I ended up looking like the old man that I am, without a shade of the mass of silver hair I had been lucky to keep right until the day of my operation. I even had a bit of colour in my cheeks, which I thought would be noticed by the ones around me.

I stood still in my room until I felt tired, then sat on the edge of the bed because it felt more casual, less committing than sitting comfortably on the chair from which it would've taken me longer to get up. It was raining heavily and the trees glistened behind a blurred curtain of water that made them look distant and inferior. I have never minded the rain, but this morning it felt wrong, ominous even. Like being born old, like starting life in the autumn, which is noticeably gliding over Denmark after three months of unbroken sunshine. It is also the autumn of my life and I should accept it, but all I could feel facing this second birth was apprehension at being launched out of hospital without a maternal cuddle, without anything to learn, without a future made of glorious dreams and determined effort. Yet, whoever or whatever holds authority over our lives has granted me some extra days, or extra weeks that will only be worth living provided I can make amends and reconstruct what I have destroyed. Learning to understand and then let go. Undoing the damage that I have done: that is the challenge now. As if.

I should've felt grateful for such a gift as soon as I opened my eyes and heard the rain tapping against the glass. Instead, I kept arguing with the weather and the seasons of my life like an idiot, hoping to reverse the course of nature as if by going back a season I could find myself healthy again, as confident and positive as I used to be. It was not the fear of death that kept me awake last night, but the cruelty of old age and disease. Nothing original, indeed.

The radiotherapist shook my hand almost euphorically when I told him that I was leaving the hospital soon after the session and that I would only be coming as an external patient. He wasn't surprised, he said, but it was great news all the same. 'That was kind of him' Grette commented when I told her about it. She was carrying my bag and I was holding her arm, partly because we always hold hands when we walk together, and partly because I needed her reassurance. If at that moment she had taken me in her arms or run her hand over my cheek reassuring me that everything was going to be alright I would've wept... It would've made me so happy.

I needed her at that moment and felt awkward in her company at the same time, as if she came from a world I was going to rediscover all on my own, and which was an unknown, narrower, emptier world than the one I had inhabited for seventy odd years. Life is tough enough before a brain tumour and I dreaded it would be tougher still after it. Going back home and living with someone else, even when that someone was the woman whose body I know centimetre by centimetre, or perhaps because of it, caused me as much joy as anxiety.

After ten days in hospital, without anybody asking me if I had paid the telephone bill or telling me not to be late from my afternoon stroll because we were invited to some dinner party at somebody's whom I had not yet met and who were going to bore me to distraction with their talks of expensive holidays and tasteless declarations of assets, was not going to be easy. I had pondered that all night, like a virgin bride in olden days must have done when she was about to leave her parents' home and move in with her new husband without knowing his real business, his real temper or whether he was in the habit of urinating into the washbasin or changing his socks once a month.

I compared myself to the unfortunate bride and knew that I was exaggerating, if not hallucinating, because I do know Grette, I do know our place, our bedroom, our life... I know what she does and that she is unflappable... I know the feel of our sheets and the smell of our clothes, but instead of finding the idea comforting and soothing, I found such certainty highly inhibiting and I remained sleepless for most of the night.

As we both left, I treaded as carefully along corridors, into lifts and out again onto the car park as over Grette's goodwill, gestures and silences. By the time I got inside the car I thought I had my fear under control, but as soon as I fastened the seat belt and Grette started the engine, I panicked being trapped in such a small space, moving forwards, unable to tolerate the movement. All I could do was put my arms round my head, close my eyes tightly and press my legs down against the seat. It felt like an eternity went by before Grette pulled up. Finally, she persuaded me to put my hands down and open my eyes, and when doing so, I burst into tears. Frightened, brain-cancered, self-pitiful tears.

Grette opened the window and I inhaled deeply the fresh damp air hoping my sobbing would not trigger vomits or worse still, a seizure. Grette's hand slid softly over my knee and her voice, gentle but crisp, reached me from some distance. Even now, I could not quote her words, I only got the essence of them, as if she had been speaking in a foreign language and I could only get the gist of her speech.

I do not know how long we were there, what I can remember is my overpowering wish to return to hospital and stay there. When the harbour slid past us, I recognized the Danish names on the boats and that was good, but it felt as though our ride had taken hours and hours, driving in circles before Grette found the entrance to our driveway.

Later on, she told me that it had taken us less than twenty minutes to get home.

Now, after an endless day, ignoring my rage and my disappointment, my wife sleeps in her own bed as if we had never slept together. Some nearby church bells strike four. The thrushes, confusing dawn with streetlights, are already singing and my happiness returns with such power that I don't need to sleep.

Chapter 19

The freedom of the sparrows

Paris, 2018

Cecille pays the taxi driver and jumps out of the car, lithe with joy, full of energy. She woke up earlier than usual and smiled broadly at herself while she put her make up on in front of the mirror. She thanked her angels for the running hot water and another day of relative peace while she sat to drink her cup of coffee and the croissant she can never resist. To counterbalance, she half starves herself for the rest of the day.

Living in Paris is to her, a wonder. A miracle. An enchantment. And the way she makes herself be aware of her good luck every morning is mainly due to a visceral apprehension, a vague yet real fear that one day her Parisian life will vanish and she will find herself back in her parents' home, as she does almost every night in her muddled nightmares. She dreams of finding that her husband, her gallery, her friends, le tout Paris she has adopted as hers, will be devoured and snatched out of her life and she will be left lying flat on her stomach in the big house in Copenhagen. She loved her city too much, but had to abandon it when she discovered that breathing its air, searching for happiness and breaking free at the same time was not possible for her. Free.

"If you ever had to choose one word, just the one, which one would it be?" one of her History of Art tutors asked the class on one occasion. Most of the students had taken a few seconds to answer. Others said they couldn't really think of just one, they needed to think harder. Cecille had not hesitated. Freedom, was her word. Freedom was her ambition, her cause and her aim. Freedom is the air she breathes.

'Bonjour, madame' she greets the cleaner as she strides over the rubbish the woman is sweeping away from the hall. She unlocks the door of her gallery and dashes for the landline telephone ringing in the little office behind the exhibition room. It's Paul. Could he come right now and try some works on the walls? He wants to see the colour himself. Cecille thinks they have already agreed on burgundy for the facing wall where his largest display will hang, but yes, he may come if he wants to. Of course, he can.

Paul is a friend. A fellow countryman who paints and sculpts and designs and puts on installations in her gallery twice a year, and only twice because Cecille and her husband want to promote other artists and remain popular in the artistic world, which is ephemeral, touchy and forever changing. Trends come and go. Protégés fall out of favour. Unknown artists become famous overnight.

Cecille and Veniamin know they have to keep abreast of these whims if they want to keep up their comfort, their luxuries, and above all, their reputation. In Paris, no less.

Cecille reads some of the emails and replies to Veniamin, who has just texted her about the Libra chair she has to go and see how it looks on this or that corner of the old lady's house. The woman is in a wheelchair and lives on her own, she has told Veniamin, but Cecille suspects that part of it is a lie, since the lady had the authoritative manner of those used to having staff waiting on them and seeing to their every need and whim. Besides, with that address... Never mind. If it means selling a piece and taking it to the apartment of the rue du Passy, she will do it and later pay the cheque into their account with glee. The artist will be delighted and grateful to have sold one more of his sculptural chairs and the old lady will be happy to have bought something so modern to shock her octogenarian friends.

'Buy me something chic', she writes to Veniamin after she types in her big hug and many kisses on her text. She sends it and wonders how Veniamin has managed to text her so early in the morning. It's five o'clock New York time. She delights in Veniamin's dedication, considering that he is not one to wake up at dawn, let alone worry about work at such time.

She replies to a few other emails and flags the ones she will answer later, once she has found the information required. Monique comes in at 10.00 on the dot, punctually, but carrying two magazines under her arm, which Cecille spots with frustration. She knows that after making coffee, Monique will spend half an hour leafing through pages of fashion and celebrities' gossip before starting to work. It is one of the habits she still finds difficult to live with after twenty odd years in France. And why haven't Jean- Ives and Sonia arrived yet.? She gets up and goes to fetch the ladder tucked behind the kitchenette door and drags it carefully to the salon. If you want something done, do it yourself, she mutters as she climbs up and starts taking the paintings down. The ones hanging on the righthand side wall will remain there for another month. The other two walls will accommodate Paul's work whose autumn exhibition will open on Wednesday. Why isn't Monique working yet? Couldn't she at least pretend?

'Bonjour, Cecille!' says Jean-Yves as he walks into the gallery, rather sheepishly, Cecille thinks.

'Hej. Did you have a good weekend? We've got quite a lot to do today'

'Bonjour, Cecille' says Sonia. 'Le métro... Emmerdant'

'Perhaps leaving home a bit earlier would help' Cecille replies before she checks her tone. She doesn't apologize though, why should she? This is her gallery. She has worked hard to get here and endeavours to keep it going and be amongst the most respected commercial galleries in the capital, which is no small job. Why would she have to make excuses for demanding efficiency?

She does not like the way her bubbly mood is seeping away from her. One day she will have no employees. She'll work by herself. She will be... free. She thinks about it and smiles at her folly, her obsession. Perhaps she really is getting old, after all. Old and grumpy, as most of her friends have confessed to becoming when they went for an after-film drink last Thursday.

She climbs down the ladder straining to hold the three-dimensional hanging without damaging it. She does not know whether she likes it or not. Planet Earth cut out in relief, in layers of forests and lakes and plateaux with people standing upside down, oceans leaking outwards and mountains going inwards, cavernous and frightening. It is disturbing and for some obscure reason, it makes her think of the works of Agnes Messager at the Pompidou. All those tiny sparrows tucked in their individual beds in pastel hued hand-knitted blankets. Are they supposed to look sweet? Endearing? Abominable? It's up to the spectator, but she read somewhere that the artist meant to represent girls at a boarding school. Cecille had been both attracted to and horrified by the creatures the first time she saw them, but then kept going back again and again to stand and stare at the unfortunate birds for the following weeks. The uniformed girls in pale blue, pink and lemon. The communal bedroom. The lack of privacy. The lack of identity. The absence of freedom. Poor babies. Dead. The babies.

'Allow me' Jean-Yves volunteers as he approaches and gets hold of the upside-down world. Cecille thanks, smiles and says she'll go and pour some coffee for him while he takes the rest of the paintings down.

When Paul arrives, they discuss the colours, put sheets of samples against the wall and finally agree on a matt slate grey and black frames for the photos. The canapés have been ordered, the wine has been delivered, the invitations were sent a week ago and the posters and flyers are hanging on every bookshop, library and gallery round the city and any other spot they were able to think of.

'Vernissages always bring in viewers with good taste and plenty of euros. This one will be no exception, you'll see', Cecille tells him.

She loves working with another Dane. Veniamin likes him too, but once made some jealous remark. Cecille reassured him by explaining that Paul could be a brother if she really had to think of a relationship that close, nothing else. Nothing different. A brother. It would've been nice not to be so lonely in the big house.

What she shares with Paul are the same things she shares with Mogens and Vekka and all the other Danes, men or women, who pass through Paris and her gallery. It is the language, the old songs, the people of a country haunted by the ghost of a king clad in armour, the sacrifice of a mermaid, the pale winters and the crystal-clear summers.

She had found her husband's jealousy upsetting, not flattering. 'It's your Russian mind', she told him and after some huffing and mumbling, they both joked and giggled at their lively exchange, but she has never forgotten his jealousy and avoids mentioning Paul or Mogens unnecessarily.

She won't tell him that she'll go for lunch with Paul. Much as she hates this game of hide and seek, she has to play it out of tact. Perhaps it's a way of lying to Veniamin, but there is nothing to hide. She wishes Veniamin trusted her and even admired her for her loyalty, for her deep, almost stoical determination to be faithful, to make him happy, to rejoice in their bliss and bend towards his every desire in the name of love. And integrity.

'You've made the wrong choice', one of her friends said when she talked about this over dinner the other day. 'French men –or women- don't expect loyalty because we don't expect to be loyal ourselves' Michelle had said, matter of fact, sipping her merlot. Cecille felt out of step, shaken and misplaced as if she had indeed made the wrong choice, but she loved Veniamin. And he her. They will always be together without cheating on each other. Surely. As she put up a smiling façade amongst her friends, she made herself dismiss the memory that came into her mind. Something she found out years ago, while she lay awake at night: that she wasn't in this world to be understood. Liked, appreciated and sometimes admired, yes, but not really understood and never protected.

They walk up to the bistro on the corner, her mind on her job, on the invoices she asked Sonia to settle and which were still lying around when they came out. Paul teases her saying that if she doesn't relax, she'll get old, very old, like his aunt Ingrid. 'I know', she giggles, 'but if I'm not on top of everything, nothing gets done'.

Paul's laughter makes her laugh. Round the corner, the gilets jaunes block their path, shouting and screaming in the name of... in the name of what, Cecille wonders. She'll never comprehend demonstrations against violence. Violence against violence. Violence in the name of peace.

'French people, so logical and philosophical, can contradict themselves very well, sometimes', she comments

'Perhaps you're being too Danish to fit into Paris after all' Paul jokes.

She stops on her heels, while some woman carrying a placard shouts abuse at her on account of her well-groomed hair and her expensive handbag. She puts a hand over Paul's arm and looks at him straight into his eyes.

'Never, ever say that to me again, please', she almost shouts so that he can hear her clearly over the shouts and the turmoil. The excitement of her early morning and the high level of physical energy she had felt, have left her. 'Sorry', she says 'But you have no idea about my motives for leaving Denmark and how much I've needed this new life'

Paul puts up his hands in apology, and then puts an arm round her shoulders as they walk in silence towards Le bistro d'Avril.

Cecille takes a deep breath and smiles, but now she wishes she could rush back to her gallery, work for the rest of the afternoon with the passion and eagerness she is known for and forget about gilets jaunes, her country, and exile. She wants the future, not the past.

Chapter 19

Ralph

'Phone call for you, sir' the girl announces as soon as I finish breakfast. It's Ralph. He is in town for only a few days. He's staying with his daughter. It's so long since we saw each other, would I like to meet him for lunch? I hesitate and am about to refuse, but being aware of my condition and that we might be seeing each other for the last time, I change my mind.

'Certainly. Of course. Would you mind coming over to mine? I'm a bit tied up here, I'm afraid.

'Sure', he says in his now American drawl. 'Mind if my wife joins us?'

'Course I don't. I didn't know... I shall be delighted to meet her. One o'clock?'

The taxi pulls up right in front of our gate allowing me to have a good look at my callers before they see me. Ralph looks shorter and fatter but that may be just the effect of not having seen him for years. Memory can be an unreliable friend, sometimes. Or foe, for that matter. The woman who hastens to hold his hand as they walk up the driveway looks like an old matron, big bosomed, grosse, grey hair in a bun. She could be his mother. Close up, I notice she is probably Ralph's age or even younger, but her whole demeanour belongs in another century. I think of my own looks with some vanity, I must admit, and find that only a year ago I must have looked better than the woman. Could I be jealous?

They met last November, got married in March. There had been no time or need to tell us all at once. Ralph knew we would all be glad for him and I lie I am, wondering whether he has prostituted himself and compromised on his principles and his good taste only to avoid loneliness and thus conquer his fear of decrepitude.

We hug and pat each other's backs and Ralph does his best to hide his own shock at seeing me in such poor form. I joke about my shaved head and my slim limbs, but as Ralph gazes into my eyes we both know I am hiding behind something bigger than a joke. It does not matter, though. Ralph's wife walks away from us, admiring the roses that are still flowering, climbing over the wall. I whisper how immensely happy I am to see him on my first day at home since my operation. He opens his mouth as if to say something, but whatever it was, he changes his mind and only points out at Donna inhaling the scent of the flowers. We all make some appropriate noises, mainly in agreement with Donna about the unbeatable beauty of a garden in summer, and step joyfully into the house.

'How long have you lived here? Did you buy it or inherit or something? You were a lawyer, Ralph tells me... What branch of Law?

'A barrister, actually'

'Are you married now?'

Donna keeps asking lots of questions and never bothers to listen to the answers. There are few things in life that irritate me more than that. It is one of the so many forms of selfishness, which I believe is the mother of all human flaws. She also keeps looking towards the kitchen waiting, perhaps, for some greasy burger to materialize, since her size betrays an appetite for bigger lunches than a smorrebrod. I do not think herring salad is to her taste, either, and as Ralph's eyes light up describing details of his new life in the States, I cannot decide whether to feel sorry, disappointed or abominably snob.

I try to be open-minded but cannot help wondering how on earth have I fallen for this man and been his lover for so many years, believing him to be one of the most exquisite mortals on this planet. Now I feel out of place in his company, as if he were someone else, somebody whom the old Ralph has met in America and who has volunteered to pass on some news during a visit to Copenhagen. If I were rude, I would ask him what has happened to the Ralph I used to know, since apart from the personal news update, we find ourselves struggling to find some common ground, some common interest to discuss.

His newly acquired American jokes are either too obvious or too brash and I feel annoyed thinking that he is telling so many of them in order to entertain me*, poor old Ole who is about to die.* Never, in any of those many moments we shared in his flat in Vesterbro did I find him boring, awkward or shallow, now here he is, unable to dive below the surface, devoid of subtlety, depth or refinement.

How can a sixty-eight-year-old man change so radically in the course of a few months, simply because he married the wrong woman in an alien country? Has he always been like this and I failed to notice? Or having noticed it, I felt attracted to his roughness as a contrast to Ulla's sensitivity, Anna's glamour, Cecille's youth and Grette's wisdom? Yet Ralph was never rough. I would have noticed that, but what I cannot recognize this afternoon is his kitsch, crass attitude.

'So, how long d'you have to wait before they tell you if you're gonna be okey?' Donna asks as I put a spoonful of raspberry sorbet in my mouth. I take my time to swallow it and then reply that I am having radiotherapy five days a week and that I refused chemotherapy.

'I guess I'd rather die than have chemotherapy. My Mom had it and she was disfigured by it, or by the cancer, I don't know. I couldn't tell which because Mom passed anyway'.

I burst out laughing. They both look at each other with embarrassment, but as I mumble my apologies now and again in between fists of laughter they also burst out laughing louder and louder and the house filled with the sound of our hysterical, tasteless mirth.

Eventually, I get up and go to the kitchen to make some coffee while they go and sit comfortably in the sitting-room. I hear Ralph admiring a sketch by Dalsgaard that Grette and I bought at an auction a couple of weeks before she went to Napoli, and I, to hospital.

For a minute, he is the old Ralph, sensitive to aesthetics, peeping into the essence of things. I remain in the kitchen for all the time the coffee-maker takes to produce a jug full of coffee. I think of all those mornings when I used to snatch a couple of hours out of my office to pop round Ralph's workshop and then disappear with him through the door that led to his sitting-room and across it to the corridor that led to his bedroom. He's been my only male lover, but better than a lover, he has been an endearing friend. A very good one. He was never jealous, never possessive, never difficult. Like me, he likes women too, but unlike me, he prefers men. Or used to.

As the water gets hot and the air becomes heavy with that sort of cozy winter smell of fresh coffee, I wonder whether Ralph indeed has such an unresolved issue with his mother, -I am getting too Freudian- that he has decided to find himself one and marry her. After all, Donna looks at him with such caring, maternal eyes that anyone would feel like an adored child under a gaze like hers.

I cover the tray with a white linen mat or however one calls those crisp covers Ulla inherited from her grandmother and I from her, and arrange the cups on their saucers, and the little spoons and the sugar pot on the tray. As I am making sure that there are enough brown and white sugar cubes in the pot, I start to feel light-headed and worry about doing something wrong or out of sequence, as if I had never served coffee in my whole life. I take the cream jug out of the fridge, put it on the tray, neatly placed amongst the saucers and then slide the jug from under the filter of the coffee-maker and serve a cup for Donna and a cup for Ralph, the steam damping my forehead.

Then there's a crash. My feet almost get burnt as the jug drops from my hand but I make it to the sink in time. Both Ralph and Donna rush in. Ralph fussing over me, Donna mentioning a brush and a cloth she needs to find somewhere, giving the spilled coffee and the glass smithereens a wide birth. I feel such a fool, washing my face and shaking in front of them.

'Hey, it's all right, Ole, it's alright', Ralph says, running his hand briefly but warmly along my back. My elbows leaning on the counter, my head still hanging over the sink, I start crying. Silently. Quietly. 'It's alright, Ole. C'mon'

The room starts spinning as Ralph turns me round to hold me in his arms. My sobbing gets louder and louder, out of control and tasteless like our laughter was a few minutes ago. I cry like I have never cried. Not since Ulla's death thirty-four years ago. What a performance.

Chapter 20

Sweden

I was readmitted into hospital the very same day Ralph and Donna came to visit and kept there for nine days, according to Grette, the doctors and the newspaper lying on the kitchen table. I haven't got any recollection of when I was taken ill or about the days that have slipped by since, except for small snippets of conversation I overheard when everybody around me were discussing my condition. They should have known better. Doctors, nurses, my sons, everybody talked over my head as if I were dead. I am starting to believe that even dead I shall be hearing what they say.

I know that Anders came with Nja and found out about their plans for the summer, and how Nja was pleased that she is not at the last stage of the pregnancy in these months of intense heat. I could not really feel such heat but at other moments, I heard Grette moaning about it. I bet she was fanning herself with one of those colourful fans she buys in Mediterranean shops.

Torben, who was the only one aware of my ability to hear, spoke directly to me, describing the lights and the shadows and the scents of the gardens and the roses I love so much. He told me that he and his partner had recently visited a friend in Sweden and were taken aback by the beauty of a bright red rose called Ingrid Bergman, in the

Swede's garden. I would love it, he was sure. Both the Ingrid Bergman and the whole garden. It was so atmospheric. Half Gustavian, half English Victorian. He thought of me then, he said.

In Sweden, amongst his friends, while they chatted and laughed and caught up with their news, walking a few steps ahead, or a few steps behind the rest, a bit apart, slightly aloof, he, my most difficult son, thought of me. He didn't tell me these details, but I could see him in my mind.

'My friend's garden reminded me of the one we had in Chelsea', he said.

Funny he would call that a garden at all, indifferent to it as he -being a teenager- appeared to be at the time. I had lugged a dozen containers upstairs and crammed them over the small roof area around the glass dome of the lift. The only access onto it was by climbing out through the windows of the corridor that linked the bedrooms on the top floor. These days the windows are probably barred in the name of health and safety, but at the time we lived there, it had been possible to create a charming haven. Every other day in the summer, either Anna or myself would fill two watering cans from the bath tap, passed them carefully over the window sill and then climb up and out rather awkwardly to water our roses. In compensation, we enjoyed the wafts of scent coming into our rooms, intense in the long, warm evenings, like the start of falling in love. It all sounds so daft now, but it felt Shakespearean then. The red Ena Harkness was Anna's preferred rose. If I recover, I will try to get hold of one of those and plant it in this garden in her memory. Mustn't forget.

There was also an occasion when I overheard Mr Henriksen ask Grette who Kar and Anna were because I mentioned their names in my dreams, rather agitatedly and more than once, along with a few other incoherences. Grette explained and he told her I shouldn't be hearing about people dying, especially loved ones, or sad news of such sort, didn't she think? I would've expected him to be less patronizing, but there you are. He has an impeccable reputation and I can certainly give him credit for his dedication, but there are times when Susan's words come to mind: Doctors know nothing. Susan is herself a Paediatric Consultant and I don't know whether to laugh or despair. I don't know whether I should buy cats or tomatoes. I like that. I don't know whether I should buy cats or tomatoes. Anna and I came across that line perusing an old volume of poetry lying on the bedside table of a Spanish hotel. We found it clever, funny, and I've been quoting the expression every time I am that confused. Grette likes it too.

Anyway. I regained my consciousness yesterday. Blandly. Indifferently. Without any feeling of elation or anxiety or even boredom as in those few days after the surgery. It might even be that all the conversations I seem to remember, never happened.

The room was a different one this time, painted yellow and with a larger window, but I wasn't too bothered by the world thriving and palpitating outside. That was yesterday. Today, I feel keener, eager and less drowsy in spite of this journey back home, which once again feels like an eternity. I wonder whether in the believers' afterlife Purgatory feels like this: an endless, dizzying journey, turning and turning, never getting to a destination. No battles and no peace either. Endless wandering.

Torben sits beside me, almost behind my head, crammed on a seat between my stretcher and the side of the ambulance, so I can't look at him easily. Every time I turn my face to him, I can only find his knees bent up high above my head. He keeps talking in a deliberately monotonous, soothing tone, trying to put me at ease by explaining that my having to lie down is only to prevent køresyge. Motion sickness.

'There's nothing to worry about. It's common and normal to feel dizzy after days and days of inactivity'.

Pure tact. He does not say "after days in a coma". When we finally arrive, the spinning ceases and I regain some balance and much calm. I demand to get up and out of the ambulance by myself and slowly, I manage to step down without falling over. The driver, a boyish-faced man, who keeps smiling and apologizing for everything he does and does not do, and a tall, burly nurse that would do better as a prison guard, try to help me along, but I refuse. The giant gives me a glaring look for daring to turn down her assistance before she turns to Torben handing over a few boxes of medicines and recite a list of instructions as if Torben weren't a physician and I were a helpless idiot.

Recognizable boxes, as a matter of fact. Some new

smertestillende to keep the pain at bay, with the peacock blue stripe running along one side and the emerald green letters above it, lively and distracting as if it were designed to provide some visual joy amidst the fatuous symptoms of death. Whether it is due to the state of my brain or to imminent madness, I must admit that I find the colours evocative of a Danish summer day along the beach, between the rows of spruce and pine trees and the sea glowing and shimmering under the sun, stretching like a gigantic whale up to the Swedish coast. Well, yes, if the stripe on a medication box makes me think of all that, then I must be losing the plot big time, as Ralph would say.

Torben opens the front door and I turn round to check that the grass has been mowed. It has, but the garden has changed. The palette of numberless hues splotched over corners and bedding is fading. I comment on this and Torben says that the temperature has been unusually high over the last few days, but that it's only the end of July and the best is yet to come.

'The best is yet to come. You sound like an amateur prophet. Or a bad politician'

'The word politician is self-describing, Far. You don't need an adjective' he corrects me, tongue in cheek.

I walk past the mirror that hangs by the coat hooks without facing myself and ask Torben to take it down, but he persuades me to leave it there until Grette comes back, in case she disagrees. She loves checking herself out every time she leaves the house to go and face the world, although she is always complaining about finding new wrinkles around her eyes. Silly girl. She always looks so sleek and smart. I'm afraid I couldn't say the same about myself, especially now. While I ponder about my decay, Torben disappears into the kitchen.

I look around at the furniture I let Grette choose when we renovated the house, the curtains we had made in London, the carpets, the paintings, everything is pretty much as I left it a week ago. No new changes have been introduced during my absence and I feel relieved at being able to recognize our rooms and feel at home after spending a few days in a different world.

Torben comes back into the room bringing a tray with sandwiches and tea, English style. We do this in Denmark too, but since he came back from London after Anna's funeral, he's been adopting some of her small gestures as if to recapture happy times in England, trying to recreate that world, keeping the only kind of maternal love he ever found, alive. It was Elba who pointed this out to me in that prudent manner she has, guessing that I would've surely failed to notice it.

Torben pours some strong tea into my favourite cup and some into his own. He seems to enjoy his food and drink, judging by the sandwiches he made and the tin full of biscuits he brought along.

'Are you comfortable?' he holds a plate in the air, waiting for me to sit upright and unfolds a napkin over my trousers, before placing the plate on my lap. He drags the coffee table closer to the sofa and sits next to me, without avoiding my eyes like he would've done in the past.

'Thank you, son' 'What for?'

'For not having a constant, stupid smile on your face, just because I haven't got long'

'You're just terrible, Dad, you know?'

'I've been told'.

There is no awkwardness between us and suddenly, it occurs to me that this will be my last chance to ask how and when did he hear about Cecille's issues. To my relief, he is happy to oblige:

'I had gone to Sweden for a long weekend. The university of Stockholm had granted me a second interview, remember? So, I decided to use the opportunity and spend two or three days in the capital. I stayed in a b&b near the Gamla Stan and strolled around the area checking up the architecture and the vibe of the place, as it were. You know how much I like people. I visited the conventional highlights and admired the Cathedral and the Viking Museum and all that. One simply has to visit those, by the way, but then on the Sunday, I spent the afternoon in the Djurgarden, lying in the sun, looking at the fluffy cloudlets fleeting about in the sky. In the evening, I sat in a fairly smart restaurant, swotting and collecting my thoughts for the following morning. I liked the city, but wasn't sure that I really wanted to do my PhD there'.

'Anyway, the interview went smoothly enough despite the stuffy attitude of the clinically immaculate interviewers.

A bony, skinny one used his hands to underline everything he said in such exaggerated way I could've thought he was Italian. You should've seen his fingers when a ray of sun fell upon the table, you could almost see the contours of the bones inside. The trio made me think of the three wise men... serious, efficient and polished, but not a spark of humour. They didn't think of me as the new Saviour, but I was proud to be there, all the same. Their letter arrived one week later and by then, I'd already decided on my future'

'I think I remember you phoning me to say so'

'The train left on time' Torben goes on. 'I had paid for a couchette and was spreading the white sheet over its thin mattress when I saw someone with pale hair walking down the corridor. It could've been any Swedish girl, really, so I dismissed any idea and carried on without bothering to look down the corridor. I grabbed an extra pillow from the empty couchette above and lay down to read my book. The sun was still hanging above the horizon, judging by the colours in the rectangle of the sky that passed by the window in front of me. I closed my eyes for a moment and when I opened them again and turned a page over, a fair-coloured halo went past once more along the corridor, above the edge of my book. It wasn't the colour, but the shape, the aura, something. I jumped up and pushed the sliding doors open. I called her name. She was surprised to see me, almost perplexed. *'What are you doing on this train?'* she asked. I explained and asked what was she doing? She looked upset, that much I could tell'.

'She'd gone to visit a friend who'd given birth to twins and persuaded her to stay one more day. The twins were four weeks old by then. She offered me a sip of aquavit from the small bottle and drank some herself, pulling faces of disgust. They were too beautiful, too sweet, the twins were. They were unbearable to look at. I should've seen them, she said, and went on talking about them for a while before she burst into tears. Really, really sobbing, so I hugged her. I remember thinking that she was going to stain my best pullover with her mascara. She kept mumbling something, but I couldn't make out what she was saying and didn't want to ask too much. She's just pissed, I thought. I was glad nobody else seemed to be coming to sleep in my compartment'

'She was twenty-eight years old. Not old, no, she could see that, but she was realistic, she had never indulged in illusions and rosy fantasies. Life was what was in front of her. There and then. Undeniable. Inevitable. Almost tangible. Things were the way they were, not otherwise, and she knew she wasn't going to have children. She didn't know whether she was maternal or not and she would never know. Perhaps it wasn't too bad when you see it all from outside, but she wasn't outside. Her heart was shattered by the knowledge that she was "a barren, useless woman", as she put it. Could I understand?'

'I didn't, of course, but I tried to make sense of what she was saying and comfort her, wondering why on earth she was confiding in me such private matters on a train from Stockholm. If she isn't drunk then she must've had a shock, I thought. She sounded really desperate. Broken. I tried to explain what was within my domain: the constant advances of science, the new techniques, the new methods. “What new techniques?” she asked. “Do you mean that Science has gone as far as to make possible for a woman without a womb to conceive? or words to that effect, anyway”

‘I apologized although I still didn’t know what it was all about. “Are you hinting at the possibility of a surrogate mother? No, thanks”, she told me, staring into my eyes as if I were responsible for her misfortune. I held her gaze, and stilled her hands, which kept wriggling on her lap. We only saw each other once or twice a year in those days and although we still felt very close to each other, I couldn’t ask about further details. She’s always been like more like an elder sister to me. One minute, warm and tactile; the next, aloof and secretive, but I’ve always been very fond of her...I thought she was having the time of her life in Paris, but obviously not. Felt sad for her’.

‘As her anguish would not subside, I tried to list a number of advantages of not having children. I attempted at reciting the Larkin poem that has become a bit of a cliché amongst the tortured souls of this world “They fuck you up your Mum and Dad”... why would she want to do the same, I giggled... She said I wouldn’t understand. “If only I hadn’t gone into hospital that day. It all went so terribly wrong, Torben! So wrong. The hospital was so embarrassed they paid me some silly money in compensation for their mistake. I gave it all away to children’s charities. Nobody knows anything about it”’.

‘I wanted to know more, of course, but didn’t pry. I only asked whether she had ever considered adoption and she said she had and then, when she calmed down a bit, she said that she could just about cope with not ever having children. What she could never do was forgive herself for making the wrong decision. It was her fault for acting irrationally. And now, her belly hurts and her heart tightens every time she sees a woman pushing a pram'

'I offered her to sleep in my couchette. I took the one above her. While she washed her face I went and fetched her luggage. It was big, red and vulgar, she joked, with a broken smile. I found it in no time so I walked to the other end of the corridor in order to take in what she'd just told me. I wasn't sure I understood the situation, but wanted to help her so much... I felt so sorry for her at that moment'.

I could barely contain my tears now that I have become a sentimental old sod and lost all control of my emotions. Torben carried on talking of her, now remembering her laughter when she visited them in London. She had hit it off with Anna and the four of them had the most spoilt weekend in town while I was away in Edinburgh. He was thirteen. Anders and Cecille, nineteen. He was in awe of her liquid blue eyes, her tinted eyelashes, her pearly skin.

'Now I think of it, -Torben says- she's always looked stunning from a distance and vulnerable in close up, like she's this sexy, attractive female and then, you sort of crack when you get close, don't you think? he asks me. He asks ME.

'Anyway, by the time I went back to the compartment, she was sitting cross-legged on my couchette, leafing through my book. She looked calmer. I left her luggage on the floor and took my washing bag to go and get ready for the night. When I returned, she was squeezing into an old T-shirt. I caught a glimpse of her long legs, her pert behind, her bare breasts. She reminded me of the sculptures I'd seen at the Museum of Fine Arts on the Saturday morning. There was room for improvement in her proportions, but she seemed to be carved in alabaster. You should've seen that... well, you have seen her, I forget'...

'She paid for her looks by falling pregnant and then had her life wrecked by some butcher who had misread her records. It happens once in a million cases, she told me, and it had happened to her. Like a game of Russian roulette. She thought it was unforgivable and so did I'.

'She made room for me to sit next to her before climbing onto my couchette and I obliged. I lay beside her and held her in my arms, stroking her head until she fell asleep, her chest sometimes heaving in an involuntary sob. Her face felt feverish and I could feel her breath smelling of aquavit hot against my chin. I also dosed off to the rocking of the train and then Cecille stirred herself and whispered "It was your Dad's baby... It was Ole's baby". That's how I found out'.

Torben repeats the words to me as if I hadn't heard them. As if I hadn't known it was my baby. I can hear the reproach in his voice and see that his self-imposed forgiveness for a matter that has disgusted him so deeply can only be due to my imminent death. It's true then. It's happening. His account of events is so vivid and detailed, so pedantically accurate, but I know there is something more Cecille has never told anyone, not even to me.

'There is nothing I can say in my defence, of course. It's such a raw wound'

'If you feel that way, imagine what it must be like for Cecille. The hospital's error was preposterous, and you, Father, really...'

Silent minutes go by. Two, five, twenty? The sun has moved and the square it paints underneath my feet becomes a thin rectangle stretching obliquely as if the sun itself were drawing light from the oak floor pulling and jerking it out of the window. It must be true that I am obsessed with light. I remember Ulla sitting baby Anders on his sheepskin rug. He would follow with his curious eyes the patterns the sun painted, his chubby hands chasing the light that spread and shrank beneath his teddy bears. Baby Anders. Baby Cecille. They used to play together on the beach, their lips almost blue in the cold breeze, always asking for more castles, for a little bit longer.

One year we crossed over to Sweden and drove to Båstad, taking the two of them with us. They must have been about five years old. They spent hours rock puddling, collecting crabs into a bucket, observing how their legs stretched and folded depending on the pressure they put on their backs. Every now and then, Anders would pick one up and throw it at Cecille, but she would outwit him by remaining calm and saying that he was being ever so silly, in that superior way that girls adopt towards boys at that age. They were happy then. Cecille didn't have to escape from her parents just yet and Anders still had his mother around. Sometimes, they slept in each other's houses, Anders at the Bossens' if Ulla and I went to the theatre; Cecille, in our home if Erika and Jensen went to the cinema.

'It was too late when I heard' I manage to mumble.

Cecille was unable to think clearly at a time when she most needed to do so. She never told me in time. I have never felt so despicable in my life.

'Don't stress yourself, Far' Torben says, springing up from his chair as soon as I stand up. He follows me round the room and stands by my side at the window as I evoke another summer, another view in another life. If I closed my eyes, Cecille would start walking up the driveway like she used to do all those years ago. It's one of the images I most vividly remember about her. Perhaps because it represents a turning point. If she had never come up to my door... If I had never opened the door... If I had sent her back...

'I should've ignored her youth and turned her down'

'What were you thinking, really?' Torben says. She was young enough to mess up and make mistakes, but you should've known better... I mean, why? Why Cecille of all people, Dad?'

My pain does not prevent me from appreciating Torben's honesty. He continues admonishing my conduct and he is right in every point, but now I feel so very tired that I have to sit down for a few minutes before I go upstairs, where once again Torben accompanies me and gently takes my shoes off.

A few minutes later I hear the gravel crashing under Grette's car tyres and see Torben leave the room through the gloomy haze of my slumber. With a heavy heart, I allow myself to fall asleep.

When three hours later I wake up and stretch to grab the cup of tea Grette must have left on my table, the telephone rings. It is Mr Henriksen, confirming what the registrar told us yesterday on his behalf. I need chemotherapy. I won't need to stay in hospital although I'll feel sick at times and above all, I shall feel exhausted. And yes, neuropathy will hit my hands and feet. Bla bla bla. It gets so bloody boring. The ironic thing is that after speaking to him, I feel so full of energy and enthusiasm that I get up and go downstairs, determined to open the mail and sort out all those papers which seem to breed when left unseen. Am I experiencing personality changes like a true victim of Glioblastoma multiforme, after all? I've already suffered some genetic alterations, Mr Henriksen said. But I have a plan and the cunning to ask Mr Henriksen to keep the chemotherapy thing a secret for a couple of days. The question is, do I really want to undergo such misery? I still have a sound mind to know my rights. Besides, what guarantees of a recovery do I have? All I hope is not to get aggressive or violent. Could that really happen? It would be ghastly!

Erika told me once how Jensen had to be tied up to his bed when he came round after one of his operations still under the effect of anaesthetics. He grabbed the nurse by her neck and tried to strangle her. Poor Erika felt so embarrassed about the incident as if Jensen's attempt had been planned in a cold blooded, clear minded fashion, that she stopped visiting him in hospital. It was only a drug induced, furtive reaction in Jensen's case, but the idea of doing something equally dangerous is repugnant to me. I told Mr Henriksen to inject me double of whatever is needed if I ever become dangerous. Or unbearable.

In the meantime, I wonder what to do now about chemotherapy, my shares and Italy. Going there would please Grette no end. They might be our last holidays. After Italy, I could go and stay with Elba and Harald, as we planned the other day.

Bloody fucking Glioblastoma multiforme. GBM, as Torben calls it, so casually and at ease with the name as if he were referring to a car make. I like it though. It makes the tumour sound interesting, ha ha. In the past, while there was not yet a single hint of my tumour, if I chanced upon an article or the odd TV programme about cancer of the brain, I used to think it was one of the most sophisticated types of this evil. Of course, I knew it had nothing to do with intellect, but if I heard that somebody was thus afflicted, I couldn't help finding it intriguing. Some years ago, I read the diaries of an English minister who, while still healthy and exceptionally fit, had had the same idea about this fatal type of cancer and without lingering on the thought and almost joking, told himself that it should suit him very well indeed when his time came. Five years later, he was dead. Of a brain tumour. Fascinating. Is my own GBM a consequence of a subconscious choice, an unacknowledged wish? Why?

My darling sister adheres passionately - everything she does is done passionately- to the theory that cancer, like every other disease and syndrome, is related to something going on in the mind and the soul. A psychosomatization of some unpleasant incident we have been unable to process and digest. (I am only quoting her). There is nothing that chemotherapy or radiotherapy can do, nothing an oncologist can do, unless the patient cooperates and contributes to his own salvation by means of a thorough soul searching until he finds the roots of the distress leading up to his cancer. Moreover, Elba would add, the organ where you get your cancer is exactly that one where your issue is locked. So, if you feel smothered by a situation you cannot control, you will develop persistent coughing, asthma... or lung cancer. If you feel that you cannot "digest" some painful setback, you will end up with ulcer of the stomach... or cancer in some part of your digestive system, or if you are lucky, with a simple vomit. "The stomach throws up what the mind cannot digest, and the words we choose to express our troubles are also symptomatic".

I can't quite follow her rationale, but much is talked about new treatments of this kind and soul-psychology-neurology these days, so I stay silent. She amuses me. 'You can laugh if you want to', Elba said, 'but mind each word you utter because every word is a decree'. Thus (I hear her lecturing me) I mustn't say that something is driving me mad because it will literally make me more anxious and stressed. Nor should I say that this brain cancer is killing me, because by reaffirming its existence, I will make it regrow, spread, take over and kill me.

'And I can choose not to let it do so, can't I?

'Exactly', Elba said, when I put these questions to her the other day. I stifled a laugh and wondered whether I was already losing my mind, but she had everything so clearly worked out in her head that I didn't have the heart to disappoint her. Let her keep her faith, I thought, and may she never ever have the need to challenge those theories herself.

It's half past ten now and after four or five of hours of sheer gaiety and good health, I'm feeling so depressed and scared of darkness falling upon us that I'm afraid of going back to sleep. Luckily, it is still daylight but the sky is now as heavy and grey as my own spirit. Where has the sun gone? One minute I am lucid, rational and in full acceptance of my fate. Next minute, I am dismayed and terrified.

'Look, darling. I've already phoned my usual hotel and they have vacancies for...' Grette tells me of her plans for our holidays. I raise my hand and she stops. She is obviously in denial, dismissing the fact that I am slightly weary of popping into town, let alone climb up and down over the bridges of Venice. Besides, I'd much rather go to France, if abroad at all, but as I might be gone in a week or two, I cannot see the point in discussing my preferences. And there is another thing I find annoying: all the time she is sitting on my bed she keeps shifting her weight from one buttock to the other, causing ripples on the mattress. It's irritating. After all, if she chose to change our large bed for two single ones, she might just as well sit on hers and leave me in peace. It's not her I am niggled about, I recognize that, but cannot help myself.

I feel guilty for being edgy and on the point of snapping all the time when all I would love to say is how much I care about her and how I value her company. My whole existence is now plagued with guilt and paralyzed by remorse. Life is becoming hell and this endless number of emotions and recriminations that fill up my days must be what I deserve, but how much longer will I be able to keep my pain and rage and frustration under control in order not to cause further offence? Is this state of mind really affected by the state of my brain? I may be fussy, admittedly, but I've never been this crazy. And I am NOT going to Venice.

Chapter 21

Bittersweetness

Cecille sounds very indifferent. There is hardly any surprise in her voice as if she had been expecting my call without feeling pleased to hear me. I ask her whether she is busy, thinking that it could be the reason for her distant tone.

'No, not at all' she says, but does not volunteer any comment. She just keeps quiet, urging me to explain the reason for my call. I know those silences. I don't know anyone else whose voice betrays her mood so clearly, but our encounters are now too few and far apart to enable me to guess the reasons. I am no longer able to work out what is aggrieving her on a day-to-day basis. We have lost each other along the way. We belong in our past, in Copenhagen. The doors of her present life in Paris are closed to me, as they probably are to the Cecille of twenty years ago.

'I'd really like... I really NEED to see you'.

'Darling Ole, you know I'd love to, but don't think I have the heart to see my parents again so soon... and couldn't be there and not see them, obviously'

'Please?'

'I'd rather not, Ole, I'm sorry. Every time I'm there, I come back home too upset and frustrated. Can't quite get over the... oh, never mind, but no, I don't think I'll go'.

'All that disdain is beneath you, sweetheart'.

I try to advise her -as if I were the ideal person to do so-

'You only hurt yourself by holding grudges against your parents. Look at how far you have got in your life, your career, just let all that stuff behind, skat'.

'Ok, leave it. Let's drop that, shall we? Are you well, though? Why do you need to see me?'

She sounds tetchy and I remain silent until she calms down. It amazes me to see how raw she still feels about all that, when she can be so mature and collected about everything else.

'Nobody has ever known how unhappy I was in those days. I didn't know it myself. I used to think there were so many more people enduring much more pain and misery than myself... I kept hoping to come out of the tunnel once I reached adolescence, once I finished school, once I graduated from university... It would pass...until it got worse. Tragic, I could say, and wouldn't be exaggerating. The years went by and the tunnel just got longer and darker. Sure, you remember...'

I do indeed. Too well, or why would I be calling her, otherwise? Too bloody wrong those days were. When she came up to me, she could no longer identify the reason for her unhappiness because her capacity to think rationally was taken over by a desperate need to be accepted and loved. She didn't feel the urge to ask for help because she didn't think she needed it. I had to be careful not to judge her parents too harshly every time she told me of their behaviour because instead of taking it as encouragement to free herself from their claws, she would become defensive.

She was too immersed in that conundrum to see that her need for them was exactly the reason for her frustration and despair. She had entertained the idea of committing suicide, she told me once, and when I asked her why, she said simply that life was too much for her. I thought she was just being melodramatic. Now I know better. That was the Cecille that could make your heart break with just being in front of you, but then she clammed up and there was nothing one could do to help her out.

And there was also the other Cecille, the one who laughed and sang and danced when she felt so much happiness that she could not contain it under her skin. We went to London, once. 'I've started to read all the ghastly news in the papers in order to stop myself from smiling too much around the house and let them see my happiness, teehee' she joked then, during the days previous to our trip.

We flew separately because her mother was going to take her to the airport and if she ever decided to see her right into the departures' hall, we would be found out. It was one of those occasions when fed up with hiding and lying, she nearly told everybody about us. It took me hours and lots of logic to dissuade her from doing so.

When eventually she agreed to keep our affair secret, she said that it was only to protect my sons from the embarrassment. No sooner she heard herself saying so, we both burst out laughing. She and my sons were the same age.

London was slipping into autumn and we walked like one can only walk in London. Endlessly. Indefatigably. She took photos of ignored sculptures in busy corners, of milk bottles standing neatly on doorsteps, of pillar boxes in autumn-coloured parks as well as of the highlights, although she insisted on seeing the collection at the… what's the name of that Gallery? We spent over an hour there, admiring this, interpreting that, analysing the other, but the main shock to her was the Van Gogh's self-portrait with his severed ear and bandage. Cecille was disturbed and upset by its poignant narrative. She had seen it in prints, but never in the flesh, as she put it. Was he being provocative? Had he deliberately set out to make a statement in front of the society which ignored him so openly? Was he waving two fingers at aesthetics? Had he expected to attract the sympathy, if not the attention, he so desperately craved? Or was he purely and simply painting what he saw in the mirror, with the same nonchalance a reporter shows us disturbing scenes or war and famines?

Cecille said that she could understand Van Gogh probably better than anybody else had done during his lifetime. Even Theo had failed him, hadn't he? Could I imagine how it must have felt not just chopping your ear off and enduring the pain, but also the torment of looking at yourself, like that, forever lonely, many times hungry, deceived by your best friend and by your lover while you fill your canvass with blue, green and as much as you can of your wretched soul? It was hard to picture such madness, wasn't it?

Indeed, I found Cecille's interpretation far more upsetting than the portrait itself, so I did my best to change the subject and dragged her out of the building kissing her repeatedly, like teenagers, along the Strand. The Courtauld. That's where it was. The Courtauld's Institute.

'This is sooo beautiful. Sheer and utter bliss' she said, referring to London as she stretched her arms and twirled on one foot like a ballerina. I hugged her tightly and then found our way up to some posh place for afternoon tea. She ordered lemon pie and a cup of Indian tea. Her brow was relaxed again and her eyes smiled freely, lively, while she kept looking around her as one does when seeing things for the first time and feeling very happy.

Then we went shopping. She bought tens of books because they were cheaper than in Denmark, she said, a cashmere jumper for herself and a Royal Stewart cap with ginger tresses attached to it for Hamlet, her teddy bear. She found the liveliness of those tartan clothes irresistible and I was touched by her eagerness to enjoy herself, and by the glow those colours gave her, emphasizing her youth and liberating her from her own inner turmoil.

She only started talking about herself when we were dining on our last evening in London.

'I was four years old, but have never forgotten. My parents thought I was asleep, or had forgotten I was there, who knows? It was after their friends left, Ulla and yourself amongst them, that they started arguing. It wasn't unusual, but that night Dad was very drunk, I guess. Perhaps it wasn't such a big issue, come to think of it'.

I remember her chin starting to tremble while she talked, but let her continue.

'A plate went crashing into a wall. Dad yelled he could not stand the sight of Mum, which was a recurrent expression whenever they had a heated argument. The actual words didn't matter much any longer, really.

I tiptoed out of my room, because I could not hear mother anymore and I got scared. Dad continued on his string of abuse, for which he had a vast repertoire. At last, I heard Mor say she wished he would have a heart attack there and then and drop dead in front of her eyes. It was the kind of mutual verbal stabbing I had already overheard on many occasions.

Dad got quiet until I heard him whisper that unless they lowered their voices, they would wake up "the little one". And at that moment, Erika replied that she had had enough of me as well, that she had had enough of my questions, my attention seeking, my crying over the itchy, sore eczema that no treatment seemed able to cure. She said she couldn't cope with her own anxieties, let alone with looking after a spoilt brat and a lunatic of a husband, who were constantly mocking her, using her, the pair of us. We may just walk out of her life. Out of her sight. Forever.'

'Mum must have been drunk, too, to answer something like that, mustn't she? Otherwise, she was always so calm, so placid. You've known her all your life. She is very sweet, isn't she? She had to have been drunk. She never was the perfect mother... She's overpowering and prone to dramatize, but she would've never meant what she said, surely...'

I reassured her and said that indeed, Erika must've been awfully drunk. Cecille wiped a tear off her eyelashes and I swallowed my own distress along with a sip of wine, then stretched over the table and kissed her eyelids, while on the table, her hands were holding her glass ever so tightly so that I would not notice she was shaking. I've never forgotten that scene. The world seemed so wrong, life so unfair, one more time.

When we went up to our room, she was bubbly again, almost skipping along the corridor, hanging on to me, telling me she was in a spell of happiness and bliss. Her joy at that moment was even more poignant than her tears.

Now in Paris, on hearing my voice all these years after that night I wonder what other secret she's been keeping. I am certain there are more demons dormant in her heart. I will not deny her then the relief, the satisfaction, of being left alone. No home memories for her. She's out of here. I should've known better than calling her like an idiot. The past needs leaving alone. That is her decision. I make light comments about something else and steer the conversation to an end. 'Au revoir, cher Ole' she says.

I hang up the receiver, thinking of all the times she called me, whispering that she would meet me in ten minutes, or in half an hour, round the corner at dusk, by the lake in the middle of the afternoon, outside some suburban station in the pouring rain, always in a different place, always breathless with excitement and fearful of being caught...

Chapter 22

Grette

'I'm closing shop' Grette announces. She's had enough of selling second homes to pale Scandinavians in sunny Italy. She is retiring. I try to dissuade her, naturally, but she has everything sorted out. Typically, Grette: unable to show any concern, any emotion, like an ice mermaid. I had assumed that she was in denial and felt upset by her apparent indifference and yet, here she is, putting an end to the business she has enjoyed for almost twenty years. She made herself a little fortune, met some interesting people – some of them, anyway- and had numerous holidays on beaches, lakes, mountains and deserts thanks to her hard work. Now she's leaving all that behind in order to be by my side and enjoy life together on twenty-four hours a day, seven days a week basis. Why make such a decision? How can she get it so wrong when she knows damn well that she will be left on her own and then won't have even her job to go back to as a refuge?

I would've rather heard that she's met somebody new to share her life with once I'm gone. Hard, indeed, but it would be easier to accept given the circumstances. Silly girl. After leaving her husband for me seventeen years ago, I could and would accept the same luck gladly. There would be some symmetry. Poetic justice, as they say. Instead, I'll be sent off with an honourable Walhalla in a totally undeserved fashion.

I remember her ex-husband's face. The poor chap's expression was indescribable. He was perplexed. Grette had been going out with me for several months but he'd been too absorbed by his warships models to notice when she was at home or when she wasn't. Too obsessed to listen to her arguments, too busy to join her in her strolls across the parks or bike rides along the canals. Grette sounded very unhappy about their lives going separate ways and their everyday comments becoming shorter and sparser as they found each other's company unnecessary, if not unpleasant. I thought she was being partial and -as a personal curiosity- tried to figure out which were her own flaws and, -as a professional-, which were exactly her motives to want a divorce. I was a barrister, family law was my area of expertise, what did I suggest?

I found her affable, in a detached, terse sort of way. Not particularly attractive in looks but there was some distinction, some class about her that was alluring. Searching for urgent answers, she started to come into my office with certain regularity, sometimes without booking an appointment. On one of her visits, I made a professional faux pas and took the liberty of asking her to join me at a café round the corner and discuss her issues there. It was a silent wings moment, something that stirred my soul long before I was aware of it. Grette was now determined to leave him. No more doubts, no more beating about the bush, she was going to break the news to him. She had tears in her eyes, but I had seen hundreds of similar cases by then and wasn't particularly moved by her distress. I had to remain objective.

Two or three months went by before she phoned again. They were still together. I wished her luck, guessing she wasn't going to pursue the demand, but she insisted. She would need a barrister. A good one.

We met at the same café at three o'clock in the afternoon. She was already there and for some stupid reason, I felt awkward turning up with snow on my shoulders and having to wipe my feet vigorously on the threshold as if this gesture made me look less composed before a conversation that had to be formal and professional. When I got to her table, she pretended not to have seen me arrive. I thought that was subtle of her.

Her husband had failed her, by not doing anything for their life together. She had felt lonely for so many years, keeping her friends at a distance so that they would not peep into her unhappiness. She had been too proud or too foolish, she didn't know which. I tried to stop her confidences but it was too late, as I was to realize months later when I looked back to the start of our affair. She withheld a tear or two while I settled the bill. It was already dark and still snowing when we left the café. She hailed a taxi and jumped into it without a word, but as I made to close the door for her, she looked straight into my eyes and asked me to get in.

We went straight to the flat a friend of mine had lent me while my house was being refurbished, and for the first time since my early youth, I felt clumsy in a woman's presence. Grette's presence. She followed me along the corridor and into the kitchen as I awkwardly offered her a coffee. She accepted, but there wasn't any. I had thrown the empty box in the morning. I rummaged into different cupboards, making excuses and giving futile explanations, but when I turned round, she had vanished.

I found her sitting on the bed, waiting for me, almost trembling with fear of rejection, she would tell me later. She undressed me very slowly, her eyes never leaving my eyes. She wept in silence when I took her.

The following weekend, she stayed with me. It was the first time she had lied to her husband. The first time she'd been unfaithful. By spending time with me, she realized her marriage had been even duller than she had believed. She didn't have a married life, only a lifeless marriage.

We toured the city in earnest as if we were foreign tourists. We visited the galleries, went to the cinema, the theatre, the Opera House. She liked the ballet. Her mother had sent her to ballet lessons, would I believe it? She had put on weight, she knew that, but her friends reckoned she had maintained some of the grace and poise she had acquired while dancing.

'Your friends are absolutely right' I said and she blushed like the little girl she must've been. Chubby, nose-freckled and rather shy.

I told her of Ulla and of my children and she told me of her husband. Of how they had met, fallen in love, married, had a daughter and fallen out of love in the course of five years. Since then, they had tolerated each other for the sake of their daughter or so they told themselves, but since she had grown up and gone to live abroad things had got worse between them and there was no point in carrying on pretending, was there? She listened attentively when I told her of Anna, -probably trying to ellicit some useful tips about how to deal with divorce and separation-, and I paid attention when she told me about her panic of the future, with a daughter living so far away and no other relative to take care of her when she would finally get old. Could I imagine? Who was going to hold her hand before she died if there was nobody else around to stop her dying in an old people's home, forgotten and neglected? She was too young to think that way, I remember saying, but she was somewhat anxious during those days and despite our expensive dinners and days by the sea, her heart was heavy with the weight of her betrayal.

We comforted each other and when we found that the situation was getting too pathetic, we ended up laughing. There are times when laughing is the last resource left. What we can laugh at, we can face... What we can face, we can conquer...

She kept a double life for several months. Daytime with her indolent husband, evenings and most weekends with me. He never asked her the name of her friend, or where she lived or where they went together. Sometimes she would drop a hint, if only to see whether he would react. He never did.

One morning, -it was July-, I remember, she put the

breakfast tray on my bedside table and told me she was going back to her husband for good. She wouldn't come back in the evening or Friday or Saturday or ever again. Dark rings under her eyes told me she hadn't slept. Her hair looked lifeless in a chignon she had tied with a printed scarf in an attempt to make herself look in control of her looks and her life. I sat up but let her go, listening to her steps going determinedly downstairs and out into the world that had brought her into my life and was now taking her away.

This is what life is about, I told myself. Arrivals and departures. Trials and errors. Comings and goings. There's no other way. She was making a big mistake, but it was her choice and her right.

Summer went by and I remained occupied, partly absorbed in some cases, partly doing my best to entertain and amuse my sons during their holidays. Sometimes, I accompanied Kar to look around for properties and tried to help him make up his mind about what he really needed. A house with a garden for the few times his friends came to stay? Three or four bedrooms? A flat in town like the one I was occupying, only bigger? Looking back, I must've been using that as an excuse to keep myself, -if not amused-, at least extra busy, cancelling any thought about the woman who had gradually, but indelibly, caused such a whirlwind of euphoria and joy and passion in my cynic, apathetic heart. The way she wrinkled her nose when she giggled, the way she could prepare a heart-warming meal out of the nothingness of my fridge, the way she made me laugh out loud again and crave for more and more of her whole being... I missed her. Body, mind and soul. Simply and madly, I missed her.

Three months later, on a rainy, dull October afternoon, I phoned her. I would take twenty minutes to drive up to her place. She could wait for me downstairs or not see me ever again.

When the taxi pulled up, she was standing in the rain, under a black umbrella printed with multicoloured butterflies and a big hold-all on her shoulder. My relief and happiness on seeing her there were almost unbearable. She told me how during those ninety-two days –she had counted them- she had dialled my number so many times and then hung up, how she had read books realizing she could not remember what they were about because she had not been able to concentrate on anything else but me, our time together and what she, by now, thought was her deep, sincere affection for me. She wanted to say all that at once, but I kept interrupting her with kisses, in the back of the taxi, like two unseasoned adolescents. I was fifty-five, she was forty-six. We were not getting any younger.

The day after, she broke the news to her husband. I watched them from a distance, sitting at a different table, in a café full of newspaper readers. The poor bloke had never had any suspicion that things had been so wrong between them, despite her many ways of telling him. I saw his jaw drop and then his head resting heavily on his hands. Shadows spread across Grette's face and I worried that she might once again give in to their routine, moved by the sadness of his solitude, but then her husband looked up, held her hand, and without needing Grette to tell me of his words later, I could make out he was saying he was sorry. He didn't fight, or plead or justify himself.

He did not blame her, he didn't accuse her of any wrong doing, of letting him down. He did what one should always do: explain nothing, complain of nothing.

Now my dear Grette suggests driving down to Italy. Italy. Italy! Bliss, she says this is. Last time we were there was for a ski holiday, which she adores and I do not because I am worse than hopeless on a pair of skis. She spent most of the day up on the slopes and all I managed was to avoid falling over.

Perhaps, I am dull and tragic and predictable as Grette tells me when she loses her cool. I must be. Who else would think of tragedy when being invited to Venice? The truth is, I cannot envisage such a tortuous journey. I tell Grette to check with Mr Henriksen whether I am fit to fly. Were I in her shoes I would probably be as keen to lure me out of my misery by booking some holidays as she is doing, but as someone sentenced to death, I feel vulnerable being away from my own stuff and all those familiar habits which are not worth preserving other than by their hyggelig, sentimental value.

Travelling round the world when one is so close to leaving it seems unnecessary, like rubbing one's nose in the vastness of a planet which has become redundant and hostile because it does not want us here any longer. Instead, staying at home on my own armchair, looking at my paintings, using my own corkscrew, my own key ring, feel reassuring. Ordinary objects that have become part of my life by dint of being mine. It would be sweeter to make the final journey straight from my Danish soil than from a country where the sun is so bright that it blinds you and whose language you can hardly speak. I just hope that Mr Henriksen will advise against travelling, but I know I'm fit enough for that.

Chapter 23

Independence regained

Everything is alright at the Morgensen's, as Tolstoi would have said. Everything is indeed going easily and smoothly, but in the wrong direction.

'You're perfectly fit to walk freely and go on short flights if you want', Mr Henriksen said. 'Within the next three or four weeks, at least'.

Ah. He may have added that I have nothing to lose, I suppose. Still. He sounded positive when I mentioned Grette's idea of going on holidays, so when she entered the room, I quickly changed the tone of our conversation so that she would not suspect a thing about our agreement. The thing is: Henriksen advises chemotherapy, but I won't have it. My choice. At my own peril. I shall die sooner, or shall I? Although it is my right to accept or refuse treatment, I've offered to put my decision in black and white in order to safeguard Mr Henriksen's reputation if ever any member of my family were to question his judgement or competence.

There is no much guarantee of the process developing one way or the other, given my medical history, my age, et cetera, et cetera, the doctor said. Also, I read on the internet that Dr such and such, who won the Nobel Prize for Medicine on two occasions, (not just one!), said that only three per cent of patients with a cancer of the very same characteristics as mine are cured by chemotherapy... I took my time to absorb that: Only three per cent of patients with cancer are cured by chemotherapy. Can this be true?

Grette almost jumps with joy and hugs me tightly when I say we can go abroad. She is almost unrecognizable since I've been feeling better.

'Oh, magnifico! Tomorrow evening we'll be in Venice, isn't it fabulous, darling? I've got thousands of air miles to use and Lotta will organize the best holidays straight away. Driving there was a stupid idea. I wasn't being sensible but oh, I'm so excited. Aren't you?' Her enthusiasm is almost infectious

'Can't we just go online and make our own arrangements? Same hotel we stayed last time, the one near San Marco, what's it called?'

She accepts wholeheartedly and jokes about my unwavering dislike for authority.

'Look who's talking', I say. We laugh, and I feel cancer-free.

In the afternoon, once we have decided on our Italian itinerary, (don't want to think about tourists and the heat steaming off the canal and the concrete) I call a taxi and drive to one of my ex-colleagues, good old Martin, who kindly witnesses my signature and gives my decision the necessary legal enforcement. So, at seventy-five years of age, I read the document the doctor put in front of me: "In possession of all my faculties, this is my final decision", and so on. I like the in possession of all my faculties bit. Being compus mentis. Such privilege! Grette stays at home, packing our suitcases and probably worrying sick about my going out on my own, but I am fine. Thin, limping and at times, slurring my words, but absolutely fine.

Martin behaves impeccably on hearing of my condition, cool, calm, matter-of-fact, but cannot help turning round to check on my step as I walk downstairs, behind him. He sees me out, shake hands and says he would have taken the same decision had he been in my shoes. I thank him and tell him an anecdote I once heard my uncle tell.

One of his colleagues -my uncle was a doctor-, had called him up to show him the radiography of a patient whose lungs were invisible under a huge, black spot. The verdict was unquestionable. What do you suggest I should tell him? his colleague said, sitting at his desk. The poor chap, he'd better shoot himself, said my uncle, half joking, still looking at the plaque, standing by the window. His colleague pulled a pistol out of his drawer and shot himself there and then. My uncle felt responsible for the man's suicide for the rest of his life.

Martin says he got the message and promises not to offer his opinion if he ever has to deal with a terminal patient again. When I turn round, some fifty yards away, Martin is still there, impeccably suited and groomed, standing on the threshold, squinting in the afternoon sun, watching me limp. Our eyes meet across some passers-by. Neither of us waves.

I weep my silent tears behind the sunglasses while I shuffle along the Strøget, leaning on my walking stick, looking for a present for Grette just as I imagined I would do if I ever came out of hospital. It feels odd, like seeing everything for the first time. With new eyes. Like a baby. I often wonder, since I've been paying attention to the human brain, whether our first experiences, and by first, I mean those from day one, are all recorded in our memory but we fail to recall them only because it would be too traumatic. Glaring light, colours, textures and sounds, noises and laughter, conversations, voices, tears, smells... New faces all the time, one after the other. Just thinking about it is too harrowing. The process must be hardly bearable, I guess. Strøget feels, looks and sounds like that.

I feel I could weep loudly or burst out laughing or scream my fucking head off. Like a lunatic. But then I think, what if I bump into some acquaintance, or a neighbour? What if people see me wandering in a daze across town and I overhear them whisper: There he goes, Herr Morgensen, the top barrister who lost the plot as well as his hair. Losing the plot. I could not stand it. Of all the intricacies and variations and complexities of the human brain, madness is the one I could not bear. I have a phobia of prisons and psychiatric hospitals, which is why I have never specialized in Criminal Law. I could not have faced the responsibility of sending people off to prison. I approve of punishing and reeducating people, but I preferred not to deal with such cases directly. So much for honesty and principles, one might think, but then again, we are all hypocrites in different measures.

A Charles Hurley QC I used to know in London got quite agitated on this account once. He had invited a few of us with wives or husbands for drinks at his country house in Henley-on-Thames. He loved to impress and certainly knew how to do it. The chap was terribly clever, but he could not hold much alcohol without losing his temper and revealing his own frustrations or whatever it was that made him feel inadequate.

Being asked about the Danish legal system and the Danes's view on capital punishment, I replied without going into too long a dissertation. I felt that the subject was too divisive and hardly suitable for a cocktail party, but some of the lawyers expressed their views and said that the death penalty was anachronistic; others, that it was unfair; others, simply waited for Charles to comment so that they could agree with him, regardless of what they thought to themselves. Perhaps, they didn't think at all. They had still to make their careers. Upsetting the boss would have been a faux pas.

I said that I disapproved of capital punishment because it is, above all, less punishing than a life sentence. Give someone a lifetime in a small jail, sometimes shared with other people without a shred of privacy, or alone and lonely, no views from his window, no going out for a pint with his mates. Not ever for the rest of his life. Ever. I could not think of anything worse, and I wasn't sure I could've sentenced someone to such a life, either.

Charles swore at me and accused me of being a right -wing bastard. I laughed it off saying that a right-wing Dane was a contradiction in terms. The others gasped, stared and said nothing. Charles's anger increased. I was patronizing him, wasn't I? I replied I was only answering his questions. He turned the disagreement into a heated argument –quite at odds with his charming, collected personae when sober- and ended up hurling the bottle of scotch at me, missing my right eye, but hitting my cheekbone rather badly.

Anna rushed in from the other end of the garden, poured the ice cubes from the bucket into a handkerchief and applied it onto my head. Then she poured a stiff whiskey, amidst the men of law who hardly moved, flabbergasted by the situation or by her intervention, and made me have one sip. She kissed my cheek better, had a sip herself and threw the rest of the drink at Charles's face. We never saw him again.

That was Anna's way of dealing with emergencies and fools. Especially, fools. God rest her soul.

God. As I realize I've been thinking of God these days, or of some god, and of some kind of after life, I mumble a prayer, asking to be free from a few fears of what I might encounter before passing onto the next life, if there really is one after all. No cancer, no prisons, no asylums. Please. My phobias could be a good topic for a psychotherapist, but it amuses me to think that I shall die before any of those creatures finds me out. They will have missed the chance of analysing me and making a small fortune along the endless years they all claim to be necessary for the exorcism of one's demons. Ha!

When Elba phoned this morning before Mr Henriksen's call, she advised me to pray for help to the Masters of the Light. I should ask them for "perfect protection of all my chakras and all my plans, including the astral plan". I wonder what the hell all that means. Her faith is really baffling, not to say extraordinary, one has to admit. I genuinely envy her for that. In fact, her words may have had an influence on my suddenly contemplative mood and I am now wandering round town with a silent prayer in my mind until I get to Amagertorv and am stopped by a group of foreign students asking for directions. I know exactly how to direct them but my speech comes out very slowly and they walk off.

I stagger on and pop into Georg Jensen's without any clear idea of what to look for, until a bracelet leaps at me, as it were, from inside a display cabinet. It is perfect. It will match a ring I gave Grette last Christmas, so I don't hesitate paying a good amount of money for it. Why would I, at this stage? She loved the design then, with three thick, octagonal ribbons of silver, white gold and platinum, one of them with a matte finish, called moon dust, according to the perfectly dressed and made-up assistant.

Grette loves these things, and now it's the season when she will be able to show off a bracelet. Especially in Italy, where it will offset her tan. Everybody is so keen on dressing up and showing off their jewels that she will feel honoured to compete with those Venetian ladies.

If only she knew how exciting it feels to be able to pop into a shop, choose a gift, hand out my credit card and carry out the transaction all by myself. Slow speech, yes, but clear minded, walking slowly but steadily… it seems like a big adventure, and to finish it off I stagger onto a bus and get myself home. It's a highly irresponsible thing to do, like playing truant at school, but it feels like real life again.

Chapter 24

Venice

We landed at thirteen minutes past six yesterday evening. The flight was good and we relaxed and chatted notwithstanding the uncomfortable seats. My head didn't spin or hurt. My eyes remained focused and my spirit, high. Only in the water taxi did I feel giddy but the discomfort disappeared once I swapped places with another passenger and sat at the front. He was more than happy to chat in his semi-fluent English with me, rather than in his native Italian with Grette. Unusual for an Italian bloke to miss the chance of chatting to a woman, but Grette didn't mind one way or the other and every time I turned round to look at her, she was fiddling with her bracelet, admiring its effect over her bluey-green shirt. She could not stop smiling, girlie and soft like she is underneath her thick layer of toughness.

At the airport, she'd been tactful enough as to make me feel in full control again by letting me check us in and then did as much at the hotel. I took care of the passports and made myself understood by the receptionist thanks to lots of nerve and a bit of my old Latin.

The room turned out to be smaller than we had anticipated, but it has got a dress circle view over the Grand Canal and a mini bar which would've been a small treasure only a few months ago before my GBM. The sunset was majestic and we enjoyed a good drink, -gin and tonic for

Grette, tonic and... tonic for me. Could be worse-. We sat on the mini balcony, loving the scene.

'Aren't we so lucky to be here in good health, comfortable and in love with each other?'.

I knew better than correcting any of her points so I kept the spell going. Half an hour later, we went down for dinner. I was glad that in Italy, as opposed to Spain, one can have a meal at any time. We were starving, and after a plateful of olives and a pack of grissini our meal arrived: lovely, fresh spaghetti alle vongole. I certainly didn't miss Denmark at that moment, which is odd because I'd been so apprehensive to go anywhere away from home this time. I love travelling but once abroad, I cannot wait to go home. Especially, since I've been getting old and the appeal of foreign places has diminished. How about that for a cliché?

This morning I got up at half past eight, having slept for nine hours without the help of any sleeping pills. A record since I was diagnosed. We breakfasted in our room, read the papers on the balcony and then went out for a stroll around town with no preplanned route. We hardly ever need one in Venice, because any corner is worth seeing. Besides, we had a clear idea of what we wanted to see.

Grette took more photos of me than usual, but I didn't say that she was trying to capture every second of these holidays only because she knows what is awaiting. Instead, I insisted she took at least two of each image so that we can have a choice and several spare ones to have them printed for the boys.

'I'll send most of them to their mobiles but we'll have some printed off for Clementina as well, what do you think?'

'Great idea'. Sadly, most of the buildings are practically impossible to photograph, unless you take it in fragments or focus on details, of course. I have taken thousands over the years of San Marco Square, what with the Palazzo, and the Tower and the imposing silhouette of Santa Maria della Salute on the other side of the Canal, but even the postcards and the guide books have difficulty in displaying the buildings in close up without pasting pieces, or concentrating either on the domes and spires or the lower half, one at a time. I would not go as far as to say that I am a frustrated architect, but I can get quite excited about buildings and the like in the same way I do about some paintings. My mother told me once that it didn´t surprise her that I liked it. She said that in her view, Architecture has to do with order, harmony, aesthetics and symmetry as much as Justice has. So here I am. Still sane, I hope, revelling in Venetian vibes. Great.

We walked for hours, visiting a few of the must-do places and then just trying to stay away from the shorted, flipflopped, baseball-capped tourists. We stopped for coffees and lunch and cold drinks at one or two cafes hidden away in narrow twisted alleys and somnolent squares. Wherever we find them, we make a point of patronizing these traditional little places run by their owners, often couples in their sixties and seventies, who have been together for longer than they can remember, and who spend their days bickering with each other in front of their customers as if their disagreements were part of the city's attractions.

It always amuses me to see how men do very little in Latin countries, compared with their wives. We would not get away with it in Denmark. Here, women take orders, prepare meals in the kitchen, serve them, clear the tables, do the washing up whereas the husbands just socialize with their patrons in their best entertaining manner. Every now and then, they shout back asking whether everything is all right in the kitchen, pretending to be the ones in charge and secretly hoping to find a fault over which to reprimand their wives. It's hilarious.

The couple running the little café-bistro, as it's pretentiously called, were no exception. The woman, -huge dark eyes, big bosom, hair in a bun, kept coming and going, wiping her hands on her apron every time she appeared, bringing and serving some dish and taking with her the used plates and glasses. Otherwise, she wasn't seen until the moment she heard a bill being asked for and realized that her husband was about to take the payment. She materialized in a flash and dealt with it herself, glaring menacingly at her husband as if to say, keep out of the till.

Later, when he offered to help because she was serving another table, she turned round and, loudly enough for all of us to hear, told him that he'd better not take cash out and go and drink himself stupid again with his friends. He mumbled something and the bickering started again. I loved it.

It was the other face of a once sophisticated city, where even the most fashion-conscious Milanesi, both men and women, swallow their local pride and come to have their suits made in Venetian textiles and spend the evening in the square, getting a darker impression of the place through their diamond incrusted sunglasses.

By five o'clock, we were back at the hotel for afternoon tea. It was a disappointment with most choices being bland, apart from two tiny pastries in the patisserie française style. Delicious, but almost invisible. Grette, forever watching her calories, only had a cup of decaffeinated coffee and then went up to have her hair tinted by the hotel's coiffeurs. I went to our room and slept like a log for a good couple of hours. I would've liked to go out alone for a while, but Grette was back when I woke up and she has been so close and warm that I considered it mean of me to leave her on her own. Instead, I pulled on a pair of shorts and a T-shirt and limped my way down to the swimming pool. I swam gently for a good quarter of an hour.

Very few things compare with being in the water, and although I prefer the cold stinging impact of the sea, I enjoyed myself swimming indoors on this occasion. It was the climax of the day. Grette watched from a deck chair, assuring me that she really didn't mind the effect of the steam on her hair. A different person from the one of my first days of post-surgery. Different from the one she had become in the last few years. She seemed relaxed and calm.

'That colour suits you beautifully' I said, and it was true. Her complexion is fair enough to take a strawberry blonde. 'It adds sparkle to your eyes'. She smiled and blew me a kiss.

Now it's ten to one in the night. Grette's asleep, next to me, like in pre-tumour days. We went for dinner at a very good, but all the same overpriced restaurant and then joined the locals and the tourists in their up and down tours in water buses along the Grand Canal. The noise was atrocious at some point, even for Grette, who has a healthy head, so it must've been very bad indeed. I put up with it for as long as I could because I love being out in this magical place in a warm summer evening, but by the time we got to Giglio, I had to give in to my malaise and suggested coming home.

Tomorrow we shall go to the Lido, have a healthy siesta on the beach and then take a good stroll along the coast, Grette said, although walking on sand might be a tad tough for me. The day after, we'll visit the Guggenheim and the one after that, we are going to collect the car she has booked and drive on to Verona and then the Lakes, having by then stocked up our boot with fancy, artificially dyed pasta dal Veneto as if we couldn't find the same varieties in Danish supermarkets. So much for EU trade. It has killed off the character of the places. Everywhere is the same. Same shops. Same restaurants. Same currency. (Good job we still keep our Krone). Traditions and local habits are gradually vanishing or merging into a characterless background in an incongruous mix where political correctness reigns supreme, annihilating identity, distinctiveness and democracy. *Vive l'Europe!*

Chapter 25

Father

All visits to buildings and exhibitions are tiring, notwithstanding the cool shelter from the baking sun that they provide. You shuffle up and down, or drag one of your legs along if your brain tumour has left you lame, looking at this arch, that buttress, this chapel and before you know it, you have spent hours on your feet, in slow motion, trying to capture and retain the whole lot in your mind's eye in order to create a rich memory of the place. Only when you come out and start walking steadily again do you realize how desperately worn out you really feel. How really pointless remembering names and dates and the rest is, but I couldn't help making a mental note of interesting pieces in every interior, though. A portrait of St Eugene next to the right-hand door of Santa Maria del Giglio, and the Via Crucis by Tiepolo hanging neatly and solemnly in the Chapel of San Polo. In Santa Maria dei Frari, I was fascinated by the wood-panelling of the choir as much as anyone else was taken by the Titian's Annunciation and the mausoleums of both Canova and Titian. Fancy having not one, but two such tombs in the same church, but what I found really touching was the portrait of St Aloysius Gonzaga in the church of Santo Stefano. Was it also by Tiepolo?

The endearing Gonzaga lad, all innocence and chastity, is portrayed with two other saints whose names I cannot remember, but I was glad to look for the first time into his face, as it were. Anna had her birthday on that saint's day. Being educated at a Catholic school, she used to say a prayer to him, every twenty-first of June. *St Aloysius Gonzaga, model of charity and purity, grant me the grace of imitating your virtues.* Something like that. She told me once that she had lain a rose on the saint's altar over his tomb at St Ignatius of Loyola's in Rome. I wonder whether she knew of this portrait here?

Grette preferred Santa Maria de Nazareth whereas I was almost scared by the overpowering mass of marble that closes in on you as you walk in, but I held Grette's hand very tightly like a frightened child, and got gradually used to its lack of light. Luckily, we were both decently dressed and therefore allowed to sit inside and look up at the frescoes on the ceiling, the blood spluttered Christ and the pair of massive twisted marble columns, while pretending to be praying, for it isn't open to the public other than as a temple of prayer. A priest, as scary looking as the gloom of the church, paced to and fro along the aisle, making sure no tourists in vests or shorts or flip flops ever entered. We lowered our heads and closed our eyes every time he went past. When Grette finally stood up, ready to leave, I felt relieved. It's got to be the most frighteningly sombre and most magnificently powerful church of all the ones we visited. A masterpiece of baroque venetianness, if such a word existed. They certainly don't build them like that anymore. Perhaps, it's for the best.

It must be the effect of so much focusing on details and recording information that I now feel beyond exhausted. We sit down on a bench. I close my eyes for a while and when I open them again, there he is.

My father looks up as I approach him, but does not recognize me. He's wearing a pair a corduroys despite the heat, and a tweed jacket, collar and tie, and apart from the fact that he does not smoke –at least not while we are looking- even the way in which he holds the newspaper is identical to Father's way of doing it. He resumes his reading, holding the newspaper now folded in half, lengthwise, with one hand -a wedding ring in his fourth finger-, an ice cream cone with the other one. I notice that he isn't wearing reading glasses any longer, which is odd. His eyes look livelier facing life as it is, without the aid of spectacles. Is he wearing contact lenses?

I go and sit next to him. It's irrational. Impossible. I check my thoughts again before uttering a word. It has to be Dad. Not even a twin brother could look so alike. I don't know what to say. A lump in my throat prevents me from uttering a single word. The palms of my hands get damper and damper and my knees shake. The man ignores me. Understandably, I suppose. If Dad wants to escape and hide away from us, he isn't going to acknowledge my presence or return my greetings easily, is he? I try speaking again, my heart throbbing, my head throbbing, pounding with the electricity of the moment. I tell him that I understand and at that, the man turns to me and looks straight into my eyes. He must be in his sixties and speaks English with a heavy accent I can barely understand. He is waiting for his friend; would I mind leaving him in peace? he says in a deep voice. Then he looks at me up and down, overwhelmed by disgust as if I were a leper or a reptile. 'You, bloody old butterfly', he mumbles.

I do not cry, as I find myself doing over anything at all nowadays, nor do I expect compassion, all I can feel is sheer embarrassment. Appalling, ghastly, new experience. New symptom. Perhaps Mr Henriksen knew this was coming and allowed me to come over before I lost lucidity. That is what I find touching and irritating at the same time: people's sympathy, people's words of compassion when in reality they don't understand about my condition any more than they do about my feelings, my anger, my happiness, my frustrations. We are individuals. We can pretend, we can attempt to share and align, tune up our thoughts, but it's hopeless. We're all alone.

Grette agrees with me, and slipping her arm through mine, we walk in silence all the way back to the room. She suggests waiting for a vaporetto. I refuse. I want to make sure I could stagger along and find the place if I happened to be on my own (Not sure now that I can).

We enter our room at twenty-six minutes past three and I head for the bathroom, amused by the realization that I've been called many things in my life, but never a butterfly. Monsieur Butterfly. Signor Butterfly. Charming.

I strip off and have a cold, invigorating shower, aided by Grette. Another humiliation. She always shrinks away from cold water and I tease her that she is not a genuine Dane. Actually, she dresses as much to go to bed in winter nights as she does to go out during the day: thick pyjamas, a vest underneath or a cardigan on top, and socks. She says there's nothing to laugh about and ridicules my observations explaining that the cardigan is made "only" of light cotton, as if such attire were the most normal thing to sleep in in centrally heated Copenhagen. It amuses me. Sometimes, I hand her her hat and gloves to wind her up and she dismisses them both pretending to be niggled by my teasing, but I am sure she would wear them gladly if I weren't around. It must be the everlasting effect of her childhood, standing in the snow, so desperately cold and starving...

When I finally collapse onto our bed, I find her lying down, a pillow beneath her legs, her eyes half closed, as tired as myself. It's not too unusual to see her like that, especially when being on holidays, as we always tend to walk for miles and miles and wear ourselves out. Yet I keep looking at her, wishing I could tell her how I feel, but fear that if I open my mouth a torrent of tears and sobbing would come out instead. I slide over the bed covers, next to her, and kiss her eyelids, her temples and the top of her nose, where she likes it, and she pulls me on top of her, gently, softly, like the first time we made love. It feels right. There's no intention of going any further. As if. Only tenderness.

All we need at this moment is to lie together, entwining our bodies tightly like we used to do until not long ago before the cancer struck. We remain like this for a long time, she embracing me, I cupping her head in my hands, gazing into her face, recording every angle, every pore, so that I can print them in my mind and take them with me in my last journey.

'You're the love of my life' she whispers. 'You're the only one who's treated me with respect and fairness... and you were so handsome!'

'Oh well, being fair is my job and handsome, my mission'

She giggles, the way she does when she is at ease with herself and the world. I tell her that she is my best love, hoping that she will stop to analyse the meaning of my words. Ulla was an overwhelming, pure love. My love for Anna proved to be powerless, however deep. Grette is the best kind of love, if not the greatest, but I don't say this out loud. What is the greatest love anyway? I heard my mother once say that one should never marry the love of one's life, because if the marriage falls apart, there is no spare, no perfect love left in our fantasies, in our speculation of what could've happened if we had married the one who we believed to be the love of our lives. One should keep that love in perfect state, in a corner of our hearts, she said, if only to go back to it in our dreams. It makes sense, I suppose. The perfect love, like the perfect place, can only retain perfection if left untouched. Trying to revisit them is an aberration, a violation of our own past and a degradation of our souls.

Chapter 26

Whatsapp

Hi, Anders. Sorry I didn't whatsapp you yesterday. I know you're at work so I'll just send you an audio message. Oh, Anders! Ole insisted on visiting churches instead of roasting by the Lido as we had planned. Fine and lively all morning, but suddenly, he announced that he was beyond exhausted (his words) even with the help of his now indispensable, much detested stick. From that moment, everything went pear shaped.

Ole spotted a man in the Campo de San Aponal and he said that he looked like his father. He couldn't take his eyes off him and the guy noticed. Luckily, he was young enough not to bother, but anyway… Imagine the man, hardly into his thirties, most probably waiting for someone, all dressed in impeccable white as if for tennis, being stared at by an old man (Ole seems to be ageing by the day).

I tried to distract him, but no chance. Couldn't suggest walking on because he said his legs had turned to jelly. His head was spinning. Kept asking what time it was, ALL THE TIME. Then, he asked me where I came from, what my rank was… When I said that he had asked me the same questions three or four times, he said he was just checking whether I gave him the same answer every time. A kind of two parallel delusions, if you ask me. Totally bizarre. He's coherent and clear in his confusion. He then said that he couldn't help feeling that either his father never died and was alive, sitting on a bench in a venetian square, or that that guy was a ghost. He himself had arranged the funeral, though… He got furious with himself for not making sense.

When the man got up and went to the ice creams stall, Ole said that his gait, the line of his shoulders, the particular way in which his knees bent… left him in no doubt. It was his father. TBH, he did resemble a young Magnus Mortensen, at least on the photos I've seen of him. He (the guy) bought himself a vanilla cone and walked back to his seat and before I could stop him, Ole stood up and went up to him. Held my breath, dreading what he would say or do next. You can imagine. I felt totally at a loss. Remained seated, watching, worrying that I would've to offer an apology to the guy. I pretended to be leafing through the guidebook, but was just keeping an eye on what Ole could be saying. Or doing.

It was all so shocking and so heartbreaking. Ole sat next to the man and I don't know what he told him but the man answered back, you can guess how. Poor Ole called me three times, shouting, although I was already running to rescue him. He threw his arms round my waist and hid his face against my stomach, like a child. At least, he didn't lost conscience of being with me, I thought. I tried to explain to the stranger that Ole has brain issues, but the guy stood up and almost ran away.

So, you see. Sorry to give you the whole scene in all its details but thought you ought to know... Will text or call you again tomorrow. Bye for now. X Grette.

Chapter 27

Water

The dream I had a few days ago about Anna finding a room for Torben in London has come true to a certain extent. He texted us yesterday to say that he has accepted a position at Brompton Hospital in London, just a few blocks from where we used to live. I guess my illness has triggered in him a determination to make better use of his profession and that the main reason why he accepted to move abroad is because it offers him the chance to be near our old home and revisit a time when he was happy and contained, as Anna would've put it. As long as some good comes out of this nightmare, I am happy for him.

I didn't phone him back to ask why or when or how he had applied for a place there, all I could do was rejoice and text back my congratulations, without showing too much enthusiasm in case he changes his mind again for the sake of being contrary. Sharp, brilliant, silly son. He could still react like a teenager towards me, I fear! And how about his partner? Will he be moving to London, too, I wonder? He never came to see me, that Samuel, and I have the feeling that their relationship is undergoing some testing times. This may be the main reason for Torben to leave Denmark, even when the other day he was going on about the beauty of a Danish dawn.

Still. He's having the same reaction, making the same decision I made when my heart was broken. I must admit I would rather he and his artist boyfriend sorted out whatever differences they may be having, but that's just my wish and it doesn't count.

With Anders about to be a father again and William brokering money far from home, news of Torben moving on for a better position comes as a joy as far as my children are concerned. Every now and then, life kisses us full in our lips. So, with that weight lifted off my shoulders, ("the monkey" off my shoulders, Kar would say) we set off to Verona, where neither of us has ever been before. We're still tired after a late night sitting in San Marco, watching the world go by and listening to the orchestras, but Grette easily finds the way out of town and drives smoothly onto the Autostrada and on to Romeo and Juliet's city.

Sitting in the car, next to her, I would like to ask Grette whether she has considered her future, but the moment might be inappropriate. I'd love to organize everything for her, introduce her to new people, other men, move house perhaps, but she won't let me. She thinks I am being defeatist whereas my intention is only to help her sort out the next chapter of her life, when I won't be around. There are times when the more you do for others the less noble, the more selfish it seems. Kar told me once that in Politics, if you go too far right you end up left, and vice versa. I see now how the same principle applies to various circumstances.

If I insist on helping Grette, she will call me a control freak, just as William says I am, so I shall have to let her live her life the way she wishes.

There was a time when life revolved around sunny days, strolls along the beach enjoying the feel of a pullover after a cold swim, mid-morning coffees with a good book, and dinners with friends. We went through life as if we were immortal, which should be the only sensible way to go about it, I'm convinced. When Ulla died, I was beside myself with grief and felt taken over by a sense of unreality.

Her death was a fluke, an unimaginable, anachronistic, heartbreaking fact, but I was still young and it didn't test my concept of eternity. It muddled up my emotions, changed my life, but I still kept going, looking to the future in between rewarding cases and well covered stupor.

Perhaps, I simply forced myself not to see that everything is so brutally fragile and ephemeral, I don't know, but what really taught me about lightness, brevity and failure was my separation from Anna a few years later. That, to me, was almost insurmountable. Being thrown out of our home and left to roam the streets of London alone, struggling to collect my thoughts, turned mortality into a possibility. All of a sudden, death became tempting. Possible. Tangible. It was at hand. It was appealing. Seductive. I revise in my mind the separations I have experienced in my life, either by death, abandonment or divorce and wonder whether Grette, driving so efficiently beside me, has also asked herself whether my departure will feel as awkward and complex as her previous divorce. I want to tell her that it needn't be so hard because she's doing everything she is capable of in order to save me the pain, the doom, the loneliness of my last days on Earth. She will have reasons to keep a clear conscience and happy memories of our life together, but she looks so cool and relaxed that I desist to raise the subject.

She looks desirable. The Venetian sun has lifted up her spirits, smoothed her forehead, bleached her hair and even brought up a few freckles on her nose. Onwards we go.

Grette wakes me up when she finally finds a place selling water. She's glad I was asleep for a while and is relieved to find that despite the dehydration, I still know who she is, what we are doing and where we are heading for. She pulls up and gets off to buy a couple of bottles from a small groceries shop.

I have such trouble swallowing my tablets that I have already finished the fizzy drink we had. Running out of water or any drink even for just a few minutes can now turn into a major inconvenience. It's humiliating. It makes me think of William telling Anders off for wasting water when people in Africa dry up along with the landscape, desperately hungry and forever thirsty. Ha. I remember their conversation now. Torben joined in, adding that we should all be ashamed, and Anders replied that he was being as patronizing as ever, despite years of practising social equality in Christiania. As far as he was concerned, Anders could not see how he was stealing water from Africa every time he had a wash or started the dishwasher.

It was a trivial disagreement, although the issue is

more than a serious one, but the reason why it stuck in my mind was only because it gave me some pleasure to see them get passionate, each of them defending his point of view like when they were young. At the back of their minds lies the certainty that they can afford to disagree without hurting or getting hurt. There is a deep, brotherly love underneath the words and the arguments, which links them and holds them together regardless of the miles between them. That, plus the fact that they still believe that they can change and save the world was the joy of witnessing their exchange.

Oh, well, I feel drained. Not unwell, just very tired of roaming, exploring, visiting, travelling. I feel as if we're living inside a travel guide book, seeing without engaging; looking without imbibing the ambiance of the places. My brain has stopped thinking of anything of interest. Instead of opening my mind to new information and to these pieces of History perpetuated in marble and stone and statues and palaces all around us, I just want to close my eyes and forget all about it. I feel overwhelmed by fatigue and indifference.

When my sons were young, we used to play quizzing one another on general knowledge: what was such country's capital, where Timbouktu actually was, who was shot on the twenty second of November of nineteen sixty-three, who was Christian IV, who discovered penicillin... now I cannot be bothered to apprehend, let alone digest or analyse the minimum dose of information.

This morning I was eager to be alive, full of dynamism and clear minded, now I yearn to go home, instead of having to dress for dinner, sitting amidst the crowds, the noise and the heat. It might not be too surprising anyhow. However trying for me or unsettling for Grette and my sons all this is, it is not yet a month since Mr Henriksen removed the GBM from my brain.

If I consider everything that has taken place since, it is enough to fill a few months in any other normal circumstance. There are phases in life when nothing seems to happen. We can feel as if time were suspended for a long time and then, all of a sudden, everything happens at once and wooosh, time disappears. Kar's funeral. Elba's visit. Torben's return. Willo's visit. Anna's death. Ralph's visit. Torben's departure... all this in twenty-six days. And the Bossens, who came that day and keep phoning to chat and check that everything is fine, by everything meaning me, my brain and my cancer. Two big losses, five significant visits. A bit of a high percentage on the doom side, but there we are. Would I turn the clock back? Of course, I would, but so many things would have to be different that it gets confusing, almost impossible to imagine what would be the entire result of, say, not having any more children with Ulla so that she does not die. How can one do that? And if that were a conceivable fantasy, - I prefer to call it a fantasy, not a notion-, would I go further back to my days of singledom, to university days? Would I study Law again? Probably. I have been good at my job, I know that. I know it as well as I know that I am not a good artist, or a good diver, or a good skier.

Grette comes out of the bathroom smelling beautifully of the bamboo and white tea bath salts and body lotion she bought in a pharmacy whose owner had the good sense of keeping its original features. A mix of Italian affluence and Orient Express styles: polished mahogany, crystal chandeliers, frescoes on the wall. A real gem.

'Are you ready? This tie looks a bit dull with this shirt, don't you think? Put on the gold one with the tiny blue squiggles. There. Much better. The contrast brings out the blue in your eyes, see?'

I'd rather lie down than bother about my appearance, but Grette is so convinced I'm looking well that I don't have the heart to disappoint her, so I lean on her arm and limp down and out to the restaurant where I try a sip of wine and then a sip of some liqueur Grette orders after dinner.

The alcohol goes straight to my head, hot and powerful. My legs feel liquid and my shoulders so heavy I can hardly move them. The headache never leaves me, no matter that Henriksen says I shouldn't have any pain. By now, I'm almost used to headaches, but soon after half past eight I ask Grette to take me home. Luckily, I succeed in getting up and out of the place without drawing attention. Hand in hand, we make our way back to our room, where fully dressed, I let myself fall onto the bed.

Chapter 28

"Carabinieri find old Viking alive and well"

I do not recall being undressed or tucked comfortably into bed. We both woke up late into the morning. I felt fresh and lucid, so I went downstairs before Grette, determined to head for the corner café where she was going to join me a few minutes later for coffee and brioches, since we hadn't made it in time for breakfast at the hotel. I felt slightly claustrophobic down the narrow stairs but told myself to think of the beautiful sky I had just seen floating above us from our bedroom window and of how we were going to spend the day ahead.

When I walked past the receptionist, I knew I was going to Gino's. We spotted the place last night on our way back.

It all sounds like sheer madness now and I find it difficult to explain to myself how can I get so bloody confused. I knew where I was. I knew what I was doing. Yet the rest of my adventure escapes me and to this moment, I cannot put a finger on to when exactly, or how the hell it happened. Is morphine to blame? Grette's face brightened on seeing me safe and sound, entering the hotel with not one care in the world apart from being slightly short of breath. It was when she ran up to me and tearfully asked where I'd been that it came back to my mind what I had completely forgotten until then.

It must have happened in a split second, because I can recall that by the time I stepped over the threshold, out of the hotel, I decided to go and visit the Arena, which emerged defiantly at the end of the street, dominating the city. I forgot about Grette. I didn't think of myself as being ill or alone. There was nothing odd about my going out on my own. I was never aware of the situation. Off I went, paid for the entrance fee, climbed up on all fours to the top step and sat there for a while, feeling the sun on my shoulders, marvelling at the way the Romans had the acoustics sorted out. Perhaps our cutting-edge designers were Roman in a previous life, now that it's fashionable and inspired to talk about past lives. I have enough with just this one, tak!

Darling Grette says she worried sick when she went out looking for me and could not find me anywhere. Luckily, her common sense told her to come back and wait in here. Otherwise, we would've missed each other for longer, perhaps for the whole day. For the night? She could've passed out with panic or worse, so she called the police. Imagine: "Wife's joy as Veronese carabinieri find mad old Viking husband alive and well". I would've sent the cutting to my ex-colleagues, or to Clementina, so that she could have a story about her crazy farfar to tell her friends.

Volete qualcosa da bere? The receptionist asks, evidently aware of my distressing disappearance. Grette, in her word-perfect Italian, asks for *un bicchiere d'acqua*. The girl rushes off and comes back in no time with two glasses of sparkling water with ice cubes and lemon slices on a gilded baroque tray. She seems happy to help us regain normality even though she does not know what normality means to us or what has altered it. I read her name on the tag fastened to her lapel. Benedetta. She could be considered beautiful, I guess, in a very Italian sort of way: ink-black hair, long prominent nose, olive skin and dancing eyes. She keeps saying *prego, prego,* which translates into Don't mention it, Here you are, or Yes, certainly, according to the context. I'm not sure I like that flimsiness in a language.

As a barrister, the last thing you want is a lack of precision and accuracy. No room for ambiguity if you are sentencing someone or defending a case, so every word is carefully chosen, its meaning considered, its implication meticulously weighed up before being uttered. I picture a defendant being read his sentence and then taken out of the Court room, as the Judge finishes the session by telling him prego, prego. It would not do.

Slightly recovered, Grette from her anxiety and myself from the agitation, we finally walk out to the café. Some Italians are already having lunch by now, but we manage to persuade the waiters to bring us a good pot of coffee and croissants, and plenty of jam. I am indulging greatly in my comfort food.

'Watch your sugar levels' Grette says.

'Lest I become diabetic? I'm afraid there won't be time for that'. She can get on my nerves sometimes.

Now, the man from the next table smiles at me, but I ignore him, still slightly clear-minded before another dizzy spell starts. After Grette told me what happened to me in Venice with my imaginary father and all that crap going on in my head, I look away when the chap smiles a second time. Then he waves. I think I blush out of embarrassment for going so definitely mad and ignore him again. Come to think of it, it is amazing how one can fold your mind in two as it were, and be aware of going mad. It is a thoroughly researched, recorded and known fact, but still baffling. It almost compares with the feeling I get when I stop to consider the feasibility of flying all over the world in a matter of hours. Even in the twenty-first century when people are already thinking of space travelling, I can't help being amazed to be able to breakfast in Rio de Janeiro and dine later in Paris on the same day, give or take two or three hours of decalage.

The stranger calls my name and as Grette turns to check which of my acquaintances might be sitting behind us in the shade of a Veronese pavement, I realize that it's happening for real. It is Lars of all people! I joke about him being our spy, or what else is he doing in Verona at the same time as us? Venice, Rome, Florence, Paris... they sound more likely places to bump into acquaintances in amongst the hordes of tourists treading along the year round, but Verona!

'Hey, great to see you! When did you arrive? I haven't seen you buying the newspaper for a while, or on the golf course, I now realize. How are you?' Lars says, and then politely shakes hands with Grette, who is somewhat taken aback by our neighbour's familiarity, because usually, it's I who chats to the people next door or round the corner. Being at work most of the time, she hardly ever sees them.

I invite Lars to join us for a coffee. He says he is with someone. I insist, assuming that someone must be his wife, but Grette kicks me under the table, so I drop it and wish him a pleasant stay in Juliet's city. 'And Romeo's', he says, now smiling at the Italian young man, whom he has evidently met and fallen for behind his wife's back. As he walks off, I jump up, catch up with him and ask him whether he has seen Cecille lately. He gives me a blank look. I apologize and hold on to a chair because the world is spinning too fast around me and then, slowly, I turn back to our table. Grette is already standing by her chair, her right hand sheltering her eyes from the midday sun, looking anxious about my condition.

We laugh about Lars's bad luck at meeting us in what he must've considered a safe town to escape to for a few days. Grette says that if she were Ole's wife and found out he was betraying her with such a handsome Italian, she would probably ask him to bring his lover home. I frown deliberately, feigning indignation.

'Perhaps, Lars's wife already knows', I suggest. 'Perhaps, they're in bed by now, the three of them, making the most of the Italian siesta and laughing at our badly disguised embarrassment. That would be enjoying life to the limit. Who knows what goes on behind closed doors? Who knows what the people behind those doors actually feel when they do whatever it is that they do in there?'

'You know what, Ole Morgensen? If you hadn't had surgery, I would say that you're pretending to be ill. How can you THINK so clearly, sometimes?'

'Only sometimes?'

'See?', she replies, laughing, and then turns round to look at one passer-by's shoes, at another one's hair the colour of cherries. People watching. In a piazza. All shapes, sizes and heights. Who are these people? What do they do for a living? Who are they married to? What kind of childhood did they have? Fascinating.

'Have you ever considered the possibility of taking two men to bed?'

She spills her coffee in astonishment and laughs dismissively at my question. 'Could hardly take one, darling!' she jokes.

'And how about living abroad once I'm gone?' I continue. 'Being nearer your daughter, perhaps?

No, she hasn't' considered that either. There are tears swelling up in her eyes. I look away.

She tells me that she has enrolled on a cookery lesson which will take place at the hotel, tomorrow morning, if I don't mind. I say I look forward to trying the dishes she'll learn to concoct and so we close the deal, tacitly, of never again mentioning her future without me, for as long as I live. For as long as I live. It will not be difficult to keep such a promise, I tell myself, while she embarks on descriptions of every Italian dish she has tried during her visits and which she intends to keep cooking until reaching perfection. Her determination is not surprising, and it's poignant to see her avoid the important issues.

I make all the appropriate noises as she continues explaining to me how much subtler and finer Italian gastronomy is compared with the Spanish or the Greek ones, and how olive oil is only good for you when raw, because once cooked, it releases all its nasty fats.

Her enthusiasm is infectious and I tease her about it, saying that after so rich an introduction to theoretical cuisine, I cannot wait to try some tangible, palatable one. Talking about food makes us both hungry, so after the coffee and the croissants we've just had for our absurdly late breakfast, we order some toasted piadini with tuna, fresh tomatoes, capers and olives seasoned with olive oil, sea salt and pepper. Heavenly.

We eat in silence because we are too busy enjoying our early lunch until a fluffy ginger cat materializes from somewhere and sticks his front paws on our table, sniffing around and trying, half coyly, half daringly, to grab our piadini. We look at it, then at each other and start laughing. The cat's appearance works some magic. Its timing is therapeutic nonsense and we laugh. We laugh for no particular reason, or because we are happy, because we have each other and are alive. Or because we are scared of turning the corner.

Whatsapp 2

Hi, Anders, Torben and William

Delighted to hear about your new position, Torben! Bravo! Here all is not well.

Your father's mind keeps wandering. One minute he's incredibly lucid, precise as ever, debating issues to exhaustion, as he's always done and the next, he's totally deluded. One minute, he evokes some distant event in meticulous detail and the next, he doesn't know who I am or where he is.

A few minutes ago, he went out on his own while I was in the shower. He got lost although not far from the hotel, thank G-d. A carabinieri brought him back because as luck would've it, another guest had seen us here before and happened to be passing by when the carabinieri was trying to speak English to Ole. I'll spare you the details.

Yesterday, after the most coherent self-analysis (he's always doing that nowadays), he went on to believe that we were driving to Verona. We had talked of going there before we came (silly of us both!) but I did not mention it again and yet…

He spent a good couple of hours sitting by the window of our room and all the time, he thought we were in a car. Eventually, he dosed off and only woke up when he felt very thirsty. This morning, he was again convinced that he had even paid the entrance fee to visit the Arena. As soon as he fell asleep, I phoned Mr Henriksen. I'm desperate to get back home, but he said to avoid flying for a few more days. Being in unusual places after weeks in hospital and on medication, these hallucinations are not totally unheard of. Don't know if I should believe him. What do you think?

I feel riddled with guilt for bringing Ole here, but he was so happy!

Please tell me what I should do. I'm honestly at a loss and don't know what to do. I'm so sorry.

Chapter 29

Paris to Copenhagen

'Tell her I'm not here'

Veniamin replies waving a finger from side to side meaning he won't lie. He has already told Erika to wait while Cecille comes downstairs, and Cecille takes her time. Perhaps if she keeps her mother waiting on the line long enough, she might give up and get lost, but Veniamin gives her a reprimanding look and Cecille gives in. This isn't the way she likes to start her day.

'She's getting on, is this the kind of memory you want to keep of her last years amongst us?' Veniamin told her the other day. She didn't reply then and even now she is not sure of the kind of memory she really wants to keep of her mother. She can't pretend her parents made her happy, or worse still, she can't pretend they ever loved her that much, can she? There is no point in rewriting history, why can't Veniamin see that?

'Hej, Mor'

'Hi, darling. How are you?'

She is alright, and how are they, mother and father? She hardly listens to the answer. Whatever her mother says, it will irritate her, so she holds the receiver far from her ear while she unwraps the towel off her head and lets Erika chatter away, asking questions Cecille doesn't want to answer simply because it's a long time since she stopped having anything to say to her mother. Then, without knowing how or why, she asks about Ole.

'Ole? What do you mean? What do you know about him?'

'How is he?' Cecille repeats, but doesn't say that she woke up early to Elba's phone call. Nor does she comment on her mother's irked, irritated tone.

'Not very well, I'm afraid'

'I'm coming over'

'Whatever for? Ole will be all right, poppet, it was just a bit of a fright, nothing else'

Cecille punches the wall in front of her. 'Stop calling me poppet, Mor, please. I'm forty-five. Stop patronizing me'

Veniamin shakes his head as he puts on his jacket, ready to go out. Cecille blows him a kiss; he smiles back and walks out.

'I'm surprised you didn't mention it before. You know I'd like to see him if... Never mind. I'll be there soon'.

Cecille has already thrown a few clothes into a bag, got the ticket, jumped onto the airplane, arrived at Ole's house... She's knocking on his door, running up to his bedroom where he doesn't recognize her, doesn't know who she is because he's too ill, hardly breathing... he is dead...

'We saw him the other day. He said you had lunch with him when you were here last month' her mother tells her before Cecille hangs up and realizes that she's still in

Paris, in her kitchen, naked, fluffing up her hair to help it dry quickly. She has to go.

The letters. The bloody letters. The bloody fucking letters. Why on earth did she give in when Ole insisted in keeping them, assuring her that they were safe with him? Even in top health as he seemed to be when he saw him, how long did she think he was going to live? Idiote, Cecille Bossen, tu es idiote'. She trips over the last step and limps along the corridor, her mind in Denmark, nineteen eighty-four.

Her mobile rings again, but she cuts off the call without a word. She rings and tells Monique to book her two tickets to Copenhagen, because she feels Veniamin's company to support and keep her calm.

Monique and Jean-Yves will manage. And Sonia. It won't be the first time they are left on their own… Besides, the current exhibition is already on, there isn't much to do for a few days. Rubbish. There is always much to do. Never mind. She needs to see Ole and gets her papers back. If someone else finds out, Veniamin will end up knowing about the whole story and ridiculous as it might be, it is her story. Only she can live with it. No one else.

If Veniamin finds out he will be annoyed and their marriage will appear to be based on her dishonesty. She should've told him, like she did Torben on the train all those years ago. Well, no, she didn't tell Torben the whole story. This is the twenty first century, for Goodness' sake! Veniamin wouldn't bat an eyelid. Or would he?

She knows it's not the fear of his reaction what kept her quiet about the subject all these years, but her determination to forget about the reason why she's always wanted to keep it a secret. Ole. Erika. Jensen. Forget the three of them. If only she could. Forget what Erika did to her and protect her from further grievance. Forget that she once loved Ole and protect him from accusations. Forget about Jensen's indifference and protect him from more hurt. Protect Veniamin from disappointment. Protect everyone to protect herself.

It's only when she walks past the mirror and catches a glimpse of herself that her mind stops racing. This is Paris. Paris, eons have gone by since those days. Relax, Cecille, relax. She has been telling herself to relax for the last twenty odd years without much success, but she perseveres until she gets hold of her present again and chooses what to wear, what to take with her and how and what to tell Veniamin. Deep breath in, long breath out. Inhale, exhale.

Perhaps she should fly by herself after all. How and what is she going to tell him to justify such sudden decision? She hates deceiving him. Would there be any interesting opening she could use as a reason for going? Any unmissable vernissage?

She'll need the suede jacket Veniamin gave her at Christmas. It's always cooler in Copenhagen despite the recent heat wave. Better play safe. Her mobile rings and it's Veniamin. She tells him about the flight... they could drive through the Danish countryside as they've been saying so many times and never got round to, they could... Is he coming?

He does not point out that she has been to Copenhagen only a month ago. Instead, he agrees to join her and Cecille knows he is doing so because he loves her. Besides, he is always telling her how good she is at PR and that wherever they go she attracts some business, and for this reason too, he follows her around, happy to be away from Paris and routine work.

Tomorrow morning, they will wake up in Copenhagen. Once there, she will face up to her past, make a mental bundle of it and throw it away. For good. Forever. Without improvement. Without mercy.

Chapter 30

Flaubert and Alighieri

I have decided I will join a bunch of Francophiles who meet once a week and put the world to rights, discuss books, films and digestive problems in Napoleon's language. Non. That would certainly put me off. In Flaubert's language. That's it. Flaubert's language. I have always liked the French language, but haven't spoken it fluently for years. Ulla and I used to communicate in broken French whenever we wanted to hide something from Anders. It must be the reason why he now cannot stand the sound of it.

I am also going to learn Italian. I have just spoken to a Signor Ragone, who runs a beginners' course twice a week and is said to be a very good teacher, according to the librarian. He asked me lots of questions, this Signor Ragone. Presumably, he wanted to know what kind of halfwit will he be lumbered with this term, but seemed to relax when I mentioned that I was a barrister. Retired, but a barrister, or the other way round, if he preferred. I could tell he was smiling at that. Was I about to move to Italy? I was not. Then, overlooking his eagerness to find out more about his future pupil, I volunteered that my fluent-in-Italian wife and I had just come back from Venice, Verona and Lake Garda (Grette keeps telling me that we didn't go that far, but of course we have. Can't see why she denies it). I have always liked the musicality of the language, I added. Besides, I need to do something to keep my brain in gear (My brain in gear! Ha!). I didn't explain further, nor did I say that I did not like the lake, its foggy dawn, its oily stillness... Its water shimmering in the sun was too glaring for me. I appreciated its beauty, the character of the walled towns around it, its silhouette drawn out by the street lights at night depicting a horizon one could actually reach by getting to the other side of the lake, but I felt too restless to enjoy it. I wish I had. I may have liked it in normal circumstances, but it didn't work.

Next time I will, Grette told me, after she brought forward the return dates. We arrived home yesterday evening and I went straight to bed. Slept for fourteen hours in one go. This morning, peace, freshness and sharpness returned.

'I wish I'd gone back and bought you the cashmere jumper we saw near San Marco when the shop was already closed for the evening, remember? It would've come in useful now the weather's changing', Grette said while we breakfasted.

'Don't worry, you can get it next time'. We smiled at each other without further comment.

At lunchtime, Anders calls for a few minutes. He has the afternoon off because he is going to take Nja to hospital where she will have a scan and they will see whether the foetus is complete, as he puts it, and find out its gender. Of course, the foetus is complete. Has to be. It is part of the symmetry of life. His farfar will go with a chunk of his brain missing before the baby is born, but he will come into the world in all his tiny, complete perfection. I try to encourage Anders, who is obviously feeling anxious, and Grette shows him a few photos offering him some distraction. After the third or fourth Venetian scene, he gets interested and says Nja and he ought to have done Venice before pregnancy. Never mind.

'You've put on weight, Dad. Tanned and mobile, looking really well. Don't you believe me? Don't you feel good, tanned and mobile?

'Extremely'.

'And you, Grette. You look relaxed and fit'.

It pleases her no end, I can tell, and I feel grateful to Anders for trying his charm on her. As long as Grette does not feel cut out of my family, as she told me a few days ago in such torrent of tears, I can go in peace.

On reflection, I can indeed see that if our Italian escapade has benefited us in anything, it has been the closeness we have rediscovered inside ourselves towards each other. I'm glad that we owe it to the holidays and not to my tumour. I can be forgiven for dismissing, for once, the beauty of the landscape or the magnificence of the architecture for the sake of recreating our story, made of fragile bits assembled and pasted onto a basis of faith, patience and optimism as carefully as we would pick up the pieces of an expensive vase and paste them together in the hope, vain or real, of restoring it to its proper shape and glory.

I had not expected to recapture the spark of our old relationship because I wasn't fully aware of it having lost its shine along the years. Neither was Grette, I think, but at some point, during those Italian evenings, we must have recognized the old feeling emerging between us and we clung to it with a new strength that makes us come up on the other side, brighter, closer, fuller. It might even be the reason why I have decided to learn Italian, or what I can of it. That way, I can revisit our holidays by means of the language.

'We'd love to come on Saturday, if that's ok? Is there something we could do? Something we can bring?'

Grette and I reply in unison. I ask Anders to bring Clementina as well and before he leaves, he tells me that Torben would like to come with Samuel, before they go to London. 'I think that Torben has already texted Grette about it, but what d'you think?'

I burst out laughing, for a moment looking at my life as if on a film in which the character goes on holidays, finds some tranquillity and as soon as he gets back home, new problems arise, doubts surface, questions emerge and his children drive him up the walls. Anders looks baffled until I explain.

'Oh, I know the feeling' he says.

'Goodness, Anders! Since when have I stopped any of you from bringing your friends home? I'll be delighted to meet the chap. Absolutely delighted. I mean it'.

Anders pats my shoulder in approval, and leaves.

Chapter 31

Confession

A beautiful August afternoon in Århus

Darling Ole

Hope you are feeling well and invigorated after your Italian holidays. Jensen and I are staying at Margrethe's here in Århus. It was her eightieth birthday last Sunday. She didn't know we were all coming to see her so it was a great surprise and we all had a good time. We ate like pigs and drank as much. Her seven grand-children were here and her first great- grandchild, a chubby baby girl, called Ava.

As you can imagine, Margrethe asked about you and family and sends her best. Yesterday, she and I sorted out some junk and papers in boxes and drawers and found old photos and souvenirs that would make you smile. There is a particular charming snapshot of you, Ernst and Elba as children. II am taking it back with me so you can see it. There is also one of your parents and our mother on Midsummer's Day, which my nephew is scanning and printing copies for each of us. You and Elba will love it!

But the reason I decided to write now is to tell you something you should know. I feel so awkward! I am a shy person, as you know, and I could not tell you all this face to face after all these years, not even at the time when ... you know what.

That's why I'm writing instead of speaking. My style is rather poor, surely, but... this is not about my grammar.

The truth is that I have always loved you. There. You know I am fond of you. I know that you feel I consider you more than a friend, a brother...but it's not so. I've always been in love with you and would've done anything to stay close, since we couldn't be together. When you had that fling with my daughter, it felt as if someone had stabbed me right in the heart. Like pouring vinegar over a wound. The night I found out she had gone to London with you instead of with that boy, Patrick, I went mad. Every time she went out, defiantly happy, I felt physically sick knowing she was going to meet you. My heart ached with jealousy as I imagined your hands over her young body, your kisses on her skin...I felt old and disposable.

I so regret not telling you about my undying love for you all those years ago, before I had Cecille, when we were sleeping together, but I didn't have the courage then. You had just married Ulla and I was married to Jensen; it would've caused a lot of harm to many people. Yet a few years later, one week before you got married to Anna, I phoned you again and again. I was ready to leave Jensen if you were ready to call off the wedding, but you never answered the telephone. I called you all day long, every day for a week, but you were not there and when you finally answered, an hour before your wedding, I lost the nerve to go ahead. It was too late. I congratulated you, holding back my tears until we hung up.

It doesn't matter now, but felt the urge to tell you. Having kept quiet for all these years was the biggest mistake I have ever made in my whole life. Now we are both old, bored, sad and bitter. (Well, I am, anyway, and these are probably the words of someone going gaga)

Tell me: Did Cecille ever remind you of me? I know she doesn't resemble me in the least, but your liaison felt so perverse. It felt incestuous and I felt so jealous. She never knew that I knew about you both until that night when she decided to tell me.

It was fate, I suppose. My shyness and my cowardice had no limits, as you can see. I have so many regrets, Ole. Worse than regrets, I'm riddled with guilt for so many things. Now my confession is useless, it goes without saying, but I hope you will understand that I simply need you to know why and how I have stayed around all these years. For all it's worth, you might think, it has indeed been Love with a capital letter all along and I would've done anything for you had you ever shown that you felt the same... We had sex a few times, yes, but I knew that you felt ill at ease with the situation.

So, my darling Ole, there you are. I'd better not elaborate any longer. I might end up tearing and binning this letter like I've done so many times over the years. I'd better seal it up in an envelope and post it without reading it again.

With all my LOVE.

Erika

PS: Jensen and I will go and see you as soon as we're back. Take enormous care of yourself.

For Fuck's sake! Where does all this nonsense come from? Why now, so completely out of the blue and pointless? Why? Why? Fuck! Why didn't she tell me all these years ago? She could've avoided so much damage! For God's sake! So much harm could've been prevented! And now... is she determined to make me lose the little bit of sanity I still enjoy? I mean, God, I despair of these people!

Why can't we have some dignity and leave things as they are? Going gaga, she says she is. Bullshit. It is just bloody tasteless crap! Oh, the meanness of the cowards! Kar had warned me about Erika's feelings, but I refused to believe it. She was just shy and gentle mannered. Not assertive enough for this world, I thought. Silly, silly, silly woman.

I don't want to think about it, but I've been unable to do anything else since I read the letter this morning. I can't be bothered to revisit all the twists and perversions of our relationship, precisely because in spite of all this, it has always been so solid, so loyal (or has it?).

Now I can't help wondering how am I going to manage the situation next time she comes round to see me. This certainly is the last thing I needed. How could I react without hurting her vanity? In fact, I do have a certain desire to hurt her. I wouldn't have got involved with her daughter if... I feel like telling her where to go and never come back. She has caused so much damage with her cowardice, her constant hiding in between the lines, but cannot fathom why the fuck she's done it.

I've always loved her in the way one cares for an unconditional friend. There was never a need to work at this friendship. We've always been together, like siblings, somehow. I am totally at a loss now.

On the other hand, and given that she is aware of the present and is not expecting to change the course of our history, I feel sorry for her. I don't want to make her feel inadequate. I don't want her to find out that her love for me was –as well as cursed- an utter waste of time. It isn't out of vanity that I want to preserve her illusion or because I feel I deserve such love. It's just that destroying the dream in which she has sought shelter from her own unhappy marriage throughout years and years would mean wiping out something good in her life forever.

She says she regrets not telling me before, but if she had really been in love with me, I would've known. She has only been in love with the idea of leading a different life. The southern belle syndrome all over again. In love with the impossible, with the unattainable. In love with love, like a teenager. Our friendship gave her dream a sense, an alibi and that is all there is to it. She kept the dream alive and ended up believing it. My mother's words come to mind. One shouldn't marry the love of our life. Wise mother.

And yet, and yet... Anna used to say that Erika could be manipulative and selfish at times, but I always took that as mere female jealousy.

Oh, for Heavens above! Life. Dreams. Love. It should be easier... but it would be a bloody bore.

Chapter 32

Serenade

The headaches have disappeared, I haven't lost my speech or vocabulary and seem to remain fairly lucid, bar the hallucinations Grette describes for me when I come to, but my physical deterioration is now remarkable. Signore Ragone had to phone Grette and ask her to pick me up, to my sheer frustration. Until now, Mr Ragone had been most impressed by my quick grasp of his language during our first lesson and when I explained that I had done Latin at school, he got excited and started to recite some Virgil by heart to the bewilderment of the other students, who have never read Latin, let alone heard of Virgil. They must've hated me.

When I related this to Grette, she said that there was no reason why these people ought to have known Latin or Virgil. I let it drop, like so many other comments I make and which fall flat on the ground because she switches on to her socialist mode. Needless to say, there won't be any more lessons.

I must accept my sentence. The road will not wind round shimmering lakes of hope and projects, through sunny glades of joy and dappled lanes of bittersweet encounters or smooth beaches of loving phases any longer. Now it is a straight, bumpy road down the steep slope of the hill. Mr Henriksen still hopes for a gentle descent. Grette hopes that I may glide down smoothly and slowly enough to be around for Christmas, and for the New Year, and for next Spring and thus ad infinitum. I just hope for the softest and swiftest option, but beggars can't be choosers.

Elba and Harald came to pick me up last Monday but they must've seen me at my worst because when I said I might delay my visit after all, they didn't disagree and after they left, instead of taking the fresh air in their farm, I asked Grette to accompany me to church, curious to find out whether I would still experience that feeling of comfort and fear and protection I used to feel in my childhood when my parents took us there every Sunday.

Erika's letter has kept me on edge because I guess there is something unsaid which goes beyond her foolishness, which may have interfered with... I don't know. Women would call this feeling intuition, I would think it's just the old barrister in me, but it might just be paranoia.

I sat on a pew for a whole service and joined the other attendants in their prayers. When they started to leave their seats and treacle down the aisle, one by one at first, then in pairs, then in groups, like summer raindrops on the garden, I feel dumbfounded by how quickly the time had gone, I stayed there a while longer.

While Grette was shopping, undoubtedly thinking of my departure and of her approaching loneliness, I rested my elbows on my knees, held my head into my hands, beneath an Annunciation, and reflected. The cancer of my brain has taught me more about my own complexities and obscurities than the best psychoanalyst could've ever helped me to unravel. As for the others... well, I have learnt more about human nature than I could've believed possible to learn. Things that were important have become negligible and those which seemed too trivial are now essential and non-negotiable.

There have been some painful findings to digest amongst the beautiful ones, such as one or two people whom I could've trusted with my life and have now failed me. Grossly. And there were a few misunderstandings which have been clarified and unsuspected revelations and confessions have come and gone and come again. And Erika's letter, of course, which keeps me awake at night not because it is absurd and untimely, but because there is something between the lines I cannot yet decipher. I know her words are only a veil drawn over some inconvenient piece of truth, but I cannot reach it and the veil remains taut and stiff over the secret. I am obsessed about it.

On the positive side, the best surprise has been my children's response to my calling. Torben's return to the family, the pipe of peace he smoked with me while he spoke and I listened; while he accused me of letting him down and I acknowledged my shortcomings. I wish it had happened earlier, though. We could've shared more, learnt more of each other, but it has been an enriching experience, all the same.

Then, there was the imminent birth of my second grandchild to celebrate. The previous Saturday, when we were sitting in the living-room after dinner, Nja let me put my hand over her belly and I could feel its restlessness inside. It immediately took me back to those days when Ulla first, and Anna later, were expecting my children. I had forgotten how violently these unknown, little people can kick inside the womb. It was an overwhelming emotion and in looking away to hide my tears, I caught Elba's eyes, who gave me one of her empathetic, wistful looks. Nja noticed my mood too, and holding my hand as well as my watery gaze for a few seconds, announced that the baby will be a boy.

'If we were royalty, he would be Ole II', Anders joked, 'but it will be plain Ole, I'm afraid'.

I said thanks in my heart for that evening while in the church and again before leaving. I looked up to the Annunciation, -pastel-hued and subtle-, like a harbinger of better days to come. If only.

By the time I came out, I had an indescribable sense of relief. A weight had been lifted off my shoulders in spite of having looked straight into the very bottom of my present situation. Or most probably, because of it. It was this conscientious, raw confrontation with reality, my reactions to it and remorse about the past that in the end proved to be a therapeutic awakening. Seeing the light at the end of the tunnel means something different now. It does not mean recovering and staying alive any longer, it just means the end of the struggle.

In the street, the shadows of the tallest buildings had already stretched over the pavements, reaching for one another as if they were scared of being left on their own during the oncoming night. Grette came to meet me and we walked up to Kongens Nytorv, proud of managing a few yards without panting. For a second, I could've kidded myself that things were getting better. Grette looked radiant in her green outfit and beady necklace.

While I meditated in church, she had found the optimism and the energy to go and buy me a couple of chocolate bars and a few books, as well as a pair of shoes for herself. She looked so happy that I didn't have the heart to disappoint her and making the greatest effort so far, I suggested eating out.

Despite being a Monday –never good for restaurants-, we dined frugally in a newly restored place which has wisely included many more Danish dishes in its previously only French menu, and left soon after finishing our coffees. I hailed a taxi and told the driver to take us home via the harbour, where I have wandered along so many times throughout my life, including the day I met Kar for the last time... The day he died... The day before I went into hospital...

A crescent moon hung low and silvery in the sky.

Grette held my hand tightly. Neither of us spoke.

'Thanks for such a lovely evening, my bee. And for every moment we have spent together' I told Grette and although she waved a hand dismissively, there were tears in her eyes.

'I could be worse, that's true'

I adore her when she jokes. She looks fine and younger notwithstanding the stressful time.

Now I am going through all the old papers I had not looked at until now and shredding as many as can be shredded. Hotel bills and brochures collected with Ulla in Danish villages, the south of France, Sweden, Norway. Cards from other women. Letters from Anna. Photos of almost forgotten uncles and aunts who only dressed in black, which none of my children will treasure; poems from my university days which I can hardly remember writing, let alone who the muse was. I empty up drawers, clear shelves and wipe out the files in my computer. All of it. I wish there were no material trace of my existence so that Grette could rebuild her life without obstacles or pointless memories tugging at her sleeve every time she looks at someone in the street, every time someone invites her out.

Sweet darling. Whenever I look at her, she looks up from her book and smiles.

A few nights ago, when she was going through the photos she took in Venice, I felt like snatching them away from her and tearing them to pieces. I felt insulted by the way she reminisced about our holidays as if I were already dead, and it was demeaning for herself to indulge in such self-pity. Where was her dignity?

I thought of my father, the way he had not slept since the night my mother died until the day her funeral took place, of how he had gone to pieces in one minute, but never allowed himself a tear when in public, never a self-indulgent word, never a sentimental gesture. He stood there, in his black suit which looked a bit too large because he had lost a whole stone in a single week, square shouldered, tall and upright as ever, in spite of the cane he used to help ease the pain in his arthritic joints. Such dignity Such composure.

I was tempted to tell Grette about him, but resisted because she must be fed up with my talk of my own family and the extensive part of my past in which she yet had no part. Instead, I mentioned Rilke. She looked puzzled like every time I bring up a subject that comes out of the blue to the listener because after thinking about it for some time, I stupidly utter only the final conclusion, the final phrase in my chain of thoughts. I apologized.

Rilke wrote something interesting about the way Northern Europeans deal with death. Nothing too deep, if I remember well, but I mentioned it in order to arouse some curiousity in Grette's mind so that she may go and read about it in a philosophical way, not just in those self-help books she has been buying behind my back and hiding under her pillow, out of tact. Recently, as a result of one of those pocket medicine readings, she was telling me how harmful morphine is. How regretful she is for consenting to my using it. Morphine. How can one explain to someone who has never experienced as much as half the pain one suffers, the insignificance of any potential damage that the only painkiller that renders the last moments of your life slightly bearable might cause? I thought about it for a while before replying, since she expected to engage me in conversation. I opted for an analogy.

I asked her whether she ever found that people, me included, actually did feel the same distress she felt when she told us, very rarely and extremely succinctly, how her parents had barely survived Dachau, and how their own parents had not. Of course not, she answered. My physical pain, my headache was exactly like that. Colossal and untransferable. If Mr Henriksen prescribed morphine, then it must be because nobody has yet come up with a better option.

'I didn't mean to irritate you', Grette said, but I was glad to have explained it like that in order to spare her any sense of guilt or responsibility. I know very well how after a loved one dies, we all tend to find every reason to blame ourselves for doing this, not doing that and all the rest.

Meanwhile, the rain keeps falling heavily, freshening up the garden, calming, soothing my anxieties. I was at last able to sit and listen to some jazz in peace. Mahler has mercifully finished playing on the hi-fi. I have always found him a bit too intense, when not heavy, in as much as I can identify his work, but Grette loves almost all classical music. She knows so much about it. It was Symphony No. 4 in G Minor, she told me, played by Daniel Barenboim. I am sure it was brilliant.

'I met Maestro Barenboim once', I say. Grette stops humming and puts her book down. 'We were both invited to Ted's yacht, as well as other friends and were introduced by our first names. Either that or I missed his surname, I don't recall. I sat next to him at table and we conversed quite openly as you do when meeting people for the first time, if they are friendly. He appeared rather shy at first, but after a glass of wine he relaxed and was very charming, I must say. Always the barrister, I asked him several questions. He said that he played music. It was due to the self-effacing way in which he said it, neither with affected modesty nor provocatively, that I assumed music was only a hobby. I didn't even bother to comment, for example, that I had been married to a well-known pianist for fear that he would take it as an intention of showing off and wishing to shine by association. At some moment, someone else must have joined us and the subject was dropped. Only after he left, Ted asked me what did I make of Daniel Barenboim. Thankfully, I never met him again. Can you imagine? I would've never been more embarrassed'

'Why haven't you told me this before? Grette protests. 'I feel so envious! Imagine! I would've loved to be at that lunch!' Her eyes light up picturing what it would be like to have Sunday lunch crammed on board a tiny yacht on the Stour, sitting next to the maestro. How she would've loved to be there.

'Will you help me choose my music now?' I ask, seizing the opportunity. No need to add that I'm thinking of my funeral.

I favoured some Chopin almost apologetically, because I think it is a rather safe option coming from somebody who, like me, loves to listen, but is hopeless at titles and composers except for the very obvious ones. Grette observes that it's probably a reaction to so many musicians around me. First, my mother, who played the piano throughout our childhood, filling the air with lively or poignant melodies according to her mood or the occasion; then Anna, who played with such feeling and talent and now herself, who listens to it constantly. I reply it has been just negligence, a kind of indifference, precisely because there has always been somebody who would choose it for me, play it for me. Anna herself composed our own piece of music for our wedding. Music is someone else's gift, even when its beauty or its poignancy pierces my heart, it still belongs to someone else, not to me.

And so, listening to this and to that, preselecting some pieces, eliminating others, we stay up until one o'clock in the morning. The rain has stopped and I start to feel light-headed with so much medication and Bach and Sibelius and Beethoven. Once again, Grette says she is envious of my luck when I tell her that when Anna and I went to St Petersburg, -still Leningrad in those days- where she was giving a couple of concerts, one of her colleagues invited us to his niece's wedding. The reception took place at the bride's parents' apartment right on the edge of the well-to-do area of the town, where the people looked exactly like one would paint the Russians. They behaved as a family like they have behaved for centuries.

Inside, the light was provided only by candles, and I wasn't sure whether it was for the occasion or for other reasons, but it emphasized the Russianness of the place and of its residents. The tables were all white linen and silver, and after eating, drinking, singing and dancing like only they can do, someone sat at the piano and recited a poem to the music of Moonlight Serenade, so beautifully, so perfectly done that everybody stood silent and then asked the man to jot the words down and pass some copies around. He didn't, of course.

Funny how something like that, which lay at the bottom of my mind, dormant and fragile for all this time, can come back so vividly after twenty-five years.

'I wish I'd been there, too', Grette says. 'And now we ought to go to bed, darling'.

I acquiesce and slowly shuffle upstairs, humming the beautiful Serenade. One more Sunday has gone by.

William phoned earlier from Dubai. He'll be flying to Copenhagen tomorrow. I need to be there on business, he said. As if.

Chapter 33

Luke

Hellerup, 2019

Cecille is here. She brought fresh figs and her husband, so that I could witness and share in her happiness. Their happiness. Perhaps she thought that introducing him to me would act as a confirmation that everything is peaceful, at last, in her life. Perhaps she just wants to reassure me that there is no need to worry about her because her present life has healed the wounds that I unwittingly inflicted upon her. Perhaps, she wants a sort of blessing from me. Perhaps, I have overdosed on morphine and am simply imagining too many things trying to find explanations and answers to what was never a question in the first place. Perhaps, I am losing the plot. Perhaps, perhaps, perhaps.

I've been asleep for a long time, apparently. Grette, may some deity bless her, behaves impeccably.

She shows Cecille and her bloke up to my room and then goes downstairs, back to Torben and Samuel, who claim to be here only in order to retrieve some old belongings from the attic before going to London. Nonsense. I may be dosed up on opiates but can still tell that they came some days ago, possibly two, or three, four?

I sense they are staying here in our house, striving not to make noises, awaiting my departure.

Cecille's husband smiles easily and genuinely. He seems sensible enough to cope with talking to a moribund stranger, me, in the stranger's house. My house. He's dressed in black trousers, black shirt and a burgundy scarf that hangs too long for someone with short legs. It's obvious that he has tried to look as if he could not care less about his clothes, but he failed. The attire is unmistakably chosen to the last detail. Crumpled linen, clean cuts. Half crisp, half bohemian. Trendy and carefully unkempt, like one of those rooms that specialized magazines describe as shabby chic. He looks exactly like someone in the Arts world, although being a dealer only makes him a voyeur of the Arts. A voyeur of beauty. A voyeur of Cecille's alabaster skin, silken hair and dark eyelashes.

'Cecille's told me so much about you'

I nearly burst out laughing, but there would be reasons to burst into tears too, so I don't. Nor do I seek to catch Cecille's eyes while Veniamin keeps chit chatting. (He looks plain French to me, without a drop of Russian blood in his veins to account for his name, but who knows). This is his first time in Denmark since their wedding and looks forward to visiting Skagen, he says. He's never been there. This morning he went to the Glyptoteket and the SMK.

I brush aside the memory of both Skagen and the Glyptoteket, and infer he has had enough of the scene in front of him and wants to get out of this room, when he announces it's started to rain. I follow both of them with my eyes, their every movement, gesture and expression. Cecille is always a fine view, but above all, I am curious about this man who has finally turned her life around. I want to make sure that there is no shadow, no mask, no smoke screen in her apparent plenitude.

What could I do if I were to detect any shadow? Nothing, of course, but at the moment, while they are both here, sitting by my bedside, holding hands and smiling lovingly at each other, I need to be sure that they flawlessly belong together, that I'm not being misled only because I'm an old man with a death sentence printed upon his cursed head.

Cecille makes her own attempts at small talk while stroking my hand, looking deeply but too briefly into my eyes. It does not matter how independent she can be, how comblée she feels, there is always something melancholic about her that makes you feel conscious of your own emotions, especially if her presence catches you unawares. She can be bubbly and playful, or fly into a ferocious temper at times, but at some point, something intense and deeply moving about her, if not poignant, touches your heart. It has always been there and it will never leave her, this aura that draws you towards her in the same way that roses make you stop and get closer to the flowers, close your eyes and inhale deeply.

She says she was here yesterday morning and the day before that and the previous one. I apologize for having been in a comatose state and she smiles palely.

Indeed, it's Thursday. I have not been up since last Sunday, when I so painfully finished choosing the music for my Walhalla. I slept through three days and night, then. Oh, God.

'I saw Elba this morning', Cecille says, and we both know what it means. I sigh the deepest sigh of relief.

This is most definitely my last chance. I can hardly speak but hang on to her hand and summoning up the last remains of courage and energy in my soul, tell her that I need a word with her. In private. Please. Her hand tenses up and a beam of apprehension flickers in her eyes. Would Veniamin wait for her in the car? He gallantly obliges. Suddenly, he remembers that he has plenty of phone calls to make, text messages to send, emails to check... He'll go to the car and catch up with all that nonsense. His diplomacy touches me. Credit where it's due and all that. I can have Cecille all for myself, not that she was ever possessed by anyone, in the literal sense of the word.

The drizzle has turned into a heavy downpour that makes the top of the trees and the sky look further away from my window. I picture Veniamin jumping into their car, trying to smooth his clothes that have got more creased as they got wet, swearing at the Danish rain, the Danish language he can't decipher and the Danish old fossil who clings to his wife's hand like moss to a rock. I could guffaw with pride, if I had the energy... or the nerve to do so.

Cecille walks up to the window and stands there, taking in the view of the garden in the pouring rain. Silently. Motionless. I know how much she loved it, but neither of us mentions it. She will evoke this small rectangle of Danish landscape later on when she'll be back in Paris, far from us and from her old self. She turns round slowly, and slowly walks back to my bed. We are only a few steps apart but her movements look delayed and deliberate, like a scene in the type of film that her adopted country favours.

She takes off her pale blue cardigan revealing an impeccably simple white shirt, and sits carefully on the edge of my bed. Her perfume, that perfume which smelt far too sensual on her when she was younger, has matured with her and like her aura, become a part of herself. I wonder to what stage of her life, to what slice of her youth is she secretly clinging every time she chooses to buy yet one more bottle of the same brand.

'What I did to you was the worst thing I've ever done in my whole life', I tell her.

She waves a hand, brushing my words aside.

'What I did to you was the worst thing I have ever done in my whole life', I repeat, and she looks first into my eyes, then down. 'I don't intend, for one second, to make you go through it again just to expiate my guilt. You know that, I hope. All I want is to get rid of all the bullshit that's been kept suppressed... all the euphemisms, the metaphors, the ambiguity... this sweeping under the carpet, just because it's difficult to face up to'.

'Your love of words hasn't left you' she says, as if to change the subject.

'Just want to tell the truth, Cecille. To hear the truth. I don't want forgiveness, but I need you to know that...'

'It wasn't easy, for sure' she interrupts me. 'I was going to leave home, leave Copenhagen and have the baby, without you finding out. I saw later that it would've been impossible for you not to know, but anyway... There's nothing else to do or say, Ole. You didn't know I was pregnant. It was... I don't know. Bad luck. You never knew what Erika did... Everything happened such a long time ago. We'd better leave it at that'.

I see the shadows in her eyes, keep quiet and then change the subject.

'I'm leaving you the Kroyer's self-portrait you've always liked so much. Please. Please, do accept it. It's only a present, not a bribe to get me into Heaven'. She giggles a wistful giggle. 'Please?' She presses my hands.

'Thank you' she whispers.

'What did Erika do?'

'Oh, forget it. I still love her too much. I miss her. She's probably the person I most love in this world and hate her as much, at the same time. Not that it makes any sense, I know'. She stretches out her arm and reaches for a tissue out of the box Grette keeps on the chest of drawers. The large sapphire on her finger is the only jewellery she is wearing. It suits her. She deserves the devotion that moved her man to buy such ring and much more.

'Once upon a time, there was a night amongst all nights', -Cecille starts, mocking her own words, her voice almost inaudible- 'I'd been particularly upset. I could tell that you were going to put an end to our affair... You had been rather distant. Not a single touch, not meeting my eyes when you spoke... I wept. I felt pathetic, but couldn't help it. We were in the car, on this driveway, about to go back into town, to my parents's house. You used to drop me in the street behind, remember? I begged you not to leave me, then. I've never begged anyone else before or since... finally, you held my face and kissed me but it was out of pity or compassion. Your heart wasn't in it, nor desire or anything else, really... You seemed too embarrassed or too detached to look at me, I'll never know which, but I knew I'd lost you. So, I made up my mind... I went upstairs on tiptoes and locked myself in my bathroom'.

'Many times, I tried but couldn't bring myself to mention it, so I just wrote it down in the simplest way I could and sealed it in the envelope I posted to you all those years ago'

'Please, go on'. I squeezed her hand as tightly as I could.

'I cried my eyes out for hours and hours, wrapped up in the tartan shawl you'd bought me in London. Eventually, mother knocked and knocked on the door until I turned the key open. I was exhausted by the upset and dizzy with my pregnancy... went to my room shivering and quivering, holding on to Mor's arm. She didn't ask me what the matter was or where I'd been that night... Nothing. No questions. She just went downstairs and brought me a cup of tea. I was about to tell her I was pregnant, but she spoke first'.

Cecille inhales deeply. Her eyes are full of tears. She looks towards the window...'Mor told me', she continues, 'Mor said she needed to tell me that you'd been together, the two of you... that she'd been young and foolish once. Dad was far too busy with other things and she'd grown lonely. You were around, like you've always been, popping in for drinks, meeting up for lunch, phoning about some business... the usual thing... And'... Cecille pauses again, takes a deep breath, holds back tears. 'And she said that you two became lovers over one summer. Mor got pregnant and your wife Ulla got pregnant too... Mor said that I, Cecille, was your own child. Flesh and blood. Daddy wasn't to know. She'd never told him or you, either'

My heart stops. After swallowing hard on what feels like a handful of sand, I manage to tell her that it is a complete, disgusting, evil lie.

'Of course, it is'. She giggles, uneasily. What we can laugh at, we can face... 'We were father and daughter, Erika told me. Why on earth would a mother say such a thing unless it was the absolute truth? That night, in my room, my hands on my belly, shaking under my quilt, I didn't doubt my beloved Mor's words'

'She's always been so gentle. I adored her. She was uncapable of hurting anyone. You know what she's like. It all sounded so true, so plausible! The next morning, I dragged myself out of bed and drove to the hospital. The receptionist wished me good luck and when a doctor saw me almost at once, I thought the angels were watching over me, after all, but their protection didn't last. They got distracted, I suppose, and the nurse inadvertently swapped my records for someone else's... I ended up with a hysterectomy. A hysterectomy. It was the stuff of wicked witches' tales. An accident like that could never happen in Denmark, can you imagine? Not in the worst nightmares, but it happened to me. "Cecille Bossen. 22 yr. old. Hysterectomy", the card clipped to my bed read'.

'Mor og Far didn't know I'd gone to have an abortion. I let them believe that I'd gone for some minor disorder and... Can't even remember what I said then. The doctor agreed to keep silent. It was convenient for him, I guess'

'Eleanor let me stay with her while I recovered. She was out working all day and it suited me being left alone. The first few days went by in a daze. I felt groggy and too shocked to feel distress. Gradually, my mind got sharp again and I concentrated on my thesis. For two or three weeks I did just that during the day and watched awful TV with Eleanor in the evenings. Neither of us mentioned what had happened. Then one day, editing my stuff on Modigliani, I came across his Jeanne Hebuterne. It touched a nerve, of course. I wailed so loudly that the old couple next door banged on the door, asking if everything was okay or should they call for the police. They didn't know what was going on'.

Every word I hear is like swallowing ground glass, and I deserve it. Careful not to pull the canula off my hand,

I reach for the glass of water on my bedside table and pass it on to Cecille.

'Somehow, everything got kind of tidy again. Raw, but tidy. I went away no sooner I graduated. Remember? I didn't want to see you. The rest is history, as they say. My history. Not yours. Not Erika's. Not Veniamin's. Don't know why I'm telling you now... after all those years. It doesn't matter anymore. I only feel anger about Mummy lying like that'.

'But...'

''course it was a lie. She told me so when I confronted her years later. All my rage, my repulsion, my resentment came out at once and I threw the conception – in painful, tasteless detail- and the abortion in her face. She was horrified and swore that she never knew I was pregnant. Only that I was seeing you and she'd felt so jealous'.

I can hardly process what she's telling me. Wonder whether I'm hallucinating, but in case this is real, I attempt to say something helpful, assuming I am making sense.

'You have to forgive her, my Cecille. For your own sake, and because you still love her so much. You think you don't, but you do'

Every piece on the chessboard had moved against Cecille on that sinister day at the hospital. And before. And after. And I was responsible, how could I not be? I was sorry beyond words.

'Nonsense. You have nothing to apologize for. I was this unhinged idiot then... My only regret is... I would've left home, gone away and have the baby even though I was so young at the time, but imagine how it feels being told that you're your lover's daughter. I panicked and acted upon my mother's revelation straight away... If I hadn't acted so impulsively... I did want a career and yet, at that time I was so irrational that even now, I think that a baby would've grounded me... See how mixed up I was? Was going to call him Luke. I was sure it was a boy'

Her voice regains strength. She sits up, almost back in control now, and I can only pray to any Mighty being that she can now move on.

'Luke would've completed me totally' Cecille says, almost whispering now. She takes a deep breath and closes her eyes. I close mine, relaxed only because of the morphine induced slumber that has kept me pain-free and sane -contrary to expectations-, for the last twenty-four hours. Nevertheless, life has suddenly got too much.

'There's no point in going on about it. Will you just hug me?'

She gently lays her head over my chest. Gently, without squashing me too hard, as if I could break. It feels so good.

'Ole'. She says she likes my name because so many things come to her mind whenever she hears it, whenever she says it. Country lanes in dappled shade. Sea breeze on the dunes. Meaningful looks across tables at the club. Winter warmth. English autumn. Summer cool. Danish light.

Cecille. Cecille...

ACKNOWLEDGEMENTS

I should like to thank the Danish Embassy in London and Rigs Hospitalet in Copenhagen for helping with my research.

To Judith Kahn for proofreading this text.

To Carina Bagge-Vestergaard for teaching me her beautiful Danish language with such dedication and professionalism. To Judith Hetebrügge Hansen for her suggestions about Danish words usage. Any inaccuracy in this book is entirely of my own.

Posthumously and very especially, to the late Rabbi Jonathan Sacks for allowing me to freely quote one of his many invaluable teachings.

To Esteban Patricio Fredez-Langan and Geoffrey Le Tot for helping with the finishing touches.

AND above all, to my husband for his constant support and encouragement.

Printed and bound by CPI Group (UK) Ltd, Croydon, CR0 4YY
16/02/2024
03704381-0001